Fool's Play

Book 1 of System Apocalypse: Kismet
An Apocalyptic LitRPG

By

Tao Wong & David R Packer

STARLIT PUBLISHING

Copyright

Published by Starlit Publishing
PO Box 30035
High Park PO
Toronto, ON
M6P 3K0
Canada

www.starlitpublishing.com

Ebook ISBN: 9781778551543
Paperback ISBN: 9781778551550
Dust Jacket Hardcover ISBN: 9781778551567
Hardcover ISBN: 9781778551604

Books in the System Apocalypse Universe

Main Storyline

Life in the North

Redeemer of the Dead

The Cost of Survival

Cities in Chains

Coast on Fire

World Unbound

Stars Awoken

Rebel Star

Stars Asunder

Broken Council

Forbidden Zone

System Finale

System Apocalypse: Kismet

Fool's Play

Fool's Bond

System Apocalypse – Relentless

A Fist Full of Credits

Dungeon World Drifters

Apocalypse Grit

System Apocalypse: Australia

Town Under

Flat Out

Bloody Oath

Anthologies & Short stories

System Apocalypse Short Story Anthology Volume 1

System Apocalypse Short Story Anthology Volume 2

Valentines in an Apocalypse

A New Script

Daily Jobs, Coffee and an Awfully Big Adventure

Adventures in Clothing

Questing for Titles

Blue Screens of Death

My Grandmother's Tea Club

The Great Black Sea

Growing Up – Apocalypse Style

Interdimensional Window SHOPping

A Game of Koopash (Newsletter exclusive)

Lana's story (Newsletter exclusive)

Debts and Dances (Newsletter exclusive)

A Tense Meeting (Newsletter exclusive)

Comic Series

The System Apocalypse Comics (7 Issues)

Table of Contents

Chapter One

The cavern was warm—a pleasant change from the snow-covered mountain meadow outside—and Fool smiled as he walked around the first bend. He couldn't remember if these were properly called "burrows" or "warrens," but whatever they were, they were much larger than they used to be.

Probably just as musty smelling though. He'd always loved marmots. The hoary marmots in the British Columbia interior were his favorites when he was a kid. He'd loved to walk around them, because they just didn't care about people. You could walk right up to them and sit next to them, and they'd keep on doing whatever it was they were doing, as if you were invisible.

He'd tried to share that awesome experience once. Decades ago, with someone he loved. She'd laughed. It had been a happy time, but all that was gone now.

So much gone and changed. The System had hit the world like a tidal wave of rage and sorrow and cleared out most of everyone's lives.

Fool had been ahead of the curve on that. He'd had a manic drive to succeed, but that turned to being manic after a few years, then he'd started to lose touch with reality sometimes. Lost his career, lost his friends, lost his family. Two decades of living as best he could after that. Managed to hold on to his car for the first six months, and after that?

When he came back to the real world, it had been a different world. He'd learned to make what friends he could. He'd learned to scrabble to survive, and to fight for a sense of any kind of continuity. Most people he knew had given up, making it day to day. But not Fool. No matter where his brain or life led, he always fought for the hope of a better future.

Eventually it came, thanks to the same thing that had taken the lives of billions of others. The System came. At first, he thought it was another hallucination. Then there was the voice, whispering a promise of what he'd longed for. Somehow it differed from the other voices, and he listened to it. He'd struggled for the first few days, then Jackal had showed up and helped Fool on his way to sanity. But that voice was still there sometimes. Only now Fool could see it was one of many Skills, assigned by the System. Sort of.

Fool knew he should use his System-assigned Skills to navigate this cave, to search for any hidden monsters or to protect himself from threats, but he couldn't bring himself to do that. He'd been gifted those Skills, and he resented that. Things like that always came with a price. And in some ways, he knew he still didn't trust that all of this was real. Some part of him still wondered if he wasn't stuck in a hallucination.

That was stupid, of course. He knew the flavors of the mind-lies, and these weren't them. These days, magic was as real as cars used to be. So were monsters. Everything had changed.

Like the Hoary Marmots. The cave was warm from them. Even as they hibernated, they still gave off heat and that musty animal smell. Before the System, they had been big rodents, about the size of a chihuahua, but a lot fatter and cuter. Now?

He walked up to the closest one and ran his hands through its fur. It was like petting a bus, but softer. He gave himself a moment and leaned into the side of the beast, letting the comfort and memory fill one little broken part inside him.

Big, soft, warm creature. A good dozen of them in this cave, all fast asleep. At least until winter ended for good. It had already started down at the base of the mountain. They'd sleep for another week or two at least.

His fingers pulled out of the fur, and the thick, downy undercoat came out in a mat in his hand. He held it up to his nose and took a deep whiff. Musky, but underneath that was the unique smell of the big creature. A delicate aroma that tickled the back of his nose and reminded him of baby powder.

The Hoary Marmots were the perfect example of the good that balanced out the bad of the System, as far as Fool was concerned. They were still monsters, giant and terrifying. The warning squeak they used to have had evolved into a shattering sonic attack that was loud enough to kill. But the System hadn't really changed their essential character that much. They still would happily ignore you if you wandered amongst them. You just really didn't want to upset them now. They sure weren't endangered animals anymore.

Fool considered the luxurious fur for a moment, then raked his fingers through the big creature's side a few more times. He stuffed the clumps into his pockets. It had much less value than an actual pelt—which could fetch an extremely tidy sum—but there were a few Crafters in McBride who could make use of even these small amounts. Especially one or two of the cute ladies. Every bit helped.

He took one more looked around the warren, but it all looked cozy and secure. Mission accomplished. He pulled the old, non-System radio out of his pocket and clicked it twice. That was the signal to Jackal that everything was okay. Then he froze.

Three clicks in his earpiece. That was Jackal's signal for trouble outside. For a moment, Fool thought about grabbing another handful of underfur, but Jackal wouldn't have signaled if it wasn't something urgent, so he turned around and started his way out of the warren.

The view outside was still epic. They were near the peak, in the Sunbeam Ecological Reserve, and from here, Fool could look down across the whole valley, and up and down the entire mountain ranges on either side. Everything was still mostly sheathed in winter white, and the air was crisp and clear. An absolute silence only added to the majesty.

Heaven.

Fool took an extra moment to take it in, feeling his nostrils and the back of his throat burn with the cleansing cold. He saw Jackal in the same place he had been before. Fool wouldn't have been able to see him if he didn't know where to look.

The big man was crouched on one of the tallest piles of rocks. His skin was almost the color of the bark on the scattered trees that clung to life this high in the mountains, and he'd chosen a darker green outfit. Hunched down low, Jackal looked just like one of the folded-over high mountain pines.

Jackal motioned to Fool, telling him to move low.

A good sign. Fool had half expected to come out in the middle of a firefight. Jackal wasn't quick to sound an alarm and was capable of handling almost any physical situation by himself.

Which made Fool curious. Something threatening enough that Jackal had wanted to warn him about it? And there was still time to head over to Jackal, twenty meters away, but he needed to stay low and not attract attention? Fool's imagination was in overdrive as he did a low shuffle over to his partner.

Trolls? Giants? Dragons? What could be in the area? Whatever it was, it was probably what they'd been sent up to find.

They'd gotten back from their most recent mission for the Foundation and were directed up the mountain right away. The water supply for McBride had been showing a spike in bacteria. Not much of a problem normally. Good old-fashioned chlorine handled most of the critters that infested the local water, and a fancy System filter the city had sprung for took care of the rest. But old habits died hard, and the worry about the usual filtration methods not working wasn't a minor worry. Having undrinkable water wasn't on anyone's fun list.

The town's water supply came from a single stream that flowed down from multiple sources in the mountains. The increased bacteria came from fecal matter, or other biological processes like decay. This was unchanged even in the System world. Things still had to break down into component parts, and that worked at the Mana level as well as the pre-System level.

So something was pooping or dying in larger than normal numbers in the watershed area. The Foundation sent teams out to reconnoiter. They had sent Jackal and Fool up to the Ecological Reserve to check on the Marmots, to see if they'd suddenly had a population explosion or if something else had moved in.

Fool made it to Jackal, who had slowly been making his way down from his perch. The look on Jackal's face wasn't good.

"Spiders," was all he said.

That was enough to make Fool's stomach lurch. He'd always had a bit of a phobia but had mostly dealt with it. And the System had honestly helped with that. The problem was that the Cariboo Mountains seemed to be a favored spot for spiders, and mutations amongst the pre-existing population had come fast and hard. And not all for the bad. Like the Marmots, the Jumping Spiders and False Widows had grown large, but not entirely vicious. Most of the other species though... larger and nastier. Big problems. The first year of the System had seen almost all local resources devoted to cleansing those infestations.

The System seemed to like to repeat itself though, so everyone knew that at some point, the spiders would flare up again. The mountain range was filled with all kinds of damp caverns, caves, and tunnels. Ample space for monsters to breed in privacy.

Fool turned and looked, then wished he hadn't.

Opiliones. Harvestmen. Nightmares.

Some part of him, deep inside, behind the gibbering, wanted to correct Jackal and tell him they weren't real spiders. And they weren't. Opiliones looked like spiders, eight gangly legs and all, but they didn't have venom, and they had one less body segment. Mostly, they were just a big fat body with a head stuck on. And depending on the species, really bizarre eyes on stalks.

But Fool was looking at one that was heavily mutated, which didn't help with its looks at all. The legs were of the usual form, all thin and gangly. The body was a flattened oval, and each segment looked like a slab of battleship armor, with a dull sheen that spoke of metal. Each segment was rimmed with spikes, for extra fun.

Big fangs. Huge. No venom dripping from them, just brute size. The thing was big enough, but those fangs were a third of the height of the creature, almost a meter long. And they narrowed right from the start, down to a wicked sharp needle point.

The real creepy thing though was the eyes. Three of them on this one. Wobbling all about on their stalks, like some sort of weird children's toy. And they had a very unpleasant glow.

"Fuck," Fool said. "This is gonna suck. Any more, or just the one?"

"Just one. So far," Jackal said.

Small favor that. Fool turned and looked again. It was a few hundred meters away, up the slope, but heading right for them. Opiliones were mostly scavengers and had a fondness for caves. So, probably, this one and its pals had shown up and discovered sleeping Marmots were a ready snack. Well, time enough to look-see at this one and come up with a plan.

Fool put his resentment aside for a moment. It was time to use his System-bestowed Skills. Talent Scout would give him the basics of the beast.

Opilione (Level 48)
HP: 489/489
MP: 121/128
Conditions: None
Scout Notes: ...

"Triple threat." he said.

Jackal nodded. "Eye beams?"

"You got it. Damage, Mana Drain, Health Drain. Armored with a ton of Health too."

"Plan?"

Fool chewed on that for a moment. He had a Skill that would help with this, and off-hand, he couldn't think of a reason not to use it. And Jackal had the perfect Skill that would put him on top of the creature. Fool preferred not to use the System Skills, but he had no problem with other people using them.

"I'll blind it, you jump on it. Between the eyes is the weak spot but get out of there as soon as you hit. Those eyes are nasty and can absolutely see every part on top. Head below after that, look for the joint between the body and head. Weak spot there too."

"Got it. Now get your armor on. Still time."

Fool swore, but Jackal ignored him. He'd really been hoping that Jackal would forget.

Fool didn't enjoy fighting. Never had. He also couldn't bring himself to spend any of the precious points that the System gave him on what he considered useless Skills, like combat ones.

But there was no arguing that the System favored fighters, and real growth came from kills. As he and Jackal had started to really push their Levels, they'd had to farm more and harder monsters to Level up. Fool had made do with buying ranged weapons when he had the funds… but now they were working for the Foundation, and money had become less of an issue. The Foundation didn't like to lose assets. So they'd "gifted" him a fine set of protective gear and some rather skookum weapons.

While Fool wasn't a staunch believer in the Foundations' long-term goals, the short-term ones worked well enough. And the gear they supplied sure helped to make the job easier.

He stopped wasting precious seconds and activated the armor. It was sort of cool: instant-on armor. That part was acceptable. The close-fitting helmet still made him gag when it wrapped around his head though. No reason for it. His vision was still good, and he could probably breathe easier through the filtered air pumps, but his brain refused to believe that at some deep level.

As soon as that was done, he pulled out his latest toy—a very nice warhammer. Modeled after a lovely historical example, but with some delightful additions. Armor-piercing and Damage buffs, as well as Speed and Accuracy. Between the hammer and the armor's buffs, he was almost as good as a fighter at two-thirds of his current Level. Almost. On a good day. For him.

Jackal had teased him about his choice of weapon, but Fool stuck to his hammer. His teenage years had been spent playing an old tabletop roleplaying game, and he'd never been able to let go of the idea that clerics weren't allowed to use edged weapons. It wasn't like his "god" cared, but Fool cared, so that's what it was.

Besides, the hammer was satisfying. He had to admit he felt a very atavistic pleasure in swinging it around. The smooth steel shaft, the finely balanced brick on the end, even the braided leather strap that kept it on his hand if his grip failed. He'd grown to love the thing.

There was no more time to enjoy the thrill, because Jackal was already moving.

Unlike Fool, Jackal had loaded himself up with nothing but combat Skills. And over the time they'd spent together, Jackal had gone from being a dangerous individual to a very dangerous individual. Fool knew he'd be able to handle the Opilione on his own.

But there was never any point in taking chances, not in this new System world. The System didn't play fair, it only played for its own ends, for its own inevitable need to spread and fill more and more. Fool was pretty sure that the one arachnid wasn't the source of the spike in bacteria. One wouldn't account for it... but a swarm might.

Best bet was to take down this one as fast as possible, before it warned its compatriots.

Fool's role in this was pretty clear, and he was ready.

"Aziz!" he shouted, sprinting after Jackal. Even running, he could target the burst of light into the eyes of the creature, temporarily blinding it.

As Fool feared, blinding it didn't stop the Opilione from firing nasty-looking rays from each eye. The Skill had an effect though. Instead of targeting them, the eyebeams spread out across the landscape. Two of the eye blasts didn't seem to do much, but the third caused epic explosions wherever it hit.

Fool made a note to not get hit by the eyebeams.

Jackal was already at the creature and airborne. His second favorite Skill. He said it was called "Death from Above." Fool always thought of it as "Scream and Leap" because that seemed more appropriate.

It was what Jackal did, after all. Not that he'd admit it. The screaming part anyway. Jackal liked to think of himself as a silent killer. He was. Mostly. He always seemed to yell like an action hero when he jumped though. Fool thought it was adorable.

In any case, it was absolutely effective. The bug, aside from the heavy armor, had a staggering amount of Health. If Fool's Talent Scout Ability hadn't identified the weak spots, they'd be chipping away its Health for a good bit and probably taking loads of damage at the same time. Instead, a single stab by Jackal's heavy glaive did an impressive amount of damage, reducing the creature's total Health by a noticeable amount.

It still wasn't down though. Not by a long shot. Fool wasn't as fast as Jackal, but he still had more speed than he did in the before times.

Which meant he was on the Opilione right about the same time Jackal was jumping off to try for the follow-up hit in the belly. The timing was about perfect. The temporary blindness of Fool's System-flashlight to the eyes had already worn off, and the giant bug was tracking in on Jackal.

So Fool whacked it in the leg with his hammer. To his surprise, he actually knocked its Health down by another good notch. The training he'd been doing must have been paying off.

The downside was that the Opilione now knew exactly where Fool was and turned all three eyes on him. And started to blast.

Fool screamed and tucked himself into a hunched over little ball, which had the intended effect. Or at least his "Oh God Don't Hit Me" Skill had its intended effect. The creature's eyes flew back up and its alien features somehow managed to look startled. It was a low-Level Skill, but it still came in handy, even if it was only good for a temporary halt to the intended beating.

The monster apparently had slightly more intelligence than Fool had originally assumed, because instead of blasting him with its eyes, it looked around for Jackal.

Fool hadn't been forgotten though. The Opilione opted to use its fangs on him.

It would have been a fair bit easier to deal with if they were actual fangs, instead of pedipalps. There were cheliricae as well, tiny little claws to shovel food into the critter's mouth.

Fool really hated the fact that he was close enough to see that. The fangs were actually stuck on the ends of rudimentary legs, which meant they could come in at different angles.

Which insane idiot had mutated an arachnid and put their fangs on legs? The damn System, that was who.

Fool bashed one fang aside with his warhammer. The other darted in from the side and slammed into his armor, which held. Barely. Damage notifications flared. The fang had skittered off, but not before ripping off an entire chunk of his breastplate. The next hit to that area would go right through.

Time to run.

Fool had just started putting words to action, feet skidding on ice, when the beast quaked and shuffled, then disgorged an entire belly full of what looked to be what it used for blood.

Suddenly, Fool was very glad for the helmet and its air purifiers, because even through them, the stench was rather overwhelming. Regaining his feet, he watched as the Opilione flopped over on its side and curled up.

Jackal smiled from where the Opilione had been standing, dropping the butt of his spear and leaning on the shaft. "Were you going somewhere?"

"Hell yes. You think I want to stick around while you play with this thing? This is your job, not mine." Fool's smile took the truth out of the words.

Jackal knew Fool would never leave him in the middle of a fight. Fool would run, but he'd always come back. That was just who they were.

It was funny, but for both of them, it had taken the end of the world for them to really find and understand what true friendship was. No way they'd risk losing that. Not after all they'd been through before, and how all that had changed once they'd found each other.

Jackal didn't laugh, but Fool saw the smile in his eyes. Made him feel like ruffling Jackal's hair. At least, until he saw one of those hairs move.

Then it was joined by another one.

And another.

"Oh shit."

"Jackal?"

"Oh shit," Jackal repeated.

Fool didn't have to ask what was wrong. He saw it for himself as he turned around.

The tension running through Jackal's body reminded Fool of a friend who had owned a greyhound. Once in a while, the dog would be let off the leash to burn off some energy, and when it felt the hand on its collar, a tremble went through it. Like a rocket made of bone and muscle, with only a thin sheet of skin holding in the explosion.

That was Jackal now.

Another half dozen Opilione were trundling down the hill toward them.

Fool felt the power leaking off of Jackal as he fired up all of his Skills and swapped out his spear for a pair of swords. Fool had already ditched the warhammer for a heavy, high-caliber rifle. He was a lousy shot, but between his pricy armor and System-add-ons to the rifle, he'd be a factor in this fight.

They didn't have to make a plan. This wasn't new to them. Wasn't new to anyone with Levels like theirs. Not on a Dungeon World, eight months after the System had arrived. By this point, you were experienced or dead.

Being swarmed and overrun? Once a week, it felt like. Sure, not usually as tough as these critters, but bad enough. They'd reached the point of Leveling where most people figured "good enough" and learned to live with the consequences. Or died. Otherwise, you were on track for more Leveling and more fights, until you joined the numbers of the dead. It wasn't sane, not really. But Fool wasn't sane, so he just smiled and started pulling the trigger.

He already knew that armor-piercing rounds were the way to go, so he'd loaded up for that. And when he landed a shot, it did a good job at knocking down Health… aided by his "No Fair" Skill that he used to reduce armor just as he squeezed the trigger.

Or at least, that was what should have happened.

If he'd remembered to activate his Skill. Instead, he'd followed his training and taken the shot as soon as he'd seen the weak spot show up. His aim had been okay, even though he wasn't really trying. He might forget to use his active Skills, but his passive Luck score was high enough that he could mostly be lazy about things like aiming.

Not always though. This time, the bullet went right where it was aimed, just a little to the side of the weak spot he'd noted on the previous Opilione. Without his "No Fair" Skill to knock the armor down though, the high-tech projectile all but bounced off the armor of the creature.

Not entirely, because it was still a fancy bit of ammunition. It cracked off a bit of the shell and took out a spattering of flesh. If it had been a normal, pre-System animal, that would have been enough to make it scream and run away.

As it was, the Opilione didn't even slow down.

They were close enough that he didn't even have time to swear. Instead, Fool had to fight against all of his instincts and settle himself. Take his time to aim, activate No Fair, and fire.

The next shot was much better. It punched a hole through the Opilione's shell, and through his scope, he saw the creature shudder.

Fool had to repeat the entire process until the magazine was empty before he brought down the first one, and he scrambled to find another target before they got too close.

While reloading, Fool glanced up to see how Jackal was doing. The big man had already taken down three of the monsters.

Jackal was dancing through the Opilione like a dervish. He'd been working on that Skill for a while now. It was a strong contrast to his normal fighting style. No scream and leap, nor stoic stand-and-take-it. Blade Dancing, he called it. It was his Class's first real multiple opponent Skill, and it was working like a charm. He was literally bouncing off of the giant arachnids, leaping up on their fangs, using them as springboards to evade the eyebeams, and all the while laying about with both swords for massive damage. It was impressive as hell to watch, and Fool found himself almost envious of the Skill.

Still, Fool had chosen his Class and Skills with care and foresight. Mostly. He was here for the long-haul, not for the flash of the moment. Even if Jackal looked totally awesome and was mowing down powerful opponents like wheat before a scythe.

Fool gave himself a brief internal shake and got back into the mission. Those spiders would kill them both if they didn't take them out quickly. He narrowed his vision down to the scope again, picking his targets with care and firing when the right opportunity came. He didn't even smile when the notification briefly popped up about the kill he'd just scored.

Only two spiders left, which meant that Jackal's Blade Dancing Skill was not in effect anymore. And now he was outnumbered, a spider on each side. Fool scanned back and forth on both the opponents as Jackal furiously blocked and dodged. The one on the left was the weakest, so Fool put his next few shots into that one. It took four more, plus a few hits from Jackal, before that one was down.

One left, and Fool was out of ammo.

But it didn't matter, because Jackal was under the last Opilione and slicing up into its weak body joint.

Fool took a quick look all around, but there were no more of the creatures about. He stored the rifle back in his inventory and sauntered over to Jackal.

Jackal was grinning. "Did we sync again?"

"Again! Nice!" Fool laughed.

Level ups for both of them.

And they'd finally broken into their next tier of Skills.

Time to make some choices.

Status Screen			
Name	Fool	Class	Acolyte
Race	Human (Male)	Level	40
Titles			
Acolyte of the (Redacted)			
Health	310	Stamina	310
Mana	760		
Status			
Normal			
Attributes			
Strength	19	Agility	54
Constitution	31	Perception	96
Intelligence	76	Willpower	60
Charisma	66	Luck	144
Class Skills			
Closseau	1	Have Faith	1
Talent Scout	2	Pants on Fire	1
Transform Object	1	Kiss it Better	2
I know a Shortcut	1	Truth or Dare	1
Dry hair is for Squids	1	Oh god, don't hit me!	2
Mint?	1	Location Scout	1
Face Swap	1	No Fair	1
Geas	2		
Spells			
Sparkles			

Status Screen			
Name	Jackal	Class	Eternal Warrior
Race	Human (Male)	Level	40
Titles			
(None)			
Health	500	Stamina	500
Mana	560		
Status			
Normal			
Attributes			
Strength	55	Agility	52
Constitution	50	Perception	92
Intelligence	56	Willpower	135
Charisma	10	Luck	10
Class Skills			
Pain don't Hurt	2	One Punch	2
INTIMIDATE	1	Mana Steal	1
Knock back	1	Mr. Freeze	1
Only a flesh Wound	2	Death from Above	2
Neo	1	Indomitable Will	2
Mestro	2	Blade Walking	2
Red Rover	1		
Spells			
(None)			

Chapter Two

The walk back was long, but at least the scenery was beautiful. The Marmots' territory was on a bit of a plateau on the side of the mountain range, and from it, you got a great sweep of the surrounding ranges. But starting back down, they swapped the vista for a more intimate, top-down view of the entire valley.

The town of McBride was off to the left, and the village of Lamming Mills was just visible to the right. Sweeping and diving across the valley floor in curves and oxbows was the Sto:lo, once called the Fraser. That had been before the System's arrival. Since then, the river seemed to have taken on a life of its own, flooding and receding, breaking its banks and moving all across the valley in defiance of geologic imperatives.

Some of the Foundation scientists thought the river was becoming near-sentient, in some sort of way related to the Elementals that occasionally tore through. That didn't seem to fit with anything else they'd been able to find in the System research they'd done though, so they had been forced to conclude that there were just some very complex things happening to the environment that resulted in the unpredictable actions of the river.

Science aside, everyone else assumed the river was now alive, and they had taken to treating it as such. That's when they'd started to call it the Sto:lo, which amused Fool to no end. The word meant "river," which was fair enough... but it was also a word Fool had learned back in his home of Vancouver, which was why he knew it was a Halkomelem word. So the locals, even in this new world of falling back on ancestral leaning, were still ignoring the actual history of the land.

Not that he knew which nation had had the most recent claim on this land. Not that it probably mattered at all. He shared the same hunch as everyone else—that this piece of land was reclaiming itself and the thoughts of lesser sentients be damned.

In the meantime, even at the tail end of winter, it was still damned pretty.

For the walk back, Jackal and Fool had swapped out their fighting/sneaking gear for more appropriate weather gear. The wind was a sharp and hard blast when it decided to make itself known. Lovely view or not, it would be nice to get back down to the old trails and the cover of the heavier woods.

Normally they'd be more cautious in the wilderness, but this area around the Foundation's secret base was routinely patrolled. Threats came from above, in recent experience, and not as much from random spawnings. Those still happened, but the Mana flow had stabilized enough in the area to make things almost predictable. Clearly some Foundation theories were working out. For a Dungeon World, the local catchment of Mana was almost civilized. Dedicated farming and working with what Mana—or the System—wanted seemed to work pretty well.

"Settle on a Skill yet?" he asked Jackal.

"Absolutely. Didn't take much thinking. I took 'The Wall.'"

"What? Why? You've already got a Heal Skill, and with my Heal added in, you don't need the Regen." Truthfully, Fool thought The Wall Skill was pretty good. It granted Jackal a short time of near-absolute Invulnerability and rapid Regeneration. But Fool's ability to throw quick Heals on Jackal was one of the few Skills he felt comfortable using.

"Can't always count on you."

"Fuck you! I have feelings, you know."

Fool wanted to be angry about that. He knew he wasn't rational about his need to feel useful to the people around, but it was still a need. And his friends should understand that. He wanted to be angry... but Jackal's smile took the hurt out of his words.

"But seriously, why not the formation-breaking Skill? That sounded pretty handy."

Jackal did that head-wobbling thing he only did when he was alone with Fool. "Thought about it. But honestly? We don't often face opponents in formation. It's not our strength, and I don't really see any need to branch out too much. Besides... how am I going to pass up invulnerability? C'mon, Fool, even you have to admit that's the ultimate badass superpower right there."

Fool shook his head to hide his grin. Jackal was a total nerd at heart. Superpowers and stoic heroes were totally his jam. "Maybe. But what about the Combat Gymnastics one? You could do more of that flippy, spinny shit!"

Jackal glared at him. "You know that's not what I'm going for."

"Right, right... Mr. Mysterious Stranger." Fool couldn't help the raised eyebrow.

Jackal turned and threw out his arms in exasperation. "Tom Cody was awesome!"

Fool grinned, enjoying the point he'd scored. "Not arguing that. Just thinking about all those other possibilities you had."

Jackal snorted and went back to walking down the trail. "Like I'm the kind to torture myself over that. Nope. I know what I want, and I got it. How about you? You going to go with that Regen Skill?"

"Maybe. Might be useful. I mean, in character too, right? Tricksters are always coming back from death." That was something Fool had been feeling some dread about. His Class was Trickster Acolyte, but all he knew about Tricksters were the Coyote and Crow tales he'd heard. And so many of them ended with the eponymous trickster dying a humiliating death, only to come back to life later. Some of the Skills farther down his Skill Tree even hinted at something like that.

"Right, so…?" Jackal said.

"What can I say? Accepting that I might *need* to Regen just sits wrong with me. Why would I let that happen? Bad luck, you ask me."

Fool couldn't see if Jackal rolled his eyes, but he could feel it, nonetheless.

"Are you sure you don't have any combat Skill in this tier? Nothing that can cause damage?"

Jackal's tone was honest, no guile in it, but Fool still couldn't help but feel as though he was being nagged by his mother. Not that he'd ever say that out loud. Especially not to Jackal.

Fool bit back the sharp retort that was boiling up and took a deep breath. He had almost thirty years age on Jackal; he was obligated to be the adult. "I have the possibility of that 'Silence' Skill, which you are very much tempting me to use right away. You know how I feel about that."

"I know. Trickster, not a fighter. Or lover, from what I'm seeing."

Fool could feel that grin, but he didn't even glance at Jackal. Didn't want to give him the chance of seeing Fool blush. "Fuck you again! It's not my fault if things keep coming up. Besides, there's that—"

"I know, the one you've been mooning over back in town," Jackal said in a contrite tone. He clearly hadn't intended to ding his friend that hard. "Pretty sure she hooked up with one of the guards last week. Told you not to let that go on too long."

Fool sighed. "Dammit! Doesn't anyone believe in romantic buildup anymore?"

"You never said one word to her."

"That's not the point! I was clearly building up to it!"

"Not everyone can read your mind, you know. You have to actually do something if you want people to know what you want. Or say something. Anything other than just sitting in the cafe, moping, and drinking your coffee."

Fool took that with the love he'd couched it in. Fool's romantic history was complicated because of things just like this. His first wife had been someone he'd spontaneously asked out, and that had been a wreck. The next person he'd fallen in love with had been a coworker he'd mooned over for almost a year before asking out.

"I really don't need another therapist at this point." Not that Fool had a current one. But he really didn't want Jackal to fill that role.

Jackal patted Fool on the shoulder. From anyone else, that might have been condescending, but Fool could feel the care radiating out as warmth from the bigger man, and he let it soothe him.

"Sure don't need any pointers on how to change a subject," Jackal said. "That said, what Skill are you looking at?"

Fool said nothing, and they walked in silence for a bit. The terrain helped, with a change from the near-tundra heights to proper forest. They were following the old road down, which was little more than a trail these days, broken with tears and cracks and new boulders, remnants of some of the larger battles that had taken place back in the early days. A new creek had forded the road at one point and provided a frozen patch of slipperiness that they both had to concentrate on passing without falling.

Time, Fool thought, to stop dithering.

He had to let go of worrying about Jackal judging him and just talk things out. Jackal, Fool had to admit, had pretty solid insight into how Fool's mind worked and might actually provide some good advice.

"I'm kind of torn. I'm leaning into 'Plane Shift,' but the warding glyph thing seems pretty handy too. But the 'Face Swap' might be neat too."

Jackal laughed. "Big green mask. I knew you'd buy into that eventually."

Fool bit back his reply. It wasn't that he hated the movie, but he was sensitive about the whole watering down of the Trickster god to being a special effects clown. It was an argument he and Jackal had from time to time, and it was usually useful. The more Jackal brought up the things that annoyed him about the way Tricksters were represented, the more Fool had been able to get a proper grasp on what it meant to him. And it wasn't being a powered-up jester. It was about being willing to stand up to authority, to be the person who was always there to undercut and destroy the Powers That Be as best they could.

Jackal seemed to pick up on Fool's mood and moved on. "I can see how it might be cool and useful. But I can really see the benefit of being able to pop into another dimension. You can take people with you, right?"

Fool pulled up his list of Skills and gave it a quick skim. None of it really made sense to him. Never really had. And He didn't want another argument with Jackal about the importance of Skill understanding, so he decided to wing it. At least there didn't seem to be anything in the Skill description that made him think it was a no-go.

"Within limits, absolutely," Fool said. "I'm really leaning into that, especially since I can also use it to send people to other dimensions against their will. Might be useful against monsters. Downside is I would have to spend some time learning about other dimensions to make it really useful. It's not even entirely clear from the description if they're real other dimensions, or if it's some kind of teleport to really distant places."

"I'm going to guess other dimensions, since we see enough monsters and I've heard of other races that come from different dimensions. It's a bit of a puzzle though. If you assume that the System has really broken space/time dimensions enough, then on one hand, teleportation should be the cheapest option. But that implies some rather hefty information processing to control. Shifting to another dimension might need some greater initial energy cost, but maybe that's lesser than the information storage or computation cost? If you go for that option, we are absolutely running some experiments... huh."

"Huh what? You've got that look."

"I just Leveled up in my System Quest again. Weird."

Fool looked at his own stats. Still at twenty percent, and that was only because he'd had to listen to Jackal ramble on. Neither of them had done any sort of actual work on the quest, but... Jackal had been someone special before the System came. Fool hadn't been able to get him to talk about it too much, but Fool had learned a fair bit.

Mostly from Jackal.

In anyone else's company, Jackal was the spitting image of the taciturn, stoic warrior. Silent. Liked to speak in grunts, but only under duress. When it was just the two of them? Jackal made up for the silence.

He'd never said specifically what he'd done before the System, but from what Fool had determined, Jackal had been a very high-level physics guy. Something to do with fields or strings or something. He'd been well-known, but also intensely reclusive, interacting with the world almost exclusively via a computer screen.

If it hadn't been for the System, they would have never met. A reclusive nerd and a crazy homeless person? Odds of running across each other were about zero. But somehow, they'd found each other in the first few days.

Fool didn't really remember much of the first days of the System. He'd just been realizing that the blue screen in front of his eyes wasn't something only he was seeing. But that memory was one he didn't want to dive into. They weren't in a fully safe space yet, and he had to keep an eye open.

"What are you at now?" he asked Jackal.

"Coming up on thirty-five. It's getting interesting now. I had a bit of breakthrough yesterday, forgot to tell you about it. Want to hear me ramble for a bit?"

Fool knew better than to think he was successfully distracting Jackal from "helping" him decide on a Skill. Jackal was offering him an out from the conversation. That was almost enough to make Fool try to continue the conversation out of spite and resistance, but he had to admit he really felt uncomfortable about the topic.

Jackal always seemed to have his next Skill worked out in advance, and that made Fool feel as though he was always on the spot. He didn't have the online gaming background that Jackal did. All his childhood game time had been spent with paper and pencil, and while it was close to the imposed System, it was different enough that Fool didn't feel comfortable making decisions about his stats until after he'd earned them, and even then, he wanted tons of time to study the potential flaws and weaknesses.

"Yeah," Fool said. "Maybe you can ramp up my completion a bit on that."

"Probably. But before I do that, how are you going to spend your free Attribute points?"

Fool cringed. No escape. "I was thinking two points into Agility. Get better at Dodging. Could use the boost for my Lockpicking and other handsy-skills."

"We talked about this. Stop ignoring your Strength. And Constitution! Things are only going to get tougher for us now that we're Level 40. Gotta step up, bro."

"Jesus, don't ever 'bro' me again. Goddamn kids. Seriously though, I'm already stronger that I've ever been, and we can both walk all day, and we never get sick. I don't need to budge that up anymore. I'm not gonna be swinging around the big iron like you, and I'm not going to need to pick up a bus or anything. Even if I'm drunk."

"One time! I had to see! Let it go. Dude."

"Bro."

"Dick. Add one to Strength and one to Constitution, and I'll leave you alone for the next Level. Deal?"

"Deal. Dad."

"You don't get to call me that!"

That got Fool laughing, and that set Jackal off laughing after a moment too. Jackal had had a brief boyfriend with a daddy thing. That had led to a rather loud and messy breakup.

Fool added a point to his Constitution, but instead of Strength, he added the remaining one to Intelligence. Had to keep up with Jackal, and it wasn't as if Jackal was going to know.

They were fortunate that the rest of the trail down was boring. No random encounters, no beasts. Just the odd bird of now-normal size in the sky. It was a good day for a walk, and freshly Leveled-up, they were in the mood to enjoy the leisure.

Jackal's System Quest theory was interesting.

He had the insight that the System was alien to our universe, because it was, as he said, "selfish." By that he meant it had a slight bias toward individual success over communal success, and he pointed out how that was in contrast to our universe.

Apparently, the structure of our society was built up from how energy attracted itself into particle, and how the particles clumped together to form atoms and other bits. Something about our universe being biased toward "Free Energy" and the elimination of surprise, but how that had stopped when the System came in.

By Jackal's reckoning, most universes would use the same setup as ours, but if a part of another universe leaked into ours, that would cause a break in the some-word-that-sounded-like-symmetry-but-wasn't.

And because it hadn't caused the complete instant cancellation of both universes, then the residual energy was busy sorting itself throughout our universe and had somehow coalesced into the System. Tons of extra energy partially explained how they could use Skills and Abilities to warp physics. It was an interesting premise, and it might have been the extra Intelligence point, but Fool felt as though it made sense. It was enough for his System Quest completion to jump to twenty-two percent, which seemed ridiculous. How long was this stupid Quest supposed to take?

At least it gave him a list of things to research when they got back to the Foundation. Look into the System origins and read some papers by a pre-System guy named "Friston."

It was, by some miracle, still dusk by the time they got back to the Foundation. It was later than Fool had hoped. By his plan, they would have set out early in the morning, bounded up the mountain, scoped out some sleeping Marmots, and been back down before lunch. And then catch a quick lift to McBride where he was for sure going to ask out... well, apparently not the person he was going to ask out. So instead, as per the protocol of no night traffic between the Foundation and McBride, they were going to have a night "in."

At first glance, the Foundation didn't look like much. Coming down the mountain, they took a right turn down a side road, just before the main one back to McBride. The road was short and led to a pleasant, eighties-style home nestled into a bunch of trees on a large lot that was divided into several terraces. The house was on the middle terrace, with a barn on the lower terrace. In the dusk, it was lit from the inside with a mix of lights and candles in the windows. It looked like a cozy winter haven nestled in the snow.

Even knowing what was inside, Fool still cheered up when he saw it. How could you not? The warm glow and cozy look of the place was all of his childhood dreams of home come to life. He didn't even really notice all the security measures silently scanning them and letting them pass. They opened the front door and stamped off their boots in the mudroom. Even through the airlock-like entrance, they could smell the redolent aroma of fresh cinnamon buns.

Jackal took advantage of his superior physical attributes to make it first through the door, and he had already stuffed most of a cinnamon bun in his face by the time Fool joined him.

"Hi, kids!" called a buxom lady sitting on a rocking chair, looking out the window.

"Hi, Gramma!" they shouted, doing their best not to spit out bits of the still-hot buns.

Calling her Gramma was ridiculous. She was clearly in her mid-thirties at the oldest. But that was her job title, and they both rather enjoyed buying into the fun of it. So did Gramma. At least this one. The previous one had been rather touchy about it, and privately, Fool and Jackal had taken to calling her Grumpy Gramma.

She'd rotated to a new position quickly, fortunately. The new Gramma was more into the role. Thus the cinnamon buns. Occasional pies. And once, a lovely hot soup with something that had tasted like turkey but clearly wasn't.

The home was as cozy on the inside as it looked on the outside, and they had helped keep it that way by carefully taking off their outside boots in the mudroom and shaking off their clothes as best they could. They'd already stored and cleaned their combat gear before starting down the mountain. Foundation had strict rules about appearances and secrecy... which struck Fool as rather idiotic. "Security via obscurity" had been a rather dated concept even before the System.

The Foundation itself could only be accessed via the house, and some smart-ass had decided that the house had to keep up as normal an appearance as possible.

But in this day and age? Who the hell had a normal house out in the wilderness?

Even with the security settings all around it, it had to look really weird to anyone spying to see people not wearing combat gear entering and leaving the area all day. Everyone wore combat gear when they left a Safe Zone, especially out in this part of the world.

Fool had given up arguing about it some time ago, but the minor irritation that sat inside him continued to keep him from fully investing in the Foundation's mission. Making the world better for everyone, post-System, was a fantastic goal, but he wasn't entirely sure the Foundation was the right organization for the job.

But it wasn't as though there was anyone else.

His discomfort was, Fool thought, a sign that Jackal was probably right in his surmise about the origins of the System. For sure, the world before the System had been full of predatory people and organizations, and they'd made an oversized impact. But they had truthfully been more than balanced by other organizations that had made life better for everyone.

Community always won out over selfishness, even if the popular impression was different. Humans liked structure, and structure that promoted cooperation won out. But since the System? The balance had shifted.

It was entirely possible now to build a perfect society and have it crushed by an over-Leveled jerk. That had always been possible, but the tendency was for the impact to be minimized. If the System had a way to corral or limit that impact, Fool wasn't aware of it yet. He wasn't entirely sure there was a solution. Jackal figured there was, but that humans would need to reach out to some of the other galactic civilizations to figure out how they'd worked around it. Of course, the Foundation figured they could work it out on their own.

The Foundation had been formed almost immediately after the arrival of the System. A group of academics had been hosting a conference on Prosociality, and their grad students had recognized what was happening almost immediately. In response, they'd made collective decisions about what Classes to choose, Skills to acquire, and since they'd been at a retreat in Well's Gray Park, what Perks to acquire. As a result, they'd put together an organization dedicated to ensuring the survival of humanity's best instincts. Since they weren't stupid, they'd sussed out the threats to that ideal.

Their response to the threats was to make a Grand Plan to bring civilization back to Earth by subtly shaping the collapse to speed up a rebuild back to what it had been. Part of that plan was to build a secret organization to manipulate events.

They'd come recruiting Jackal less than a month after the System arrived, and by that time, Jackal and Fool had already teamed up. They'd found Fool's Skill set to be potentially useful, so he'd been recruited too.

And Fool had been happy for that.

He absolutely shared the ideals of the Foundation. He and Jackal had already been building a community in their little section of Vancouver. Moving on to something bigger that could make more impact had sounded brilliant. It was probably still a good idea, but he wasn't entirely convinced the current management could pull it off. But it was still early days.

Which meant the primary mission for Jackal and Fool was to do quests for Credits. The Foundation needed a lot of funds for their plans, so they had a lot of teams out doing tasks for pay. Every time they came back from a mission, they could see that the Credits were being put to good use, but at some point, the Foundation would need to actually get around to doing the work. The System seemed to have a way of steamrolling everyone's plans if they didn't get off their asses and get it done first. Either by invading aliens or waves of monster attacks.

Fool resisted the urge to hug Gramma as they headed down to the basement. Not that Gramma would mind so much, but Fool was pretty sure she'd respond by pinching his cheek, and that just seemed like a little too much.

"Fool?" she called as they started down the stairs.

"Yes?"

"Don't mean to ruin your good mood, but I wanted to give you a heads-up. Professor X wants to talk to you right away."

Fool groaned. Professor Xi was the mastermind behind the entire organization. They called him X because he liked to sit in a chair with a blanket in his lap, and the rumor was that before the System, he'd been in a wheelchair. Getting called in to talk to the boss was never good, and he had a bad feeling about why…

"Your cat," Gramma continued, "seems to have shit on some of his files."

Fuck. The cat. He'd forgotten about the cat.

Chapter Three

Getting to the Director's office was a hell of a walk. The tunnel from the basement of the house led straight back into the mountain, then took a few sharp turns before joining the main Foundation complex. Which was absolutely huge.

McBride had eight hundred people in residence and a big percentage of them were actually Foundation employees, but the facility itself had almost another two hundred people living full-time inside. Part of that was due to intense recruitment, but McBride was one of those rare towns that had actually grown in population after System activation. It was because of a quirk of geography. McBride had started out as a small village, but the surrounding area was unusually dense with farmers and back-to-earth folks. They'd been better prepared than most for an apocalypse, and McBride had already had community facilities to serve the extended population.

Fool had no idea what the folks in the Foundation did but crafting and planning and other activities seemed to take up a lot of their time.

There was also, he knew—from painful experience—an efficient set of combat simulation and training rooms. And a Shop even. Somehow, they'd arranged that.

Fool and Jackal offloaded all their loot from the Opiliones as soon as they arrived. The official summons arrived the moment they left the Shop.

Ms. Chemero had apparently drawn the short straw of delivering the news to them. She was rather an officious terror to deal with, which suited her title of "Corporate Compliance Officer." Fool expected she enjoyed delivering orders to people.

She hadn't added more detail to the summons at least. Just a brusque "Director wants to see you" and an about face. They didn't have to scramble to keep up with her, at least.

Fool had to admit that the points spent on Strength and Constitution had a benefit. Chemero clearly worked out and was a fast walker... but she wasn't a Combat Class. Entirely corporate in all her Skills. Fool felt as though they were supposed to be struggling to keep up with her. Chemero liked to power trip and making them uncomfortable would be one of her happy points. Not that Fool really minded. She might be a horrible person, but the power trip walk kinda worked for him. He was happy to enjoy the view.

Until he heard Jackal trying to hold back a laugh. When he turned to glance at Jackal, he was looking right at Fool, who realized that maybe he'd not been as discreet as he thought. He glared at Jackal, but that just made him snort out loud.

"Something funny?" Chemero stopped and turned to glare at them.

Jackal's face turned red, and it was up to Fool to reply. "Sorry, I was just making faces at Jackal. We had a bit of a moment in our last scrap, and I couldn't resist making fun of him. Keep going, we're following you."

Chemero held her stare a little longer. "You might want to keep a straight face for this, you know. Director's got a serious job for you."

That surprised Fool. "Job? I thought we were in... I mean... any idea what the job is?"

She shook her head and started back down the hall. "None at all. Although I will say, you should be pretty happy with it. Rumor is we're moving to the next phase, and I know you've been getting restless."

Fool glanced at Jackal, who shrugged and walked after Chemero. Fool stuck his tongue out at Jackal and joined them.

"Neat!" Fool said. "Definitely been looking forward to that. When did the rumors start?"

"Couple of weeks ago." Chemero didn't even slow down. "Maybe if you'd spent more time paying attention to what we do around here instead of mooning about in McBride, you'd have heard them yourself."

That got Jackal actually laughing, and Fool spent the rest of the walk glaring at the floor.

"Fool! Control your goddamned cat!" the Director yelled.

Fool shrugged, palms up. "It's not my cat! I don't control it. Have you tried talking to it?"

The Director didn't react at all. He just sat in his chair, hands on the desk in front of him, and stared at Fool. Fool could see one of his fingers twitch a bit, as though he was thinking about jabbing it at the Trickster Acolyte across the desk from him.

"Don't start that shit with me again," the Director said, leaning back and letting out a near-growl of exasperation. "You know we checked it out. It's a normal house cat. It doesn't goddamned talk at all. Stop with your pranks and keep the thing in your quarters, like we've told you again and again. For God's sake, can't you find someone in McBride to adopt it? This is a research facility, and as we've said time and time again!" At that, he lost some of his control and the finger leapt up from the desk, jabbing in Fool's direction. "NO pets. Surely you can find a lonely kid in town who'd be happy to have an actual pet."

Fool was wise enough to shrink back. He had found it useful to pretend he was being influenced by the show of authority. Sometimes. "C'mon, that's the whole point! Do you know of a single other house cat that's come through the System unchanged? That's an aberration right there. And it's not my pet. It just followed me, and I don't even know how."

The Director was back to sitting still, but his fingers were drumming silently on the desk. He stared at Fool for a moment then shook his head. "Can you at least get a litter box for it?"

"I don't know where it sleeps!" Fool was at least being honest about that. "Where would I put a litter box? It never even shows up in my quarters!"

"Meow."

The Director jumped. "What the hell, did you bring it to this meeting?"

The damned cat had jumped right up on the Director's desk, and from out of nowhere, as far as Fool could tell.

The thing had been a nightmare since the last mission. Fool knew he had to take care of it... somehow. The cat clearly had a mind of its own. It has been assigned to him by his own personal deity in exchange for saving Fool from a powerful mage. Worse, it talked. At least it did when it was alone with Fool. Once, in front of Jackal.

Not that it had much to say for itself. It tended to ask brief questions and not respond after being answered. Typical of a trickster god, to drop a massive puzzle in his lap and have that puzzle cause problems for him.

That had been how Fool had gotten caught up in all of this in the first place. Right from the start, at the System Activation, that quiet, oh-so-helpful voice had gently guided and teased and cajoled him into making the choices that had led to his current Class. And gave him a structure to let his various mental health conditions stop being a hindrance to being present and engaged in the world in front of him. Fool didn't mind the results, but the method still left him a little touchy.

"No," Fool said. "I keep telling you, it shows up wherever it wants and does whatever it wants."

"Meow," the cat said. It was looking right at Fool, and he was still a bit surprised to see that it had a normal cat mouth, which it closed after its outburst, with a single lick of its lips.

Fool shook his head. "You shut up. You heard the boss. Poop outside."

The cat said nothing, just looked at him and wiggled its butt. Which should have been the warning he needed. It sprang at him, claws outstretched. Fool yelped, but it was too late to react... and unnecessary. The pounce ended not with claws in his face, but with a nimble landing on his shoulder and a purr-y head-butt.

Fool sighed and looked at the Director.

The Director looked at Fool, no change in expression at all. His eyes shifted sideways to the cat, then back to Fool. "Moving on then. I'll read your report later, but what did you find in the Ecological Reserve?"

"Opilione," Fool said. The cat's tail had somehow wound around his neck and was tickling the edge of his nose. He tried to keep a straight face.

"What the hell is that?" the Director said. "Some sort of new alien spawn?"

Fool shook his head, which resulted in a stray cat hair going up his nose and ferociously tickling him. "No. You know, harvestmen? Spiders that aren't really spiders? Scavengers. Mutated. Very big, shoot death rays from their eyes. Only one kind so far, but we ran into a half dozen. They aren't big enough to tackle the Marmots, but they might be feasting on the Fire Elk, or maybe they're getting lucky with the hibernating Marmots." He managed to get all that out before sneezing.

The Director ignored Fool's sneeze, but Fool could almost feel the silent chuckle from Jackal.

"Spiders." The Director leaned back in his chair and looked at the ceiling for a moment. "I was worried about that. We've culled most of the major mammalian threats in the area, so the System was either going to spawn something new and alien or get to mutating insects or arachnids. Ha! I win my bet with Souza. She was leaning toward insects, but I bet that the local mountain climate was more favorable for arachnids. They've always been the dominant species in the area."

"More efficient," Jackal said.

The Director chuckled, then leaned forward and nodded at Jackal. "Exactly! I felt safe with that bet. Thanks to your last paper, I figured that the System would react to our culling of the more aggressive lifeforms not with a new alien species, but with a mutation. I'll split the whisky with you."

Fool tried not to grimace. He really had no idea what they were talking about, but the Director looked to be in a better mood, so he figured now was a good time to keep the topic moving. And away from the cat, who was now purring and actively running its tail under his nose. Clearly trying to coax out another sneeze. Fool did his best to ignore it.

"I heard a rumor about missions?" Fool asked.

"Mm. Meant to ease into that. But yes, thanks to your take from the Prince George job, and a few other team's successes, we were finally able to complete the latest quest. Because of that, we could activate the Foundation's next Ability: a machine to scan for those individuals, like yourselves, who are key to our next steps. Gentlemen, we are now active on Phase One!"

Both Fool and Jackal hissed out a triumphant "Yessss!" with celebratory fist clenching. The Director smiled at their understated enthusiasm.

"We got the machine up and running this morning, and we got our first hit a few hours ago. The first person of interest to us is only a short distance away, in the village of Valemount. You two happen to be free, but I'm also pleased to report that the machine says you're the best team to recruit our target. So you head out tomorrow. In order to keep our usual low profile though, you'll need to make the trip on foot."

They groaned at that. It would have been a pleasant drive on the highway in pre-System times, or even on foot it would have been about a sixteen-hour walk. Two days' walk at a good pace, with some lovely camping overnight. Now? It could be as long as a week, and a hard, hard slog.

The road was mountainous, with steep sections… but worse than that, it ran alongside the Sto:lo, which meant dealing with the creatures that roamed out of the river. At least the lethal threat level was mitigated by the Tete Jaune Cache Fort, which was probably one of the sturdiest forts in the whole Rockies.

It had to be, since it protected all of BC from invasion by the stupid high-Level creatures of Mount Robson Park and Jasper National Park on the other side. The Tete Jaune Cache Fort was home of only the bravest and stupidest and had a massive turnover rate… but those who lasted were Leveling faster than anyone else in North America, on average. It was the grind that true adventurers craved, and the Fort was also showing signs of becoming a premier tourist destination with off-worlders. Word was one of the major Guilds had already bought the Fort, and others were buying up the nearby land. It was likely to hit Town status soon.

If the beasts didn't wipe it out in the next monster horde rush.

Either or.

Fool would be happy to be in and out of the Fort as fast as possible. After that, Jackman Flats had its own issues, but nothing better or worse than any other part of the Cariboo. No idea what to expect in Valemount though. They'd only had sporadic contact with the village since the System arrival. They knew it still existed, and occasional travelers had reported going through it, but the exact situation wasn't something Fool had looked into recently.

In any case, they should expect to be on the road for a week. A long, hard week with more than a bit of a fight all along the way.

"What's the target? What do we know?" he asked.

"The machine is still in the translation process, so we don't have any details until we learn to use it better. But this is our first find, and it's urgent. The individual identified is mid-Level, female, not native to the area…" The Director looked off to the side, his fingers tapping on the desk again. It almost looked as though he was typing, and Fool wondered if it wasn't some sort of Skill the Director was using.

"By our predictions, if we don't find her, she will be dead before two weeks have passed," the Director continued. "The machine predicts that if we can save her and recruit her to our cause, she'll be worth a one percent increase in our chances of succeeding. Small, but on a global scale, that's a tremendous increase for us. For perspective, Fool, you rate an increase with us of about a thousandth of a percent."

"Love you too, Professor X," Fool said.

The Director bolted upright in his chair, fury across his face. "Don't call me that."

Fool grinned, and Jackal stopped the brewing spat by abruptly leaning forward and raising his hand, almost like a referee halting a bout.

"How do we ID her?" Jackal asked.

"We haven't learned how to find that information yet, nor have we learned how to phrase it to the Shop to buy it, so we don't really know. But we were able to generate a sort of compass from the machine, a portable communicator that connects directly to it. You'll be able to use that to get closer to, and eventually identify, your target."

"And what," Fool said, "are you holding back from telling us?"

He didn't see any sign that the Director was holding back information, but somehow, the cat seemed to be trying to tell Fool there was more information. He couldn't really say how he knew that, but there was a sort of urgent pressure. The cat reinforced that with some sudden sharp claw action as soon as he asked the question.

"Nothing." The Director looked a little perplexed.

"Oh. Uh. Sorry. I thought maybe there was more."

"Not that I'm aware of. You should have everything you need to do your job. We'll obviously keep you informed if we find anything new, and the team will work on this through the night just in case they can find out anything more. Do you need anything else, or are you good to go?"

Jackal cleared his throat. "Was there anything odd that's not related that we might want to know?"

The Director smiled. "Well. Not really. It's silly. But… the machine seems to have embraced human archetypes pretty strongly, and it uses them to build metaphors for conversation with us, to describe what it sees. And in this case, well…"

He looked almost shy, but mostly amused, as he continued.

"It says that your job is to rescue the Princess."

"A princess? I mean, maybe a real one?" Jackal asked as he and Fool walked down the hallway.

"It's the System. Anything is possible," Fool said. "I mean, I'm pretty sure Canada doesn't have any hereditary royalty. Outside of you-know-who. But maybe the System does something to reactivate lost hereditary genes? Would that make sense?"

"Hard to say, but I don't think so. We've run across aliens and humans with titles before, but those seem to be System-assigned. Those aren't hereditary, from what I know. Maybe it's a Class?"

"Or they come from Europe? Or hell, maybe it's a metaphor and the machine is being cutesy," Fool said.

"Maybe. Be kinda cool to rescue a princess though. Kind of a childhood dream come true; I have to admit."

Fool glanced at his big friend and smiled. "Yeah, but is this gonna be a Princess Leia kinda rescue, or a dragon-slayer type rescue?"

Jackal chuckled. "Oh nice, Fool. Way to wreck the dream. I'm pretty sure neither of us are up for dragon-slaying just yet, and now I'm imaging some over-powered alien out there with a frikken Death Star."

"Right." Fool rolled his eyes. "That's a thought to fall asleep to, I guess."

"Not without a stiff drink," Jackal said, gently knocking Fool on the shoulder. "Or three."

Fool nodded. "Mess hall is still open. Wanna see if we can fleece any more techs out of their money?"

That got a chuckle out of Jackal. "I think word has spread about the chess thing. Could try Go. Haven't played that with anyone yet."

"Poker?" Fool offered.

"Now that's a possibility," Jackal said. "It's also the one game you can play and sometimes win on luck alone, so maybe you can make some money instead of just me."

"Not my fault I suck at games," Fool said. "I mean, honest games anyway. Not my fault no one else can handle games with some proper spirit to them."

"Cheating," Jackal said. "Not spirit. Cheating."

"Ha. Quibbling details."

Jackal smiled and shook his head. "So... where did the cat go?"

That made Fool stop. The cat had been on his shoulder when they left the Director's office, and he could have sworn until a second ago that it was still on his shoulder. He would have felt it jump off.

"Did you see it go anywhere?" Fool asked.

"Nope. One second it was there, and the next second it wasn't. And to be honest, I don't really remember the last time I saw it on your shoulder. If I think really hard, I remember it being there, but somehow, I don't 'feel' like it's been there."

Fool paused for a moment to think about that. What Jackal said made sense. There was a strange sensation of "feeling" as though the cat hadn't been there for a while, but he could, with effort, dredge up a memory of feeling the claws and weight of the creature shifting on his shoulder moments ago.

On a hunch, he ran his hands over his shoulder, where the cat had been.

Nothing.

"Well, it's not invisible," he said. "At least, not invisible and still on my shoulder."

"You're the expert on this kind of thing. Some kind of illusion or mental manipulation?"

Jackal had a point with that, Fool had to admit. "Maybe, but I don't think so. Something else is going on here. Maybe we should go talk to the Witch?"

"You mean Dr. Edwards? I believe 'Metapsychic Researcher' is her job title, not 'Witch.'"

"Semantics. Same thing," Fool said. "Let's have her run some tests. She'll be able to tell if we've been manipulated."

"Semantics?" Jackal said with only a hint of a smile. "Really? Did you spend a point on Intelligence instead of Strength?"

Fool did his best to look shocked and hurt. "Hell no! Would I lie to you?"

"Nothing. You're both clean, aside from the residual influence you two keep on each other," Dr. Edwards said. "Somehow. Pretty sure that's just you being your weird friend selves with each other though."

Fool stuck out his tongue at her. Despite what he'd told Jackal, he rather liked the older woman. She was a short, roly-poly woman with a long grey ponytail. She was also one of the people who'd embraced the arrival of the System as a justification of her lifetime of research. Edwards had gone from crackpot studying the fringiest of fringe sciences to someone people turned to because she had even the slightest idea of what had been going on.

She'd freely admit that she knew nothing about what had actually happened, that the reality had nothing to do with what she'd been researching. But as she put it, the archetypes tracked. Her theory was that much of human mysticism and "other-worldly" experiences had resulted from long ago contact with System-affected aliens and that had actually primed us at some level to be ready for the arrival of the System. She believed that we'd lost an essential edge when skepticism forced people to turn their backs on things they didn't have the tools to understand.

She'd actually spent a fair bit of time with Fool when he was in the Foundation proper, helping him try to understand his unique Class and Skill set.

When the System had arrived, Fool had been living on the streets for over a decade and was only a barely functional schizophrenic. Or has had been explained to him, not actually a schizophrenic, but someone with a host of psychiatric disorders that had expressed themselves as schizophrenia.

All of which meant that Fool had spent a sizeable chunk of his adult life engaged with hallucinations.

When the System came, it had seemed normal for him to make a contract to be an acolyte of what sounded like a god. Why not? It offered protection and clarity and a chance at a better life, without really asking for much in exchange.

He'd accepted and been rewarded with a massive slap of clarity. Enough to help him and the fellow members of his homeless encampment rally together and survive the first few hours. Well, a larger portion than would have anyway, what with mutated rats, cockroaches, and the occasional fantasy monster choosing to get vicious and hungry.

Normal System Healing and upgrades, and a few more discreet visits to the Shop, had returned Fool to the state of being a competent, socially functioning human being. Sanity... wasn't something he was entirely ready to embrace just yet.

But one essential question had stuck with him, and that same question had intrigued Dr. Edwards. The System had shown them how psychic powers, magic, and advanced science could all coexist... but that still didn't really explain what in the hell the being that had called itself the God of Tricksters really was, and what its connection to Fool really meant.

Edwards's theory was in line with her explanation of everything else. The god was probably an ancient and extremely high-Leveled sentient that had tapped into a level of System integration that was beyond what they could imagine currently. It certainly sounded possible and gave Fool enough of a grounding to move forward until they could learn more. He'd occasionally had nightmares he'd made a pact with some sort of hideous demon, but that was mostly a result of the few years his parents had forced him into Catholic school to get past his learning issues.

Fool looked around Dr. Edwards's lab, half expecting to see the stupid cat again. When he was sure it wasn't around, he asked the question that had been on his mind.

"So… the cat showed up the last time I made a bargain with the Trickster. I figure it's some kind of test, or quest, or something. Any idea what that might be?"

"Nada," she said. "If I had to guess, probably some sort of debt that the Trickster owed someone else? Like a pet-watching service for another acolyte or something? Is that likely?"

"Maybe. No idea. I know that most of my Skills are a 'boon' from the Trickster and fit into different categories… and most of them honestly feel like variations on different kinds of bargains. So it's possible. At least as much as anything else."

"Better keep the cat safe then. Sounds like your god is depending on you. I mean, still a chance it was just some sort of random creature that showed up and connected to you, but as far as I can tell, it's a normal cat."

"Aside from the disappearing thing," Fool said.

"Aside from the disappearing thing." She sighed and walked over to her office chair and sat down. "And the circumstances of how it showed up in your life. Does that sound like the kind of coincidence that would happen, or is it more likely to be direct intervention?"

"Occam's Razor says it's the Trickster getting me to do something. Just wish I knew what." Fool watched the doctor. Was it his imagination, or had she added a little extra sway to her walk? And now she was idly running a hand down her crossed legs, which led Fool to realize she was wearing seamed stockings.

"I bet," she said. "But sorry, that's out of my league. You'll have to work out the whys and whats of that cat on your own. I'm guessing that's the point. All cats are a puzzle, but yours just might be a literal puzzle you have to solve."

Fool sighed. None of this was going to be easy. But what was these days?

"Dinner?" Dr. Edwards asked.

That confused Fool for a moment, because her tone of voice was rather more intimate than he'd have expected.

Then he realized she was looking at Jackal.

And Jackal's smile back at her let Fool know all he needed to know.

As he watched the two of them walk out arm in arm, he noticed that the roly-poly figure of the doctor moved with a rather alluring happiness, so maybe Jackal was a more perceptive person around women than Fool had given him credit for.

He snorted and got up, heading toward the canteen instead of the mess. He knew when to let his friend have some privacy, and besides…

Fool had some research to do. Maybe the library had some books on feline care. Or feline psychiatry? That might be more useful.

Chapter Four

The morning started with a pleasant walk, if a bit tense. The road from the Foundation to McBride ran along the Sto:lo river, and that wasn't a walk to take without care. Fool and Jackal were careful to stay on the side of the road farthest from the river, and even so, they still tended to jump with every errant splash or gurgle.

And there were a lot of them. The spring melt wasn't in full swing yet, and the river was at its lowest winter level. It wasn't frozen anymore, but there were still ice chunks everywhere, and the occasional ice dam. The crackle of noise was almost constant. There was no easier route though. The road hugged the river all the way to McBride. River on one side, mountain and forest on the other. The river was clearly the more dangerous threat, but the line-of-sight benefit provided by the road made it a marginally preferable path to trying to cut through the forest.

They had the advantage of scouting reports from the overnight patrols. They'd reported a clear road all the way into McBride, at least from the mountains. And they had an up-river specialist with tripwires in Lamming Mills, counting anything that might come downstream. No alarms had been triggered, so aside from random spawns, they'd be okay. And those had become more rare as the Mana flows in the area had stabilized in the last while.

So they had no real reason to stay on edge, but they'd become an experienced traveling team on the old roads of British Columbia. Even in safe territory, they weren't going to let their guard drop. If nothing else, it was practice. Best to get the rust off before they hit Yellowhead Highway and all the fun that promised.

"Thalassocracies," Jackal said.

Fool glanced at him and found his companion looking out over the Sto:lo. It reminded Fool of taking road trips in the before times. The best part was always the conversations. And with that single word, Jackal had given notice that he was in the mood to talk.

Which was a treat for a few reasons. To Fool, the most important reason was that it was a little touch of trust that Jackal showed him. For all that Jackal lived up to the stereotype of the taciturn and stoic hero, when he let his guard down, he was almost the complete opposite. But he only let his guard down around people he truly trusted.

That was the reason Fool's heart sprang a little with that word. The other was that Jackal always had something interesting to say.

Fool had always considered himself smart when he was younger. Read a lot, studied all the time, could run circles around his teachers and classmates. But Jackal was on a whole other level. At least Fool knew what Jackal was talking about. Thalassocracies were governments by oceans. It was a term used in some circles to describe countries like Portugal and Spain when they were at their peaks. And the Nordic countries... Vikings.

"All right," Fool said. "This should be good. What's that got to do with a frozen river?"

"Nothing," Jackal said. "It's an interesting context though. The System ripped our world apart, but the actual issue long term is the rest of the galaxy, right? They've got the power, and we've got nothing to stop them from exploiting us. Eventually, the Earth just gets chopped up into pieces and what's left of our civilizations fades into the history books as we become a glorified Mana-mall for the rest of the universe."

"That's the plan. And that's what the Foundation is trying to stop. So what's this got to do with seafaring nations?"

"I think it's a bit of weakness. Like, the aliens we've run across already have come in and set up strongholds. It's akin to the Portuguese *feitorias* that they used to set up throughout Africa and Asia. Little fortress factories for processing local goods and projecting power and influence. They've got the whole universe and what amounts to a massive tech advantage over us. Near-instant, or super-fast, travel. And communication at the same speed. Can't beat that, right?"

"Gotcha, it's like the Viking raids in Britain," Fool said. "You can't see where they're coming from, so when they show up, it tends to be in overwhelming force for the local area. Can't chase 'em down and keep them from raiding unless you spread out your army or invent something new to travel or communicate."

"Right. But with commerce and politics instead of raiding. Mostly. Some alien overlord has the funds, they buy your area through the System, and suddenly you have a new boss and have to live under their rules. That's the whole world, right? But it's not absolute control. Same weakness as the thalassocracies had. You can only control what you can easily reach. They set up towns and cities and Shops, build walls for safety all around it, but they don't really control the land between. The System puts a hard brake on projection of political power. In this case, you can only extend power to the reach of your gun. Granted, they have big guns, but it leaves holes for us mice."

"The river. Gotcha. Rivers used to be used for good transport. Fast and cheap. BC was built along the rivers, so that makes sense. But rivers aren't passable anymore, if you're thinking about 'River Power' and going all Atriedes on everyone."

Jackal smiled as he stepped over a snowdrift. "No, not… not yet, anyway. But I can see why the Foundation chose this area to build in. This whole area has been historically a bit of a forgotten area, even though we have this big, wide river. Why is that?"

"Because it's a dead-end branch of the main river?" Fool said, kicking a hole in the snowdrift as he walked through it.

"Source, not dead end. But basically, yeah. Most of the use of the river that we know about really starts much farther away. Probably because it's nothing but oxbows from here til it turns south again. But from Prince George down, there's a reason the highways follow it. It's not just because it's the flat land. It's the path of trade. And the System doesn't work so well at that level… at least not the sentients using it currently. They stick to the faster and more modern travel methods."

"Not something we can beat with rivers," Fool said. "I gotta admit, I'm not really seeing how this can be an advantage for us."

Jackal walked with a jaunt, skipping past some of the larger snowdrifts. Fool got the idea he was practicing some of his combat footwork. The idea was solidified when Jackal jumped the next drift at an angle, then did a spin and looked back over his shoulder at Fool.

"Me neither," Jackal said. "It's just a thought right now. But it explains why the Foundation set up shop here. There isn't a hell of a lot to attract attention along this part of the river. Just enough residual civilization to explain our presence, but nothing worth someone coming to fight for it, now that it's properly owned. And if we can build an economic flow along the river, that'll let us spread and get some control right under the nose of the System. Maybe. If the Foundation is that ambitious."

When Jackal turned to face forward again, Fool scooped up a handful of snow and kept the conversation going. "Ambitious, yes. Not sure about the timeline though."

Jackal nodded. "I assume they aren't going for the Asimov 'thousand-year' timeframe? Have you heard anything concrete about that?"

"Not really," Fool said. The snow was just the right amount of wet and was packing easily into a nice ball. "But from the little snooping I've done, they do plan on laying low and watching things fall apart for a bit, so yeah... your theory checks out on that."

"Hide out and preserve what we can. Thus the Princess."

Fool nodded as he paid more attention to Jackal's steps. "Thus the Princess."

"Got a plan for rescuing her yet?"

"Ha!" Fool reflexively tucked the snowball behind his back at the slight emphasis Jackal had put on *plan*. "Not really. I mean... the usual? Head into town, act like Adventurers looking for adventure, either lie low or cause some shit depending on what seems to make sense and wing it from there."

"That's the usual, all right. Got an escape plan in mind? I mean, we're looking at walking back this way with a Princess. If she's a literal princess... shit, what does that mean?" Jackal stopped and turned back to look at Fool. "Are we kidnapping a child? I didn't sign up for that."

Fool dropped his head back with a loud sigh and looked at the clouds. "Really? C'mon, this is why I said we'd wing it. If she's a kid, we'll scope out the family, take them with us. No guarantees of any kid being with their birth family these days though. They might not be the best of people. We'll cross that bridge when we get to it."

Jackal turned around and walked again. "Good point. But I'm not seeing a kid making the trip back on foot. Or, just spitballing here, if it's an elderly princess type. I mean, age wasn't mentioned."

Fool tried not to let himself focus too much on the back of Jackal's head. "Steal a car, I guess? Got money to buy one? I'm pretty sure Valemount has a Shop. If not, I've heard that Tete Jaune Cache has one now. Might not be able to access it though. That offworld Guild is rumored to own the place, and they might have rules about that."

"Right. So. Wing it. The usual."

"Yup."

"Just the way you like it."

"Yup." Fool was grinning. It wasn't that he enjoyed being in danger or was any kind of adrenaline junkie. He just really liked to solve these kinds of puzzles. Especially if he wound up looking like the good guy. Always a good outcome. He cocked his arm back. The snowball was ready...

"Hey," Jackal said.

Fool froze his arm in place. "What?"

"What'd you do with the cat?"

"Ugh. Talked one of Edwards's students into taking care of it while we're away. Said they could try running some experiments on it." This was his chance. He'd picked up Jackal's rhythm, but he knew Jackal's Perception would probably pick up his attempt, so it was time for the distraction. "And what's the deal with Edwards anyway? You showed up looking a little tired this morning."

One more step, and he started the pitch...

"Did you know she used to be a world-class fencer? Incredible legs."

Fool faltered and the snowball flailed off to the side, not even making a splash as it plopped into the bank of the river. "*Dude.* She's old enough to be your grandmother!"

Jackal didn't even stop. "All ladies need love, Fool. And nobody really sees themselves the way they look on the outside. You want to be happy? Try to see how people see themselves at their best on the inside and treat them like they look like that. Trust me. Some amazing lovers out there, and people look right past them."

He should have expected that. Jackal's background gave him a lot more insight into people than Fool expected from most people. Fool had to admit that he didn't think of himself as being his age either. He didn't mind the grey hair when he saw it in the mirror, but in his mind, he was still the fresh, capable youth of his early days. The aged body was a shell that felt like a poorly fitting coat. He kept expecting he could take it off some day.

Jackal, of all people, could probably see what was behind that coat more than anyone.

"Fair point. I'll keep it in mind." Still, Fool wasn't sure if he was quite ready to be that open-minded. He just had certain… preferences. A kind of look he was just a sucker for. Couldn't see that really changing.

But three years ago, he couldn't have seen himself being an Acolyte to a Trickster god, so who knew what the future would bring? He had no problem admitting to himself that he wouldn't mind being as happy as Jackal always seemed to be.

It only took them an hour to reach Koeneman Park. At the guard station on the bridge leading back into McBride, they spent a little time chatting with the guards, seeing if anything had changed since last time they were in town. Nothing had, and once they were sure no one else was on the road or approaching from either side, the guards let them into the underground part of the station.

There, Fool and Jackal changed into their proper adventurer gear.

For Jackal, it was his usual Renn-Faire-inspired outfit. All leather and ruffles, with the near-swashbuckler hat and cloak, a long rapier at his side, and a buckler balancing it out on the other. And some knee-high biker boots. Bit of a contrast normally, but Fool had to admit that Jackal could pull off the look. On anyone else, it might have looked silly, but Jackal had the looks and demeanor to make it look all Aragorn. Rough and tumble pretty. With an extra dose of tough guy.

Fool had on his favorite outfit, shiny and gold, with a million pockets, and loaded it with every gadget he could get his hands on. He liked to be conspicuous. It made it easier to disappear when he took it off. He threw a big parka over top, and oversized mukluks with Vibram soles. The warmth wasn't needed. His outfit, like Jackal's, had been System-enhanced in the Shop to keep him comfortable in almost all weather. He liked the look though. Snow season was over, but it was still on the ground, and he wanted to feel cozy.

The final touch was a prepared pack for each of them, full of travel essentials. They could use their inventory for gear, but the road south was true wilderness even before the System, and now? If they made it, they'd need their inventory for loot.

They each took from the packs the special wallet that was included with each mission. It had complex locks on it, but even so, it went into inventory. When opened, it gave them each access to a stash of funds. Emergencies only, of course. And while Fool might have been tempted to stretch the definition of "emergency" from time to time, that he'd had to raise some of those funds himself kept him from being too frivolous.

Usually.

Most of the time.

Okay, some of the time.

They gave each other a quick once-over, double-checking everything out of hard-won habits. Once they'd confirmed it was all in place, they climbed back up out of the underground room, waved goodbye to the guards, and set off south, down the Yellowhead Highway to Valemount.

They'd rough it overnight, camping in a potentially-still-intact safe-ish spot, and the next day they'd hit the fort in Dunster, which was maintained by Foundation folks in the guise of Good Samaritans from McBride, doing their civic duty to keep the road as open as possible.

The stretch after that would be sketchy… the hardest part of the trip. After Dunster, the mountains pressed closer, and the road got pretty rough. The walking wouldn't be as easy, and they could expect many attacks. There was still trade along the road, but only sporadically and usually via heavily armed convoy. Individual travelers were not often foolhardy enough to make the trip.

But the worst would be when they got to Tete Jaune Cache. There was an oversized fort there and for good reason. The highway split there. In the before times, it had been a beautiful, scenic drive through the mountains to Alberta. Now? Mount Robson and Jasper Park were combined into a zone of alpine madness, home of the fiercest and most high-Level monsters. The Fort was the only thing keeping Valemount and area from being completely overrun.

Some wag had named it "Beau Geste," but Fool figured Fort Zinderneuf would have been better. Or even "Fort Whisky" because it did seem to be constantly on the verge of being overrun by bugs. Or wyverns. Or trolls or demons or whatever had bred in sufficient numbers up in the park.

The Foundation had tried to hold it, briefly, with folks from Valemount, but the turnover rate had been unsustainable. They'd used quests to man it, then hired mercenary companies, but the cost was crippling. It made sense to sell it off to a Guild. The right off-planet group was probably more than happy to farm the critters that came down the pass and could provide people of high enough Level to survive the experience.

Meeting them would be interesting. Hopefully, Fool and Jackal would be able to rest and recharge at the Fort. If they couldn't, the Foundation had hidden a number of caches along the route, so they'd have supplies if they needed.

The fun part would be surviving to get there.

At least, once they were past the Fort, the road to Valemount shouldn't be too bad.

Fool woke early with a start. For a moment, he was frozen in fear, struck with the dread thought that something was outside, that a random noise had awoken him. But as his head cleared, he remembered the dream.

A flash of his old life, memories of fleeting happiness. A home, a job, a car... big paychecks and the warm joy of waking up next to a loving wife.

That had jolted him awake. The sweet, calming relaxation. He shuddered at the recollection. Waking up had been a mercy.

He might have been okay. The dream might have veered away into a direction different than memory. That wasn't a chance he wanted to take though.

He rolled his shoulders and blinked rapidly the way he'd been taught, trying to clear his head. The memory was fine, but how long until the history of reality pressed against him from his subconscious? The thought of being helplessly asleep and having to recall how his life had etched itself into acid lumps of destruction was enough, even awake, to banish all thoughts of sleep from his mind.

Jackal was still asleep, and Fool wasn't worried about that. Jackal would sleep through all of Fool's personal attacks, leaving him his privacy. At least he faked it well enough. He'd be the first awake if there was an actual problem though. They'd had that happen often enough, especially before they were able to acquire camping gear that let them sleep through the night. Fool really didn't miss having to take turns keeping watch through the night.

Although they would, as they got closer to Tete Jaune Cache. The gear the Foundation had provided them with was loaded with sophisticated alarms, but the threat level as they got closer would be too high to trust any device.

Clearly, Fool wasn't going to be getting any more sleep tonight. Besides, the tent walls were already starting to lighten, so sunrise was probably soon.

He'd always hated to sleep with his clothes on. It was even worse now. It made him feel as though he was roughing it on the street again, crashing when and where he could. But the System had a knack for late-night surprises, so on the road, he'd learned to compromise by stripping off his shirt and rolling his overalls down to his waist. The shirt would go under his pillow, and he had no problem fishing that out now and slipping it back on. Sitting up also reminded him that his bladder clock would have woken him up soon, if his errant mind hadn't.

Slip-on, instant-fasten boots were his favorite purchase from the Shop, and he relished the joy of not having to do up laces on the floor of a tent with a full bladder.

A moment later, he was outside. It was a clear day, brisk and cold, but not as cold as yesterday. For a moment, Fool imagined he could smell the lazy heat of summer on the wind. He looked about, and the perimeter was undisturbed. The snow all around their makeshift campsite only showed their own footprints, and nothing else could be seen as far as the eye could see.

He glanced up again, as he had on leaving the tent, but the skies were also clear. Good enough. He stumbled out of the campsite, the pleasurable cronking crunch of the snow under his feet drifting through lonely mountain air as he walked away to empty himself.

Sweet relief. Fool leaned back, looking at the sky and the flicker of stars still showing.

And then his stream stopped. He froze. In a sudden, sure sensation that something was watching him.

Carefully, slowly, he titled his head back down. Nothing was visible. No creature, no person, no glowing eyes. The world was silent, not even the sound of tiny birds or night flyers looking for the day's rest.

That was odd. The change from night to day was usually noisy and busy as the shift of creatures switched around. He steadied himself and tried to narrow down where the feeling was coming from.

Behind.

It was behind him.

Slowly, carefully, he zipped up. Turned around.

Nothing.

They were on the side of the highway. It hadn't been plowed since before the last snowfall, when the last convoy had returned back to Valemount. But the last snowfall had been light, just enough to reveal any footprints. And there were none other than theirs.

The tree line on the opposite side didn't show anything, and... the watcher didn't feel that close, now that he looked.

But he was clearly being watched. All the hairs on his back and arms lifted, and his gut suddenly felt hollow. Something big. Something scary. Something that was sharing the valley with them and knew where they were. Whatever it was, it was far up the mountain. Didn't mean much, because these days, big things could move fast.

Fool reached out with his Talent Scout Skill. Sometimes he could get a read on people out of sight using that, but usually only if he'd already been tracking them and if they were within range.

Nothing. He made a mental note to reconsider upgrading that Skill later.

Then the feeling of being watched disappeared.

Gone, in an instant.

It left Fool suddenly feeling awkward and a bit silly. And his bladder reminded him it was still in need of emptying.

He knew the feeling hadn't been in his head, but the sudden change made him feel as though he'd been overreacting. He turned back and finished his business with only a small part of his mind still on his surroundings.

He heard Jackal stirring, so he knew the feeling hadn't just been in his mind, and now he'd have someone watching his back. A fresh surge came from his bladder as he relaxed even more.

A few moments later, Fool was setting up for their breakfast, and Jackal stomped over to the same place Fool had been, to do a repeat act.

"Any idea?" Fool asked.

"Was hoping you'd seen something. Felt big. Figured it was something flying overhead, or you'd have yelled out."

"Nothing. Seemed to be up the mountain though. Ways away."

"Maybe later today then?"

"Maybe. Dunno. We'll be at Dunster Fort soon enough. Can see if they've been noticing anything. Hope it's not something new."

"I haven't heard of anything new in the area, but Mount Robson Park has been seeing a lot of action. Heard a rumor of a Mountain Giant, maybe a Dragon of some kind. If it's big and bad enough, might be scaring some of the local wildlife out of range."

"Fuuuuuuuck. That's a lovely thought. Let's hope not."

The park had been home to some rather frightening beasts—one of the reasons that no one was surprised a Guild had bought Tete Jaune Cache.

The surviving locals from Tete Jaune had Leveled up fast and fierce in response to the beasts that came down from the mountains, but they were more than even rapid Leveling could deal with. And those had only been the comparatively lower-Level creatures.

Rumor was that the sky around Tete Jaune Cache was often filled with roars and thunderous crashing, even though the park proper was more than a day's walk away. Not a place either Fool or Jackal wanted to go. Nor did they want to tangle with a creature that could only be driven away by such titanic battles.

With luck, they'd reach Dunster Fort with no problems and they'd find out more information there. Hopefully, they'd never run across their unseen watcher.

Suddenly, Fool was wishing he had put more points in Luck.

Chapter Five

The Fort itself wasn't in what was left of Dunster. Thankfully. The former almost-a-village was a barely standing collection of empty buildings now. They'd drawn the short straw with the arrival of the System and the community had vanished within a day, and not in a pleasant way. Fool had started to skim the reports from the first expedition to the area that the Foundation sent, but he'd stopped after the first paragraph. Details were not a thing he cared to know, not for that level of human suffering. It had happened, they were all gone, and he was happy to let their souls have some peace in rest.

The Fort itself sat at the intersection of Yellowhead Highway and the road leading down to the former community. In the before times, it had been the site of a summer farmer's market. It was hard to imagine what the area would be like in the summer, but Fool looked around and tried to.

Like the rest of the valley, the area was, on its own merits, beautiful. The Rockies on the left, the Cariboo on the right. Fool couldn't quite see the highest peaks from this low in the valley, but the mountain ranges rose with a presence on both sides, giant walls sloping down to the valley floor with a dramatic presence.

From Fool's viewpoint near the Fort, nestled up on the Rocky Mountain side, the valley was broad and full of promise. He could look down the length of it and see the end of the valley, where it split off into three new mountain ranges: the Purcells, the Monashees, and the Selkirks. They started to split just past Fool and Jackal's destination, Valemount.

The Fort itself was passingly impressive, if small. Somewhere hidden in it was the original building, which might have been a gas station or something. It was hard to tell, as it had been rebuilt into a much more "modern" style fort. It sprawled over the highway, with gated entrances and fences controlling traffic, and mean-looking turrets on the corners. There was a watchtower on one side, and Fool waved at the watching sentry, who nodded back.

They'd signaled the Fort when they first caught sight of it. The Foundation had sent word ahead, but you never knew. Didn't want to be shot out of hand.

Also, it was the first chance for the Fort to warn them off if there was any reason for them not to approach. Either unexpected visitors or monsters attacking. With no problems in the area, the Fort opened a small sally-port on the gate's side for Fool and Jackal, and one of the Fort residents waved them in.

A few minutes later, they were sitting in the Fort's lunchroom with bowls of hot chickpea curry in front of them and a pile of samosas in the middle of the table. Fool was left to do all the talking, because Jackal was busy stuffing his face.

Channa masala was Jackal's comfort food, and no one in McBride offered it. One of the Fort residents had been a local who'd brought his surviving grandmother with him, and she spent her time cooking for everyone. Fool wasn't entirely sure that Jackal hadn't agreed to this job just for the excuse to eat her cooking.

"We haven't seen anything," Balvinder said. She was the boss of the Fort, and she reinforced that impression by leaning against the wall and watching them eat. "But yeah, we've been feeling the presence of something stalking the area the last few days."

"So no threats?" Fool asked.

Balvinder shook her head and crossed her arms. "Wouldn't say that. Just no threats we think are related to that presence. But yes." She was looking off to the side, clearly thinking. She let out a little sigh. "There's been a bit of a migration lately, so you want to keep your eyes open until you get to Tete Jaune."

Fool caught the subtext. "Oof. That sounds lovely. Flame Elk or something more fun?"

"I wish. I've been craving elk meat lately. No, bit worse than that. Spiders."

"Ah. Shit. Yeah, we thought that might be happening. Theory was that spiders would be the next wave of mutations to try to fill in the ecological gaps. We tussled with some giant harvestmen up in the Sunbeam Reserve couple of days ago. Have they made it down here already? Or did they come from here?"

"Huh. Haven't seen those yet. No, two species you want to look out for. Jumping spiders and ones that look like giant black widows, but I've been told they aren't. Still. Creepy shits." She shivered. "The jumpers are big. Car-sized. They seem to be opportunistic hunters. They won't hunt you down, but if you see you and you aren't too far away, they'll pounce."

She got a little animated at that and leaned forward off of the wall, using her hands to mimic something pouncing. It was absolutely adorable. She had quite the twinkle in her eyes too.

"And they can jump a long way," she continued. "If you see one, don't wait to see what it's doing. Run and find cover. If they land and can't see you, they'll go off looking for something slower. Much better than trying to fight them. Tough, tough spiders. No real weakness, just gotta wear 'em down. No special attacks other than the jump either."

"We can deal with that. Hiding's my middle name," Fool said.

"I've heard that about you."

Balvinder gave Fool a look, and he wasn't quite sure how to interpret it. The twinkle seemed deeper, and he felt himself blushing. Mostly, his reputation within the Foundation was good, but some people seemed to be very offended by everything he did. He had no idea why.

Her look was more... intrigued. Well. She was pretty enough, if you went for very large and strong women. Which Fool did.

"Hope you've heard good things," he said. And he couldn't help it. He added the smile.

Fool had spent a lot of points on Charisma. It just made life easier, especially when you spent most of your time trying to convince people that you were all that. At the same time, he'd always been careful not to take advantage of his attractiveness.

He'd always been on the good side of looking, but he'd had enough heartbreak to know it sucked, and he preferred not to be the cause of it. But he'd been spending time learning to be charming without overwhelming, and he'd practiced just the right smile for when he wanted to be seen as a nice person.

"I've heard a lot of things about you, Fool," she said. "Some of it's been good. Some."

Fool found himself blushing a little. She seemed to have some hidden depths herself. He found himself wondering if he could spin up a reason to spend the night at the Fort, but Jackal delicately kicked Fool in the ankle with the point of his pointy boot, so he changed the subject.

"Uh… spiders? Another kind?"

Balvinder smiled. "Yup. The widows. False widows apparently, if you care. They've been building webs all over the place. Keep away. Odd ducks, these ones. Not that big, maybe dog-sized, and you can walk right by them, and they won't care. But sit down, turn your back on them, pause anywhere near the nest? That's the end of you, unless you have very high poison resistance.

"The weird part though? The last patrol swears the spiders were trying to talk to them. But they couldn't hear anything, if that makes sense. Still, they said they could hear what almost sounded like voices in their heads."

"Oh. Lovely. Psychic spiders. That sounds… interesting."

"We've already sent word to the Foundation to send some experts down to check them out. See if it's some sort of Fascination power that's not working right on humans, or if it's something else. In either case, best to get past them if you see them, but from what we've seen so far, no real need to attack them unless they're in a place you need to rest in."

"Fair enough. Nothing else?"

"Not so far. Honestly, if you can avoid the spiders, you've got a clear path to Tete Jaune. If you leave right away, you'll make it there before dinner tomorrow. The roads are a bit more clear. That new Guild has been a lot more proactive about patrolling and keeping lines of communication open."

"Right, new Guild. We've been hearing rumours. Any idea who they are?"

"Mountaineers Guild. Seem like good enough folks. And by that, I mean they don't seem to give two shits about us, once they'd checked out the area. Fun mix of folks though. All kinds of aliens. Woulda loved that a few years ago. Used to dream about making alien contact." She leaned back and laughed, and Fool found himself smiling along with her.

The world really had changed.

And maybe… they could leave a few hours later? Just long enough to maybe talk Balvinder into showing him around some of the more secluded parts of the Fort? Maybe her room or a forgotten storage area?

"You suck, Jackal," Fool said.

"Sure. You'll thank me when we're cozy at Tete Jaune Cache for dinner tomorrow. I'm not keen, and I don't think you are either, to spend any more nights in the open than we have to, not with whatever it is out there. And we're sleeping in shifts tonight."

Fool wanted to argue with that, but he really couldn't. The best thing they could do was get back on the road as soon as possible. And as much as an overnight stay at Fort Dunster had been showing the potential of being more than a little interesting, getting to Tete Jaune Cache quickly was a higher priority. If the System, or something, was pushing new monsters into the area, it wasn't going to go away. The System didn't reward passivity. So there they were, on the road again right after eating.

Still, Fool let out a huff, for the principle if nothing else. "Right, agreed, but we couldn't wait one hour? Or two?"

"Dude. C'mon," Jackal said. "You really aren't pining for your lost soulmate in McBride much, are you?"

That hit a nerve, and Fool found himself sputtering out a reply. "I never even asked her out and you told me she found someone else, so why are making this so hard for me?"

It was true, he'd never asked out the waitress in McBride. He'd never really spoken to her, aside from the occasional small talk when they ordered food. But nonetheless, Fool had developed a crush on her, which Jackal had called him on. Fool had to admit though—he'd have nursed that crush for as long as he could have gotten away with it. Years, probably. And never said a word to her.

Hopeless crush. Just the way he liked them. And Jackal knew how much harm Fool did to himself with that, so he'd been making a point of getting Fool to be better.

Fool let out a sigh. "Dammit, she was so pretty."

Jackal stopped, turned, and looked at Fool. "You know you do this once a week, right?"

It took an effort of will for Fool to not cross his arms and pout. "Now you're exaggerating."

"I am, but I made my point, didn't I?" Jackal didn't wait for a reply before starting back on crunching through the snow toward Tete Jaune Cache.

Fool didn't dignify that with a response. He told himself that he could have, but he needed to keep his wits about him looking for the Jumping Spiders. He didn't think they'd be that hard to spot, but apparently, they were black and white, which made for damned good winter camouflage against the snow. Higher in the mountains, the evergreens would make them stand out a bit more, but down in the valley, the trees had a higher percentage of aspens, and the barren winter trunks were almost tailor-made to hide black-and-white critters.

They'd been walking for hours and hadn't seen anything yet though. Fool was just starting to feel optimistic when Jackal cleared his throat.

"How big did she say those spiders were?" Jackal asked.

"Car-size. Why?"

"You ever see a car that big?"

Fool spun to look where Jackal was pointing. About fifty meters away, nestled up against a stand of fir trees, was the cutest looking tank-sized spider Fool had ever seen. Its gigantic eyes were looking right at them, like big sad puppy dog eyes. Big sad murder-puppy dog eyes.

"Shit," Fool said.

"No cover. Plan?"

Fool took a quick look around. Like most of the highways in the BC interior, the Yellowhead was raised on a bank that ran through the scenery. That gave him a thought, but there was no time to think it through, because the butt-wiggle the spider was doing was clearly a sign that it was about to jump at them.

"Over the side!" Fool yelled and sprinted for the edge of the road without waiting to see if Jackal was following. He was hoping there was a culvert at the bottom, and they could hide in that.

As he slid down the snow, Fool saw he was almost right. There was a culvert about a half-kilometer up the road. No way to make that in time. During the slide down, he'd unclipped his warhammer from his belt and hefted it in both hands, looking back up the slope.

Jackal came barreling over the side. Not a second too soon.

The spider landed with an enormous explosion of snow and the tearing sound of metal as the guardrails on the highway gave way under the impact of the beast. The spider skittered for a moment, and Fool had a vision of it tumbling down on him and crushing him with its weight.

Or not. He had a crazy moment of wondering what the impact capacity of his armor was and whether it could handle a falling bus-sized spider. He was about to pull up a menu to check before he caught himself.

Jackal slid to a stop next to Fool, and they both watched the spider.

It wasn't jumping right away. It was still, but clearly looking down at them. Two figures against a white backdrop… that was it, Fool realized. The white snow background was probably making the spider pause while it tried to accurately judge the distance to them…

It didn't pause long. Fool didn't even see it jump; it was so fast.

Fortunately for him, it was aiming at Jackal. Fool only took an incidental blow from one of the legs, but that was enough to send him spinning away. It was one of those weird combat moments when he wasn't really aware of what was happening. He just found himself suddenly looking at a totally different view. His armor lit up with damage notifications, but it still held.

Jackal was screaming something, and the Spider had him in its jaws. It looked as if one fang was all the way through Jackal already and the other was working its way in, while Jackal tried to slash it away with his twin swords.

Fool bit down on the flash of rage that filled him when he saw that. Jackal could handle it. And if he couldn't, Fool leaping in like the fighter he wasn't would do more harm than good. Instead, he reached for his Skills.

The spider had Buffs for Speed and Armor Penetration.

75

That gave Fool the opening he needed, and he quickly Debuffed the Armor Penetration. And then, despite himself, he sprinted forward.

The brief confusion of not being able to stab through Jackal's defenses caused the spider to pause long enough for Fool to Debuff its Speed. He then leapt in with his hammer and tried to cause enough damage to distract it.

Everything shifted, the world spinning around him.

Then everything was white.

It took Fool a half-breath to realize what had happened. He was face down in the snow. The spider must have batted him aside, even with its Speed removed.

Fool groaned and rose. He knew better than to shake his head to clear it, but the temptation was fierce. Instead, he took a deep breath and clenched his hammer to help him focus. He'd once again earned his moniker.

The battle was still going on. He couldn't have been down for more than a few seconds.

Jackal had somehow freed himself, but the spider had knocked him onto his back and was about to stab down again with its fangs—fang. As Fool watched, Jackal, with a burst of Speed and Gymnastics, spun about and lopped off one fang.

Fool hit the beast with another rapid Debuff, alternating between removing the Speed and Armor Penetration. At his Level, they didn't last long, but he couldn't think of anything else to use his Mana on. He longed to get in and be of more help to Jackal, but that wasn't his strength. Fool wasn't built for this kind of combat, but taking away some of the spider's advantages should let Jackal get the upper hand.

"Keep going! You're knocking down its Health! Not much more to go," Fool shouted. Jackal didn't need the morale boost, but Fool used his Show Must Go On Skill to give that to him anyway.

The spider was slowing down, so Fool darted in and landed shots when he could. He didn't have the raw power or exceptional Skills of Jackal, but his Perception and other Skills gave him a knack for diving in at the right time to drop some hammer-weight onto the beast.

Fool giggled a bit as they wore down the spider. He was starting to see why Jackal specialized in this. There was a certain kind of gross, physical joy in combat. The kinetic sway of the body, the thrumming crack his hammer made on impact, even the sound of his breath gasping inside his helmet. And there was a degree of mental game as well. Judging the timing of shots, darting in and out… it was almost fun. If the fear of death didn't overwhelm all of that.

Jackal finally landed the killing blow. He'd made his way up to the back of the spider and, with luck, managed to find the heart of the beast. He stuffed both swords into it, backed up with all of his extra damage Skills.

Fool almost lost it when the spider died. He'd been expecting the traditional fall down or roll over, and instead the damned thing appeared to get taller for a moment. Fool was steeling himself for some sort of notification about an undead spider or a new spawn or something, when the creature toppled over. It had risen because its legs had contracted. They had eventually pulled all the way in, at which point the beast finally flipped over.

Fool laughed. The classic dead spider look, all curled up on its back. It was absurd, given the size of the thing.

Jackal watched him laugh for a moment then looked at the dead spider and chuckled. Then he set about looting it. After a moment, Fool sat down and made repairs to himself and his armor.

"That was fun. You okay?" Fool said.

"Better than I looked, I'm sure."

"Kinda looked like you got bit clean through."

Jackal looked at Fool, and he had the grin of a kid on Christmas morning. "I thought for sure I was a goner! If it hadn't been for the new Skill, I might have been too."

"I forgot! Invulnerability. So what did I see?"

"Went through the armor and gear. Must have looked bad from your point of view. But not a scratch on me... at least not from that attack. Wore off pretty quick. The recharge is going to be killer. I have to watch that in the future. Saved my bacon though, for sure. How you doing?"

"Bit of a concussion from being batted about, lost some Health even through my armor, and my armor's going to need a day to regenerate, at least. Let's not run into any more of those things."

"You sure? Nice bit of experience, and the loot's looking pretty rare. Bet we get a pretty penny for this!"

Fool shook his head. And then regretted it.

The concussion would heal faster than before the System, but he was still in for a headache for another ten minutes. He had no idea how Jackal seemed to relish this kind of risk. Fool loved risk too, but the risk of pulling off the perfect scam on some deserving knob or walking away with something you got for a usurious bargain... or for free. Or a stolen kiss that came with a pleasant blush.

That was worth anything.

Nearly getting pulped by a spider, by an attack that was little more to it than brushing off a flea? Not Fool's idea of fun. He rolled his shoulders but didn't hear the creaking of bones he expected.

He couldn't see anything down the road at least.

"Let's rest for a bit," Fool said, "then push on, yeah? I figure this fella was big enough to eat anything else in the area, so we should be good to rest a bit here. Kinda tempted to push on through the night though. Gotta admit, not a fan of walking through the territory of more of these things."

Jackal nodded and fingered the gaping hole in his armor. "Could do. We can make it through the night for sure, and the snowpack gives us more light to see by. As long as we stick to the road, we should be okay."

He stopped to struggle out of his armor, and Fool sat on a nearby rock. He was going to help, but Jackal found the latch he was looking for and shrugged off the damaged breastplate.

Jackal kept talking while he pulled out a repair kit. "It's going to be harder to see these things in the night. Black and white against snow? Nighttime with less color contrast? Might be better to find a hidey-hole to spend the night in is my guess."

Fool nodded. He'd been thinking the same thing himself. Pushing on through the night wasn't making sense anymore. "Fair enough. We should get moving pretty quick then. I suspect if those other spiders are around, they'll be taking up residence in all the good hiding spots. Jumping spiders hunt other spiders, so any hiding spot that's good for us is also going to be good for them."

"Lovely." Jackal slapped the repair patch on his armor. "Shall we get moving then?"

Fool took one last look around. It looked safe enough, but he hadn't seen anything before the giant spider had suddenly appeared either. And being below the highway was creeping him out. Who knew what was on the other side, or waltzing down the road? "I think that might be a safer bet than still being on the road come nightfall."

By the time they found a good spot to tuck up for the night, it was far into dusk. As Fool had been afraid of, the other spiders they'd been warned about were more prolific as they got farther down the road. At least they weren't aggressive.

They hadn't gotten close to any of the webs, just to be sure. Not that either of them were in any mood to get that close. Neither of them were arachnophobes, but there was something heart-stoppingly unpleasant about the web-building spiders.

The False Widows looked oil-drop black in daylight, but they had distinct patterns across their abdomens. Spots, stripes, one even had what looked like snowflakes patterned on it. It was hard to describe a spider as beautiful, but these came close. They were, somehow, more disturbing than the Opiliones or Jumpers, probably because they looked more like a normal house spider, but at a size that was more jarring.

Had they been larger, like the jumpers, they might have flipped over into a sense of unreality. But being sized somewhere between a large cat and a dog? That just triggered something in the spine.

They seemed a bit social as well. Fool and Jackal never ran across more than one in a web, but more than a few stretches of forest featured clusters of webs, the shiny black bodies populating them. And the occasional web featured a webbed-up bundle of something larger than the resident spider, which spoke well of the efficiency of their poison.

Fool had run one check on the False Widows to see what Abilities they had. They had Enhanced Poison, Heightened Senses through the web, a hypnotic Ability with the patterns on their back. That was all somewhat expected. The resistance to psychic attacks and other manipulations was surprising. It was either randomly assigned by the System on mutation, or something in the evolution of those spiders had made them need that.

The oddest thing of all was that when he ran his check on the first spider he saw, it had quivered in its web and adjusted its facing. Fool could have sworn it was watching him, and that kept him looking over his shoulder for the rest of the day.

They set up camp in a culvert under the highway, free of any spiders they could see, and packed up snow on either end to keep up the illusion. They left air-holes in each pile. Their System-purchased camping gear was supposed to work even in low-oxygen and low-pressure environments, but they didn't want to test that.

They ate a quick meal then went to bed, intending to rise early and push on through to Tete Jaune Cache to reach the Fort before lunch. With the snow packed around them, they decided it was worth the extra rest not to take turns on watch through the night.

The voice woke them just before dawn, whispering in both their ears.

Chapter Six

It was, as Fool had feared, one of the False Widows. Neither he nor Jackal doubted it. Mostly because the voice they heard was clearly in their minds, and somehow… it tasted like a spider. It said only two words, but they came with a sudden, hard impact and an overwhelming sense of urgency.

*Wake **up***

Neither of them said anything, but they dressed and armored up as fast as they could. Fool made sure his warhammer was hooked to his belt, but he also pulled his rifle from storage. And a few pistols with their associated holsters, which he added to the specially made connectors on his jumpsuit. Plus a few grenades for extra fun. The sense of threat was growing.

Jackal had his spear in hand, and that was probably enough for him. He also had that nice Ability to pull out weapons at need in mid-combat, so he was covered.

"Shall we?" Fool asked.

Jackal nodded, and they walked toward the plug of snow. They could somehow sense the agitation of the spider on the other side.

"We're coming out! Stay back!" Jackal yelled, then kicked aside the snow. It didn't take long to clear a path out.

The moon was still in the sky, bright and sharp. The sun wasn't close to the horizon, but there was a brighter blue glow showing around the rim of the mountains. One of the False Widows was outside, staying a respectable distance away. In an arc behind it were three more.

Fool's stomach clenched right up at the sight of them. "What do you want?" He had no idea if they could hear him or not, but they seemed to be waiting for him to say something.

Danger. For all. Prepare.

Fool glanced at Jackal, but Jackal shrugged.

"What kind of danger?" Fool asked.

LISTEN

Fool had no idea what that meant, but he stopped, slowed down his breathing, and tried to listen… for a crunch on the snow, for a bellow, for voices, for wind, for anything.

There was nothing.

Something?

Fool couldn't quite tell, but something… something felt wrong. It was almost like…

It comes

…something familiar, something…

Flee

"Oh, shit," Jackal said.

The spiders burst away back to the tree line. All the hair on Fool's body stood up.

There was nothing to see, no sound, no nothing.

Whatever they had sensed that first night was back and coming for them. The focus of its attention was so fierce that Fool felt as though the surrounding air was shaking. They both got notifications of Mental

Influence being resisted, but it didn't help with the atavistic screaming in their hindbrains.

The urge to dive back into the culvert was almost overwhelming. Fool felt himself taking a step in that direction, but he stopped when he imagined himself being trapped in one spot. Better to be out in the open, he reasoned. Better to be able to run in any direction.

The worst part of waiting was knowing that it was coming, but not being able to see it. The rise of the highway above the culvert was working against them now and meant that when whatever it was came upon them, it would come from above and they wouldn't have much time to react.

Fool glanced at Jackal, who nodded. They took off at a sprint toward the tree line, following the spiders. There was a slight chance that this was a trap set by the spiders, but Fool, at least, would rather be suckered by the spiders than deal with whatever was coming at them.

The air split with an odd ripping, keening wail that ended in a series of explosive barks. It was on the other side of the highway. It was scenting for them, but Fool didn't think it had found them just yet. Somehow, they scraped out a little more Speed, plowing snow up around their passage like a train through a reluctant drift. Fool felt the snow pooling around his feet, going into his boots and leaving a band of cold where it melted. Each breath was harsh, sucking in frosty air and expelling hot, humid breath that misted in front of him.

They were almost to the trees.

Almost...

The wailing shriek lit up again, but this time it came from the culvert. The creature must have scented them from inside it. Fool started to pray to his god that the creature would think they were still in it, but then stopped.

Best save his prayer for when it was needed. As bad as this creature seemed, Fool was still more afraid of having his god hear his prayer.

Now, what kind of Acolyte did that make him?

They didn't make it out of sight behind the tree line. They heard the shriek, but this time there was no highway between them and it. The force of the sound was enough that they could feel the pressure of it buffeting their backs, almost making Fool stumble. Jackal had no problem. Annoying Agility bonuses.

As one, they spun to face the entity.

Rising over the concrete guides on the side of the highway above them was a slick black snout. A snout the size of a car. As it got closer, the snout rose and revealed a mouth with rows of sharp, white, peg-like teeth, then a crazed eye, darting all about. Impossible! It was the head of an orca.

It crested up over the guides and started to crash down the side of the road. It stopped short, hanging over the edge for a moment, close enough for the two friends to see that the orca had legs... thick, clawed legs. They looked like the hairless legs of a grizzly bear, only there were six of them.

The creature locked eyes with them, and its head dropped low, like a wolf. A rumbling growl shook the air. They saw its tail whipping back and forth. Right behind the tail arched a dorsal fin.

Fool took the time to take a quick read of it.

Orcabear (Level 27)

HP: 273/284

MP: 139/154

Conditions: Enraged

Scout Notes: Sonic shout, Increase regeneration, Vulnerability: Fire, Hangnail (Left foot)

"Sonic Attack, Regen, vulnerable to heat," he shouted at Jackal.

"I got nothing for that. We're going to have to wear it down!" his friend replied.

The Orcabear was pacing a little, side to side. That wasn't a great sign. It wasn't the usual "dumb beast" monster. This one knew they had weapons and Skills, and it was being cautious. But it wasn't going away. It was giving every sign of being a creature that had Leveled up by piling up Adventurer corpses.

There was nothing to lose though, so Fool did the first thing he could think of.

He flung a grenade with as much force as he could. Before the System arrived, he'd never been an athlete of any kind. Tossing a heavy grenade, he'd have been lucky to throw it far enough to avoid the blast radius. Never mind with any kind of accuracy.

He felt a brief and satisfying rush as the grenade easily lobbed right at the Orcabear. Every point he'd spent on building up his physical Stats continued to be rewarding. He had to admit, making the distance on this throw wouldn't have been possible without Jackal's constant pestering.

The grenade arced up, coming right down toward the wailing and hissing beast.

Bull's-eye.

Or would have been, if the creature hadn't casually stepped aside at the last second, confirming its experience with Adventurers.

Fool hadn't chosen which of his four grenades he was going to throw. One of them, he remembered belatedly, was a thermite grenade, System-strength. He briefly hoped that he hadn't wasted that on a throw the creature had dodged.

Then night turned to day as a massive BOOM echoed off the mountains and a chunk of the highway turned to rubble.

"I told you no more plasma grenades!" shouted Jackal.

"I thought I'd gotten rid of it!" Fool shouted back.

The Orcabear was screaming but righting itself. The blast had knocked it over and looked to have singed off the hair on one side of its body. There was a ripple of burned tissue along its side, but even from this distance, Fool could see that the damaged tissue was knitting back together from the edges in.

"Oh, good," Jackal said. "You've pissed it off."

The beast leapt over the railing and thundered toward them.

They split, Jackal to the right and Fool to the left.

The first thing Fool noticed, as the Orcabear charged, was that it wasn't very fast. If anything was going to keep them alive, that was it. The two of them moved quickly in combat, and they might have a chance to keep out of this thing's major attacks. Fool wasn't too worried about the Sonic Attacks… both of their armors had been hardened against that. Well, Fool's armor had been hardened. Jackal was just sort of hardened in general.

The Orcabear didn't hesitate in making its choice, veering right for Jackal. Worked perfectly for Fool. He paused to glance at his grenades and identified the thermite grenade before he shuffled it to his right-side hip pocket. It wouldn't be strong enough to one-shot the Orcabear, but it might give them a bit of an edge… as long as he didn't waste it.

That done, Fool sprinted after the creature. Jackal was already engaged with it, and from the red Fool could see on the snow, the Orcabear hit hard. Jackal was probably saving his Invulnerability for the bites and relying on his Regen and other Buffs to carry him through most of the claw attacks. Fool didn't think that strategy could last long, not with the amount of blood already on the snow and the occasional cry of pain erupting from his friend.

Apparently, Jackal agreed, because he switched to a more defensive fighting style, suddenly leaping higher to avoid the swipe of the claws.

That was a bad move, and Fool cringed inside, thinking of all the nature footage he'd seen of orcas tossing around the carcasses of seals. Sure enough, as Jackal came down, the Orcabear's mouth was ready for him. The beast was slow on covering ground, but fast with the teeth. It reared up and caught Jackal by one leg before it ragdolled him all over the place.

Fool damped down his panic.

He couldn't see a spatter of blood, so Jackal must have activated his Invulnerability. Which meant he only had a little time to survive before the Orcabear worked through his defenses. It was thrashing him around hard enough that Fool didn't think Jackal would really be able to come up with a plan to counter it.

Which meant it was up to Fool to distract the beast.

He didn't remember what rounds he'd loaded the rifle with, and he had no time to confirm or choose. His default load was a 1-2-3 mix of sabot, slug, and explosive. He'd learned that from someone. It was enough for most creatures.

Fool dropped to a knee. He was far enough away that he could place his shots, and just close enough that he remembered to switch to the dot sight instead of the distance optics. Right behind the eye seemed like the place to aim. Watch it whip its head down, then start to whip back up, time the travel and drop of the shot.

Fire.

Again.

Again.

Three shots cracked out, so fast they almost sounded like one long rolling rip. The first punched a neat hole just behind and above the eye, the second tore a chunk out of the space where the upper and lower lids joined, and the third blew a big hole that left a ragged chunk of eyelid flapping loose.

A wail ripped out of the Orcabear again, and it let go of Jackal on the upswing. He went sailing up and off into the distance. The beast didn't turn toward Fool right away. Instead it twisted its body, shrieking the whole time, and slammed the wounded side of its face into the snow. The impact was hard enough that Fool swore he felt the ground around him shaking.

He didn't stop shooting, emptying the rest of the extended magazine into the creature, stitching down its body as it writhed on the ground. None of the shots seemed to have the same effect as the one near the eye, and Fool came to the sickening realization that the rifle wouldn't be of any real use other than as a distraction. His singular hope that he'd be able to keep up firing into the eye to try to damage the creature was dashed when it lifted its head from rubbing it into the ground and revealed a completely intact orb.

This thing Regenerated fast.

So unfair.

Fool ran.

He didn't think he was quite fast enough to reach the woods before the whale would get him, so he dropped another grenade on the ground as he ran, hoping he'd set the timer right. He was still holding on to the thermite grenade. The time wasn't right for that. Maybe if he could make it to the trees.

Fool was about ten seconds from the tree line when the grenade went off with a muted *thump* and the Orcabear screamed. It sounded as though it was right on him, but Fool didn't bother to turn and see what had happened, just kept sprinting for the woods.

There was a faint glimmer of webbing in front of him, and the brief flicker of an oily black body shifting away. Fool didn't slow, but rolled down and forward, just missing the web. No idea if the spider had let him see it on purpose, though he'd thank them later. Probably.

He wasted no time getting back on his feet. He had no illusions about the trees or the webs slowing down the Orcabear, and he could see fleeing spiders in all the trees ahead of him.

All he had to do was get out of view of the rampaging beast for the briefest moment. Just one moment.

Fool had no way of knowing if it was watching him, but he didn't hesitate. A quick dart to the right, behind the largest tree he could see, and he slammed himself up against it, in what he hoped was a blind spot, and activated his Geas Skill.

A tree. He was a tree. Just a tree. Trees don't move, they don't think, they just are.

The mantra repeated itself over and over in his head as the Orcabear entered the woods with the sound of splintering trunks and shaking Earth.

Trees, Fool added, don't piss themselves.

The Orcabear was beside him in a moment, stopping, questing about. Its thick blubber side was towering above him, only inches from his shoulder.

Trees don't look.

Trees don't make eye contact.

Trees don't scream.

Its gaping slash of a mouth opened, and Fool was horrified to see that its teeth had what looked like bloody shreds of flesh still in them. Jackal hadn't gotten away scot-free.

Trees don't feel rage.

Trees don't scream and leap, they don't seek vengeance.

Trees just are.

A low moan came out of the Orcabear, rising into a wailing crescendo as it raised its head, echoing its rage off of the confining blue shield of the sky.

And then Jackal was on top of it, screaming, driving his spear down into its back, almost an arm's length in.

The Orcabear exploded into motion, and Fool was battered aside as it spun about. He only caught the very edge of the creature's motion and managed to get his feet back under him. He used the momentum to let him kick off a tree and grab a branch just above his head.

Jackal was putting up a good fight, judging from the roaring and crashing all around, but Fool figured that would only last until he lost his balance on top. Fool might have better odds outrunning the Orcabear in the trees, but it was still not the best place to be.

Fool took the time to work himself up the branches until he figured he was out of easy biting range, then he fished out the thermite grenade. Now all he had to do was hope that somehow Jackal managed to bring the beast back toward him.

He took the time to look around. The False Widows had warned them and didn't seem much of a threat. He was hoping he could somehow rally them to help with his scheme, but a quick glance showed him they had completely vanished into the depths of the forest.

It was expected, but it still hit Fool with a flash of despondency. There was no escape. The Orcabear was too big, too strong for them to kill. They might be able to dodge out of range of its attacks for a little while, but eventually they'd tire. The valley was a death trap for them and the perfect hunting ground for the Orcabear.

Fool wasn't ready to give up though. Something always happened, something always made things work out their way. He'd learned to accept that, and this damned Orcabear was going to learn that too.

"*Jackal!*" he shouted. "Bring it back here!"

There was no answering shout back, but Fool could still hear the crackling of wood, the shrieks of the creature, and the occasional screaming invective from Jackal. He'd have to trust that his friend was on the way.

Fool's nerves got the best of him, so he climbed up one more branch. And then stopped, because this branch was thinner than the others and was bowing precipitously under his weight. The smell of shattered wood and exposed sap was all around him, reminding him of the consequences of being the monkey that climbed too high.

Jackal came back, probably faster than either of them had really wanted. He was too busy being a projectile to complain though. Fool could just make out that most of Jackal's body was intact, but there was a lot of blood. Mercifully, he missed the tree trunks and plowed into the snow.

Fool wanted nothing more than to jump down and make sure Jackal was still alive… but he knew he was. He'd know, in his soul, if Jackal was dead. As long as Jackal was a little bit alive, he'd make it. Fool had to believe that. They'd both been through enough rough scrapes before, had faced the reaper and skipped the invitation.

But this Orcabear had them not just out-Leveled but outclassed too.

One last try.

Another otherworldly wail ripped through the trees, and the beast charged toward Jackal's unmoving form. It was going to pass right under Fool.

He set the fuse to a half-second delay and pulled the pin.

Stared down the Orcabear as it charged.

Considered making a prayer to his god.

At the very last second, its liquid black eyes looked up and noticed Fool.

It was too late for it to stop, but it slowed enough that it would slide to a stop just past Fool and chomp him out of the tree a split second later.

Fool almost hesitated. Almost. He had the crazy thought that maybe he could time it just right and drop the thermite grenade down the beast's mouth.

Cowardice wasn't something he'd attribute to himself, but it touched him in that moment, because he knew if he waited that long, he'd be in the beast's mouth while the grenade was going off. Common sense. It was just common sense that made him drop the grenade right when he'd originally planned.

The timing was perfect. The sleek metal device seemed to float down, and every second slowed to a wounded man's crawl. Fool tore his eyes away from the scene just as the grenade touched the side of the charging beast. He could actually see the blubber slightly deform as the grenade's weight hit, and then the flash.

A little too slow turning his head, and the bright light filled half of his vision.

In the resulting shock, Fool didn't hear the explosion or the scream of the Orcabear, and he couldn't see the direct effect. But he could smell the horrific stench of burning, rancid oil.

The tree shook and rattled, and Fool almost fell out.

His eyes cleared just enough to see the monster thrashing about in pain. It was missing a leg, and the whole side of its body was a raw, ragged red mess.

Even with all that, Fool saw that it was already Healing, and its hit points were ticking back up. Between all that he and Jackal had been able to do, the Orcabear wasn't even down to half of its starting Health.

No help for it then. Fool started to reach out to his god, to make his request for help, to bind him to another unbreakable contract at the whims of the unknown that he worshipped.

And before the thought had even half-formed, a bright ruby-red beam lanced out of the dark and tore right through the Orcabear. The beast screamed and spun itself into a tight little ball, quaking.

In terror, Fool realized that maybe his Skill hadn't told him everything the Orcabear was capable of and that it seemed to have one last terrible attack left up its sleeve.

But then another red beam lanced out, and another.

And the impossible happened.

The Orcabear turned itself once more in a spiral, and with another wailing shriek, it tore off through the woods. Fool heard trees breaking in its passage for another moment, then eerie silence all through the forest.

He sagged into the tree, the relief inside him so sudden and vast that he felt a single tear slide down his cheek. More welled up behind that, but he choked them back before he lost himself to shaking and sobbing.

Later, he promised himself. Later, he'd find a quiet, private spot and let out all of that. Later.

Later was a possibility now.

"Jackal?" Fool yelled. He wasn't that surprised that his voice cracked.

No voice replied, but the muffled groan he heard was all he needed to know. Still alive. They'd survived. Again.

Ten minutes, unless the monster had some kind of Debuff. Ten minutes and Jackal would be right as rain. Of course, so would the Orcabear.

The System giveth and the System taketh away. Mostly lives.

The white blob in his eyes, remnants of the flash, was still obscuring most of his vision, but it was fading fast. He blinked a few more times, then looked back up the forest in the direction they'd come from, back toward the highway. That was where the beams had come from. He could just make out some figures walking toward him.

A group. All they had in common was that none of them were human. Aliens, all of them. And all sporting abundant weaponry and armor. All of them looked tough and competent.

Fool leapt down from the tree and stood to face his rescuers as they slowly made their way around the shattered tree trunks.

"Nice work with the thermite grenade," one of them said. It was a short humanoid, almost human looking, and clearly female from the revealing cut of her armor.

Fool had seen a lot of creative choices in armor. The System allowed for a lot of leeway in practicality, if you were willing to spend. Her armor was mostly functional-looking, if aggressively modern. Except for the deep cut down the front of the breastplate. It would have looked fine on a nightgown. On armor? She pulled the look off, at least.

He pulled his eyes back up. She was cute and still smiling at him. That made him feel foolish for staring, and he could feel his cheeks redden.

"Thanks." Fool didn't know what else to say for a moment. He really wanted to be sure these were rescuers. He'd heard about alien slavers.

"Probably you'd be dead otherwise. Probably we'd all be dead. Our lasers did the most damage to the Orcabear, but even with the group of us, it's no sure thing. We've already lost one party to it. Figure your thermite was what made it decide to book it. Figure we owe you for that. Call it even for the rescue then," she said, leaning on her rifle and looking slowly around the woods.

"Uhh... sure. Thanks? How... what brings you here? Were you hunting it?" Fool asked.

"Yah. You need Healing? Can do cheap."

The rest of the group stayed silent, but they weren't just standing around. They split into quadrants and took up positions all around them. One of them was walking toward Jackal.

"No, all good, but let me check on my friend," Fool said and sprinted ahead of the alien to check on Jackal.

It didn't look good. Jackal was missing his right arm from the elbow down. And most of his torso armor was gone. Both his legs looked crushed too.

Something inside of Fool was screaming and crying, but it was deep down in some lost part of him that he was pushing farther and farther away.

The alien didn't ask but knelt down beside Jackal. Fool couldn't get a good read on it, aside from it being a biped. Its head seemed to be mostly nose, with what seemed to be tiny eyes and mouth below. They had what Fool assumed to be a medical scanner out and grunted in surprise when they ran it over him.

"What?" Fool asked. "Good? Bad? How is he?"

The alien shouted something back at the woman who was striding over.

"He says, 'Tough.' Your friend is very tough," she said. Her rifle had already disappeared, and she stood over them, hands on hips. With Fool on his knees, they were eye level to each other. "He said he's Healing. Some poison is slowing it down though. Our Healer is helping him with that. It will take time. And once that is done, his own Regeneration Skill will recover the limbs."

Jackal's eyes flickered open, and he managed a weak smile at Fool. A wave of relief silenced, for the moment, the screaming part inside Fool.

"Thanks again," Fool said. "That would have been too close for me to think about. You and your team came just in time. Lucky you found us."

"No luck. Followed. Led us right to you."

"Followed? Who'd you follow?" Fool asked. Maybe the Foundation had sent out another team?

"This your cat?" the woman asked.

And with a meow, the cat leapt up on her shoulder and blinked at Fool.

Chapter Seven

The newcomers wasted no time in rigging up a travois and bundling Jackal into it. They were quick and competent at it, chopping off branches from fallen trees and weaving them together into the carrying rig. Fool was baffled. The contrast between their high-tech gear, clearly of alien origin, and high System Levels had him expecting something more modern for rescue gear.

That was explained quite quickly when he learned who they were and why they were here. The new Guild that had purchased the Tete Jaune Cache Fort was the Mountaineers Guild. They were a Galactic Guild of suicidal maniacs. At least that was how Fool interpreted it. Their purpose was not just to climb mountains, but to climb them with no System-enhanced gear at all. Or even boosted Stats, as they didn't want to damage the peaks—most Leveled up Strength Skills were enough to crush rock, after all. They still used Class Abilities when appropriate, so it wasn't entirely suicidal. Just mostly.

The Guild had come to Earth to climb peaks that no Galactic had ever climbed before. They planned to hit all the mountain ranges on Earth that they could, and the Fort had given them a great opportunity to set up a base camp for both the Rockies and the Purcells. They planned to be in the area for at least a few years yet to come.

The hobby was a risky one for more reasons that just the sporting chance of falling to your death. Mountains that were challenging to climb also tended to be popular with the more rare and dangerous monsters, so Mountaineers Guild members had strong Levels in combat, and some pure Combat Classes tagged along for the chance to fight the worst monsters. The Guild also attracted a fair number of older, retiring Combat Classes. As a result, the Guild was small but punched way above its weight class in terms of Levels.

With the exception of the rescue group. They were the advance Guild team, tasked with setting up the area for regular Guild members to come and try the mountains. And do explore tourism potential.

They'd been tracking the Orcabear for a few days, without really knowing what it was. It had been tearing up most of the Mount Robson Park entrance and driving out lesser monsters in waves. They'd figured it was best to kill it before it Leveled up too much.

After this encounter, they were putting in a request with the Guild for a heavy-hitter or two to be sent their way.

The leader had filled Fool in on all this as they made their way back to the highway, after stopping to retrieve Fool's and Jackal's gear from the culvert. By the time they climbed up the sides back to the highway, Jackal had started to stir.

Fool went to check on his friend, who was moaning and thrashing about in the travois.

"Jackal, how you doing, buddy?" he asked.

"Fool?" Jackal replied with a weak voice. His eyes flickered open and, after a moment, settled on Fool.

"You just rest. It's all good. We're in good hands, heading to a safe spot. Just get some sleep, okay?"

"You suck at fighting," Jackal muttered before his eyes closed again.

Fool waited a moment until he saw Jackal's breathing slow down and steady before he got up. Somehow the cat had appeared on the travois and was settling into a nap on Jackal. Fool looked at it for a moment, but it seemed appropriate. He nodded at the stretcher-bearers, and they walked down the road toward the Fort.

The rest of the group was already on the road, having already determined somehow that the Orcabear wasn't coming back anytime soon. The leader was waiting for Fool, so he walked over to her.

"This is what you humans do, right?" she asked, holding out her hand.

Fool took it and gave it a shake, wincing as she nearly crushed his hand. Fortunately, it seemed to be an unintentional thing, and she withdrew her hand promptly after the single shake.

"Lexi ShiningMoon. You are Fool? Why do I only see one name for you? Thought you humans did two or more."

"Bit of a story," Fool said. "It's just my name now. It's unusual for some humans to have one though, yes. Bit rare here in this part of the world, but we're complex creatures."

She gave him a bright smile. "Has meaning, yes? I only see one, but that would mean your parents did not think well of you."

Fool sighed. "My parents gave me a different name, but everyone stopped using it a long time ago. My name has meaning to me that's different. It's sort of, uhm… rakish? Does that make sense?"

Lexi frowned and made some motions in the air. She must have been making adjustments to whatever was helping her with translations, because her language skills immediately got better. Her smile got brighter and had a touch of predator in it. "Sure! You're pretty enough. Might be fun too. We'll see what the night brings."

That made Fool raise his eyebrows a little. It's not that he was opposed. It was just a bit sudden. If it was actually an offer. Might have been an issue with whatever language upgrade she had installed. Not something he was really going to worry about just yet. Might be she was just learning English naturally. There were crazy people all over the galaxy, after all.

Sometime while the fight had been going on, the sun had finally broken over the mountains, and the sky was showing a vibrant blue. The mountains were glistening with the angle of sunlight on the snow, in a way that always reminded Fool of wet metal.

Fool took that as a reminder that things weren't always what they seemed and to keep an eye open as he fell into step with his rescuer.

The Fort was only a few more hours down the road, and maybe he'd learn something on the way.

By the time they made it to the Fort, Jackal was conscious. His new Regen was kicking in nicely too. Fool wasn't sure why, but he thought the cat might have had something to do with that. It hadn't stopped purring the whole time it had been curled up next to the giant warrior.

The Fort, when they got to it, looked to be in the process of heavy refurbishment. It wasn't likely to stay a fort long, from what Fool could tell. He wasn't sure how the System managed such things, but the cluster of buildings all around the Fort proper sure weren't part of the planned setup.

The Tete Jaune Cache Fort had originally been some sort of motel or something, off of the Yellowhead Highway. The humans who'd claimed it must have been the original owners or passersby on the highway, because it still looked like an eighties campground office with a restaurant attached. Someone had added a few throw-back wooden towers and a rudimentary wall around the Fort, but Fool could only see bits of that, thanks to the more System-modern sloped stone walls with parapets.

But the clusters of houses outside the walls of the Fort? They looked like some sort of warped love child of the stereotypes of western-style log cabins and the classic Bavarian Bauernhaus. Fool found them sort of cute. He asked Lexi about them and wound up getting a detailed talk about how the Guild tried to keep to local traditions and how they'd researched all about human Alpine culture.

She was quite clear that a central mission of their Guild was not just to challenge themselves by climbing the peaks, but also to preserve the natural state of peaks as best they could. They were committed to keeping things intact for future climbers.

Lexi kept looking at Fool as she said these things, clearly expecting him to agree. He nodded and listened and eventually figured out that she'd been reading a lot about the reasoning behind why the parks had been built in the first place, as well as some of the writings of more prominent outdoors people, and assumed it was a universal human trait. Fool wasn't going to correct that.

They were greeted warmly by the resident Guild members, and they bustled Jackal off to a recovery room for further treatment at very reasonable rates. There wasn't a Shop, but they had a Crafter skilled enough with gear repairs that they were able to restore some of the durability of Fool's gear.

Jackal's armor was beyond their abilities, and Fool had to talk Jackal into storing it aside until they got to a Shop for repairs. They'd have to rely on Speed and Stealth to overcome any more issues on the way to Valemount. That was fine with Fool. That was how he preferred it anyway.

Fool was tired after the walk and the long, unpleasant adrenaline dump after the morning combat, so he found himself a chair to sit in next to Jackal. He knew his exhaustion was more mental than physical, what with the System refreshing his Stamina, but he knew better than most that the mental was just as important as the physical. If not more.

Slumped in the chair, with a sunbeam coming in the window and lighting up half the room in a golden glow, Fool figured that would be a great place to take a nap. As he curled up, the cat jumped on his lap and butted him in the head, full of purrs. He scritched it behind the ears and rubbed it under the chin. It blinked at him, purring louder, and a fat bulb of drool plopped down into Fool's lap.

"Thanks for showing up," he said. It really was a cute cat, with deep green eyes.

"You're welcome," the cat said. "Couldn't let you get killed before the fun started."

"Not worried about yourself?" he asked. "Leaving the Foundation wasn't the best idea. Lots of things out here that can kill you."

"Not worried at all. Nine lives, remember? And you know cats don't travel the same way you do."

"Right. Through walls and all that?"

The cat looked up at him and bumped his fingers to remind him that he'd stopped petting it. "Sometimes, Fool. Sometimes. Now go to sleep. You need the rest."

"Sure, kitty. Sure. Maybe you'll still be here when I wake up?"

104

"Maybe."

Fool drifted off, the warmth of the sun and the cat curling up in his lap overcoming any remaining desire to stay awake.

When Fool woke, night had already fallen. Jackal was still sleeping, the faintest snore coming from his giant form. Fool was amused by that. Jackal in movement didn't always seem too large. He wasn't proportioned like one expected from such a large human. There was no bulkiness, no overwhelming mass of muscles or super-broad shoulders. Just a normal, if very athletic-looking, person. But lying on the bed, sprawling out a little? Jackal covered almost all the surface of the bed. His one leg still on the bed carried its foot off the frame.

His other foot was on the floor. As big as he was, Jackal was only sleeping on half of the bed. The cat occupied the other half and was sleeping completely sprawled out, with its front paws shoved against Jackal's hips. Fool snorted at that.

And then looked back again.

Fool didn't think it was possible that such a tiny cat was able to physically shove such a large person off of a bed, but he was starting to think anything was possible with the critter. There was no denying it was cute though.

Seeing that the window shutters were mostly closed and no one else was in the room, he took off his ragged armor and put it neatly on the other bed that had been provided for him. His golden overalls were still mostly intact, and he pulled a jacket out of storage to tone down the look a little. There weren't any mirrors to check his look in, but Fool assumed he looked good. He generally assumed he did.

Fool half expected to find the door to their cabin locked, but it opened easily enough.

There was a guard outside though. Fool nodded at him, and the guard pointed him toward a larger building nestled right up to the wall of the Fort proper. This one leaned even more into the Bavarian theme, with white walls and dark brown timbers crisscrossing the front. Out front, it had a small area with a low picket fence. Visible through the large windows, was a scattering of tables and chairs, all candlelit. And judging from the happy, smiling faces inside, it was either a pub or a restaurant.

That brought a smile to Fool's face. Obviously, the Mountaineer's Guild was planning on staying a very long time and had no qualms about setting up for a larger presence. Fool had expected a robust but stark Fort, and the chance to eat a proper meal in the middle of the journey struck him as the most pleasant possible thing.

As he got closer, he saw Lexi sitting at a table inside. She must have had some way of seeing outside the reflected light on the windows from inside, because she waved at him as he got closer.

As soon as he sat down, Fool asked her, "Isn't this a bit... extravagant?"

"Guild requirement. Mountaineering is a dangerous life, and Guild members don't have a long lifespan. So we try to live as full a life as we can. The first priority in any new location is to set up a place to celebrate life. And honestly, it's not that expensive. We split the cost with a restaurant chain that uses our branding on more civilized worlds. They get the cachet of what we do for advertising, and we don't have to front the capital costs. Plus Guild members get a nice discount. So dinner's on me."

"Sounds brilliant. What's good?"

"We've been trying some Earth foods. Working our way through the local Alpine cuisine. I've tried something called spätzle, and schnitzel, and nachos. All pretty good. But that peppermint mocha stuff is vile beyond belief. What you humans can stomach is pretty outrageous."

Fool smiled. "Maybe later I'll see if I can introduce you to eggnog. I have a feeling you might prefer that. But schnitzel sounds good. Beer?"

"The Guild has its own brew on tap. Hope you like it strong."

Dinner was pleasant. The potato side was a normal potato, but the meat in the schnitzel was something purple with brown streaks in it, with a bright green gravy. It tasted great though. It had a musky, almost cardamom bite that took some getting used to, but worked well with the crunchy batter.

Fool had played it smart with the beer and asked for a sip of Lexi's before ordering. She'd knocked back a large schooner already and ordered another for herself. Fool asked for a snifter's worth and was carefully sipping at it through the meal. System-developed beer could really kick one's ass, having to get through abnormal Constitution bonuses and poison resistances. He was only a quarter way through by the end, but his head was spinning.

Lexi had spent most of the conversation regaling Fool with tales of peaks climbed and tough situations. They'd had a brief digression on geology, as Fool had heard rumors of dormant local volcanoes showing signs of coming back to life.

Lexi had shared that there was a theory that Dungeon Worlds, due to the high uncontrolled Mana levels, might suffer from tectonic issues, but that it might also be some kind of new Monster or Elemental activity. She didn't seem too concerned about it though, so Fool relaxed.

"When did the Orcabear show up?" he asked.

"Best we can tell, a couple of weeks ago. Came down from the deeper mountains and drove a whole lot of critters before it. Those few weeks have been nonstop attacks. We'd been expecting something major to break through soon. Actually, we'd been hoping to send up a team to kill it before it got this close. Looks like we're out of luck." Lexi sighed and ran a hand through her hair, pushing an errant lock out of her eyes. "We've used up the funds for shipping in new Guild Members til the next quarter, so not much to do about it. Honestly, we thought we'd be able to recruit locals to help hold the Fort while we sent out a party, but even at a good rate, we got no takers."

"From Valemount? That's surprising. They don't have a lot of people, but I've heard they've got a good chunk of high-Level folks. Surprised they didn't want to take the chance to get some Leveling Up done. Have they got problems coming from the other end?"

"Not that I've heard." Lexi was looking off to the side. Something was on her mind. "The road south from them hasn't been heavy on spawns and is being controlled by another group with resources. But they were pretty clear as to their reasons for not helping. Credits weren't going to change their minds, not in the amounts we could offer."

Fool looked at her. They'd spent a few hours talking since the morning, and she hadn't really struck him as the kind to hold back. But she was clearly hesitating to share something with him. And he had a terrible idea what it was.

"We're heading into Valemount tomorrow, looking for someone. Is there anything we should know?"

Lexi blew out a big breath. "Someone close to you?"

Fool shook his head. "No, it's a Quest. Not someone we've met or really have any idea about."

"Hmm. How much do you know about the Valemount folks? I've been assuming you humans are all pretty closely connected, but now I'm wondering."

"Never been. Don't know anyone there. I'm from McBride, and even before the System arrived, I never really traveled down that way. If I ever needed anything, I'd head up to Prince George. I drove through once, a few years ago, when I went to Vancouver. That's it though. There used to be regular travel between McBride and Valemount, but that stopped a while ago." Fool shrugged. Hopefully her language pack had local body language in it too.

"No one in McBride really has any connections there," he continued. "Anyone who lived between there and us moved to McBride as soon as the System arrived. It was the closest town with all the facilities. It's how we managed to get our Village status so quickly. McBride actually has a larger population now than before the System."

Lexi's substantial eyebrows flew up. "You're kidding. That's… unheard of. How the hell did you manage that?"

"A bit of luck, but mostly geography. The whole Robson Valley is really weird. The population, historically, has been really spread out and very independent-minded. There's also been a lot of resources in the area, but not a lot of city center, unlike the rest of the province. So things got a bit spread out." He mopped up a bit of sauce with a forkful of potato. It really was a fantastic meal.

He took another sip of the beer before continuing. "But people still have the needs of bigger communities, like hospitals, schools, community centers, that kind of thing. The government's solution was to build

McBride into a regional hub for facilities. Basically, the town had the capacity for at least double its population. So in a way, it's not that it grew, it's that the System seemed to think it was underpopulated. When people flooded into it as a natural gathering place, they found that most of the stuff they needed was already there. Made it a lot easier to rescue more people. Plus, the roads at the time were packed with tourists, backed up because of a landslide." He felt as if he was rambling a bit, but Lexi encouraged him to continue with a nod.

"Pure luck, really," he said. "But it gave the town a hell of a head start. But no connection to Valemount. We weren't even really sure they'd survived up until about two years ago, and even though we've sent regular patrols, it's mostly been supply runs. No real population exchange or anything."

Lexi chewed her lip while she thought about it, and Fool took the opportunity to look at her a little differently. He was finding her oddly attractive. She had a really animated way of moving her hands when she talked, and when she was distracted and thinking, the way she was now? She had a habit of running her tongue behind her lips and nibbling on the inside of them. Fool was finding the thought of kissing her more and more entertaining.

"Okay," she said. "We've only run across the convoys, and they don't really stop. We went down to Valemount shortly after we arrived, after we bought the Fort. I'm not gonna say they ran us out of town, but they really seemed like they wanted to. Not very friendly people at all. Pretty sure that was because we weren't human though."

"Ah," Fool said. "Yeah, I guess that's not too surprising. The province has always had pockets of folks who came to mountains to stick to themselves, as a way to practice some of the worst of human behavior out

110

of the sight of others. It's not surprising that some of those may choose to use the System arrival as an excuse to focus their bigotry on a new group of people."

Lexi nodded. "We get those kinds too. It's why we kinda rolled with it. Assholes gotta be assholes, and sometimes they band together. Or just wind up in charge and bully all the others. Not sure what you got to deal with in Valemount, but assholes for sure. I mean, I'm assuming your assholes are like ours? They don't really play favorites with anyone who doesn't toe their line?"

"Got that right. I was afraid of that. They don't like you. They probably aren't going to like Jackal or me either."

"Shame. Hope you can get your friend out without any issues."

Fool shrugged. "Not a friend, but I wasn't planning on staying longer than it takes to resupply, make contact, and get them back home."

They were interrupted by a waiter bringing them their dessert orders. Fool had learned from the Guild beer and carefully asked Lexi what the dessert menu options were and how they tasted in comparison to everything else. He'd opted for something that sounded like ice cream… but when it arrived, it looked like cabbage soup. Bubbling cabbage soup. Lexi was munching on what looked like a bowl of grasshopper heads in syrup. Smelled good, at least. His dessert smelled like raw sewage.

Lexi laughed when she saw the look on Fool's face. "Just try it. I know it smells like death, but it tastes great. Trust me!"

Fool frowned but scooped up a spoonful and brought the spoon up for a deeper sniff. It still smelled vile, but there was something under the sewer stench. A bit of anise? Another sniff, and it smelled more like cinnamon. He decided it was best to be a bit brave and to stop sniffing, so he took a delicate sip.

He almost spit it out. The initial taste was in line with his expectations, but then it changed. There was a whole gamut of flavors, but either his brain or tongue rapidly overloaded and settled on one. It wasn't anything Fool had tasted, or expected to ever taste, but it settled somewhere around a very strong, floral vanilla. It wasn't bad, so he tried the whole spoon.

"Good!" he said. "This is good. Weird. But good. I like it."

Lexi tilted her head and looked in his eyes as something burning unlidded itself further. "Feel like trying something else different?"

Fool's legs were still a little weak and shaky when he got back to his cabin later in the night. Jackal was up, reading a book he'd found somewhere, and looked at Fool when he came in. The cat was still napping, this time on Jackal's lap.

"Looks like you had a good night," Jackal said.

"Yeah. Different. Good different. I like this new world. It's weird, but it keeps being weird good."

"I see." Jackal didn't bother to hide his smirk. "I'll pass on the details, thank you. I got caught up on the whole Mountaineers Guild and the Orcabear and all the rest from the gentleman assigned to stand guard for us. Anything else you learned I should know about?"

"Valemount's likely full of racists. Speciests. Whatever. Might just be alien-haters, but I'm going to assume that the mentality sours everything." Fool dropped into the other chair with an audible sigh.

"That's been my experience," Jackal said. "Granted, I'm a little biased on that front. But you never know. It's not going to take long for a

'Humanity First' mindset to set in. Might even get some of the more open-minded racists to start seeing past skin color and maybe start to see people as people."

Fool just stared at him.

"Fine," Jackal said. "I knew it was what you were going to say. I thought I'd save myself time arguing with you. See if you wanted to start from the other side this time, maybe."

"Not tonight, but thanks?" Fool said, shaking his head. His friend, he thought not for the first time, knew him too well. "In any case, I suppose we'd best keep an eye out for things to go sour on this. Or not, I suppose. Is it sour if we need to put some people in their places?"

"I think we can always plan on doing that when the opportunity presents itself."

The two smiled at each other. Both of them, in their past lives, had dealt with more than their share of bigots of all kinds. That was the thing about being on the lowest rung of the ladder. All the masks people wore came off because people stopped worrying about who you'd complain to.

"So," Jackal said, "do we have a plan yet, or do you need more data?"

"More data, but here's my plan for now. We come in as Adventurers on our way south, maybe some story about going to Vancouver for family. Maybe we say we're looking for people to travel with us? Give us an excuse to walk around town. Maybe we'll stay more than a day, depending on what we find out about our target."

"Start with misdirection. Got it. If we get chased, make them go south first. Do we have any contacts or people of note to look for in Valemount?"

"No one from the Foundation. And apparently Valemount is run by a 'Sheriff' these days. Didn't get a name."

"Sheriff?" Jackal asked, putting aside his book. "Like an American? Or a corrections officer?"

"Not sure, but there was a Provincial Courthouse in Valemount. The one thing McBride didn't have. So it could have been an employee there. It might also just be a System Title or Class. We're going to have to wait and see on that."

"So the usual then?"

"That's our specialty, Jackal. Carefully unplanned mayhem."

"Except you always plan it. It just never works out."

"Just like I plan it."

Where Jackal got the peanut to throw at him, Fool had no idea.

Chapter Eight

Fool and Jackal arrived at Valemount just before dinner the next day. The journey had been uneventful, thankfully. Jackal had still been moving a little stiffly in the morning, mostly from the psychological impact of his injuries. The actual damage had completely Healed overnight, including regrowing limbs. But the mind took a bit to catch up from the seesaw of losing a limb, and then having it back again.

Fool didn't envy Jackal that adaptation process, but from what Fool could tell, his friend was handling it pretty well. The long walk was probably the best thing for both of them, giving them a chance to emotionally recover from the encounter with the beast.

They hadn't run across anything that dangerous before. Scarier, for sure. There'd been all kinds of terrors unleashed on the world, but the two of them had always seemed to be one step ahead of everything they faced. Even higher-Level monsters or human opponents, they'd always come out ahead, if not with ease, then with a surety that came from confidence in their Skills.

But the Orcabear, despite their best efforts, had torn through them. Their best attacks and setups had amounted to nothing more than irritations, and that had dented their confidence.

As much as Fool liked to think he was resilient, always bouncing back from the constant swarm of life's problems, he had to admit that the thought of the trip back and possibly facing that beast again? He wasn't too stuck up to admit he was afraid of that outcome.

Jackal didn't seem to care too much, because when Fool admitted his fear, Jackal shrugged it off. He expected that the Mountaineers Guild would hunt down and kill the Orcabear in the next few days. Even if they didn't, they'd planned to hunt it until they did kill it, so it wasn't likely to be anywhere near the road on their way back.

Fool rather hoped that would be the case, but he still wanted to run some tactics by Jackal. However, after a few hours of back and forth, they hadn't been able to come up with any workable solution that didn't fall back on the one thing Fool wasn't willing to do—call on his god for help.

Fool sulked for a bit after they'd run out of ideas, but Jackal brought him out of his burgeoning slump by asking him how he'd managed to hook up with Lexi. And talking about how he'd had a nice dinner with her and been swayed into going back to her place and finding an absolutely lovely connection with her dramatically improved Fool's mood.

"Looking forward to the return trip then?" Jackal asked.

"I suppose. I mean, I don't know if she meant it to be more than a one-time thing… I don't even know much about their culture. Or her. Or… yes. Yes, I am. I want to learn more, and I'm hoping that there is more. Happy?"

He could hear the grin in Jackal's voice. "I'd like you to be happy. So I expect I will be, yes. I'm looking forward to actually meeting her properly, I have to say. I only got to really see her this morning, but she was busy prepping for the next hunt."

"Yeah, she was looking forward to killing that thing. If they can manage to skip actually engaging with it until they make it to McBride, they should be able to get enough reinforcements to take it out."

"That was a pretty clever recommendation you made, and nice job phrasing it to keep the Foundation secret."

"It just made sense. The usual cover story of how the place got big because of its location and blind luck will also explain how McBride will be able to spare a few high-Level hitters to help them out on the hunt. And I'm sure Professor X wouldn't want something like the Orcabear in the area either."

They were close enough to the entrance to Valemount that they both stopped talking for the last bit of the road. It was like McBride, sitting in a valley with mountains on either side. The difference with Valemount was that the valley ended just past the town, the start of another mountain range closing off the valley.

The town used to look like a small cluster of motels, gas stations, and fast food joints just off the highway, with the bulk of the town a bit hidden away. Now, the remaining forests on this side of the town had been torn down, apparently used to build a wall that entirely blocked access to the town from the highway. And stopped anyone from continuing down the highway.

That was all it took for them to fall back into their "mission faces," with Jackal being the strong silent one and Fool the smart and charismatic leader. And, Fool thought, it was really only Jackal doing the acting. That made it easy.

"Identify yourselves!" a voice shouted from on top of the walls surrounding the town.

"Fool and Jackal. That's our names," Fool replied.

A head stuck over the parapet. Looked like a young man wearing a baseball cap with what looked like a police insignia on the front. "Valemount is a closed town. What do you want?"

Fool looked at Jackal, who shrugged. Closed town wasn't a phrase they'd heard before.

"We're just passing through. Coming down from Prince George on our way to Vancouver to join our families," Fool said.

"That's stupid. It's the long way. Why come this way?"

"Used to live in Blue River. My house is still there, wanted to see if anything was left. Can we come in? We can walk around, but we'd love to rest a bit, buy some supplies. You got a Shop? We've got some drops we can sell too."

The head disappeared again. Fool took a look around. If they weren't going to be let in, they'd have to find another way to access the town. It didn't look as though it would be too hard. The wall wasn't as big or tough looking as walls they'd seen in other places. In Fool's experience, there was always a way in.

The head stuck back out after a moment. "Wait there. Someone will come out in a moment."

It took another five minutes before the gate opened. A beefy man in uniform came out, and as he got closer, Fool could see that it was indeed a provincial sheriff's service uniform with sergeant stripes on the sleeve.

"Sheriff Barnes," he said and held out his hand to Fool.

"I'm Fool," he said, shaking the Sheriff's hand. "And this is my traveling companion, Jackal."

Jackal held out his hand, but the Sheriff only nodded at him. Jackal took it in stride and put his hand back and returned the nod.

"You folks planning on passing through? Not planning on staying, is that right?" The Sheriff had that sort of steady eye contact people used when they wanted to appear extra tough. Fool had seen it on many, many cops in his past life. But never on the good ones. Never on the actual tough ones or competent ones. Just on the bullies.

"That's right," Fool said. "We're kinda anxious to get to Vancouver. Finally Leveled up enough that we figured we could make the trip safely. Hoping we can spend the night, head out tomorrow. And access your Shop, so we can sell some of our loot."

"What kinda loot you got?"

"Uh…" This, Fool found, was the important part. The Sheriff was absolutely being rude in asking, but they'd been given a selection of loot drops to use as trade goods to give them cover. Valuable trade goods. The trick was to make the Sheriff think he wanted them, so some hesitation would serve to make him think it was more valuable. And that maybe they had more they could be talked out of later. "We managed to cull a small herd of Flame Elk on the way here, got antlers, hooves, and fur. Hoping we can buy goods in the Shop with that to finance the rest of our trip."

"Flame Elk. Hm." The Sheriff made a show of thinking about it, but the greedy flash in the man's eyes had told Fool all he needed to know. "Tell yah what. We got some Artisans in town might give you a better price on those. I'm letting you in overnight, but you gotta be gone before noon tomorrow, understand? And you'll be staying in the Super 8 Motel overnight. You can hit up the merchants between here and the Shop, at the old IGA on 5th.

"But you stick to that street, you hear? We catch you anywhere else, you're back outside the walls right away. If we're in a good mood. Y'all gonna play nice?"

"Absolutely," Fool answered for both of them. He was finding it hard to keep a straight face, talking to someone who was clearly Canadian but seemed to be intentionally using some sort of hybrid Southern American way of talking. There was more than a hint of meanness in Barnes's face though, and that kept Fool on task. "We're really just looking for a place to rest up and recover for tomorrow. Are there any good places for food in town we should look for?"

"Pub just inside the gate a bit. It's close to the Super 8, so you can check in first." Barnes started to turn around, clearly not interested in them anymore.

"I suppose there's no rush on that. Not a lot of tourists these days?" Fool couldn't help but try to be a little annoying.

Barnes stopped and turned back to look at them. His face was a lot less friendly than it had been a minute ago. "Ain't no proper hotel no more. People trying to make a living, sticking together cuz it's safer. That's the place in town that's got room for you, so that's where you go. Check in first before you do anything else. I'll have one of my Deputies check in on you later, make sure you got it all settled up." With that last pronouncement, he turned and trudged back to the gate.

"Shall we tell them you sent us?" Fool asked after him.

"Whatever," the Sheriff replied, not even turning around.

Fool glanced at Jackal, who was giving him that special look that said, "Why the hell are you trying to make the bad man angry at us?" Fool raised his eyebrows and smiled, and the two of them followed the Sheriff through the gates into Valemount.

It looked pretty much like one would expect a small town to look these days. It hadn't been much even before the System. Most people would either pass by or stop just long enough to get gas. Valemount was in one of the prettier parts of the province, at the end of the Robson Valley and Jackman Flats, anchored at the far end by the start of three of the more spectacular mountain ranges in the south of British Columbia.

But the town itself? Nothing special.

Roughly eighteen blocks. Bigger than McBride, with the same small-town grid and sprawl layout. One major retail row, and the usual facilities running parallel to the highway. A couple of no-name motels with a fast food joint or two. Inside the town, Fool knew without even looking would be one or two smaller hotels, maybe a pub or restaurant for the locals. Maybe both. A bakery or a coffee shop and a grocery store. A bookstore if they were lucky.

Would have been a nice place to grow up. Fool knew that from experience. Nice, but boring. Before the System arrived.

Now? Most of the buildings were still there, but some were clearly gutted. Some had burned down. The place looked empty.

The Sheriff turned off as soon as he passed through the gate, heading into a small shack and slamming the door. Fool looked back at the wall from the inside and saw three more men in the same uniforms, looking down at him. One of them was scowling at them, but the other two smiled and waved before turning to look back over the wall.

The wall itself didn't seem to cover all the town from what they could see. At least not the part that was clearly System-bought. Fool could see, farther down the way, scattered mounds of garbage and debris that had been turned into bulwarks, with short, squat towers near them. Cheap, but effective.

The other side of the town was covered by a creek, and these days that was pretty good protection. You never really knew what was in the water anymore, so you really only had to worry about things coming out of it once in a while. Fool figured there were a few more squat towers on that side that he couldn't see.

Maybe a dozen towers. One or two people per tower. Couple of shifts, probably long ones. Fool ran the math in his head, trying to figure out how many troops the Sheriff had. Maybe twenty or thirty?

Depending on whether the remaining townsfolk participated in the defense. They probably did. So maybe as few as just the ones they'd seen. Probably a range between eight and thirty townsfolk helping was Fool's guess.

Which, he thought, was not good news. Not that there were so many defenders. That made sense in this day and age. What bothered him was that he felt it necessary to try to determine how many of them there were. Something was starting to feel rotten.

Best to get the "Princess" as soon as they could, then get the hell out. Tonight, if he had his druthers. He didn't relish the thought of falling asleep here.

Not at all.

He glanced at Jackal. "Clear?"

Jackal shook his head once. Fool didn't bother trying to clarify if they were being followed or just being watched from some vantage point, but he trusted Jackal. No point in pulling out the tracking device just yet then. Best to check in to the motel, get to their room, and use the privacy of that to figure out what was going on.

But for sure, his instincts were on fire.

Fool's original plan of laying low and figuring out what was going on before making a move was completely out the window. The new plan was to identify the target ASAP, make contact, and extract immediately with as little notice as possible. He wasn't in the mood to tangle with a B-movie wannabe bad guy, which was clearly what the Sheriff intended to be.

The motel was only a few blocks in, just past the pub Barnes had mentioned. There were even a few cars left in the parking lot. One was stripped down to the frame, and another was a shell, what was left of the windows covered in the smoky residue of the fire that had gutted it.

They crossed the lot, opened the front door, and stamped their feet clear of snow as they walked in.

It was like stepping back in time. A normal, regular motel office. There was even a fax machine on a small table to the side that had clearly been obsolete even before the System.

An elderly lady sat behind the front desk. She hadn't even looked up when they came in. Something on the desk in front of her was occupying all of her attention.

Fool and Jackal looked at each other, then back at her, then walked up to the desk.

"Hi, we'd like a room?" Fool asked.

With a sigh, the lady closed her crossword book. From the quick glance Fool got, it looked as though she'd been using a crusty old bottle of Wite-Out to fill the inked-in squares. Made sense... it wasn't as if anyone was likely to be publishing new crossword books for a while. Maybe there were Galactic ones, but they would likely be a pain to use. Then again, the Shop had everything, didn't it? Perhaps you could buy a crossword book there.

Might be a thought and a bribe for the old woman if he needed it.

She was a very worn old woman, with the kind of eyelids that drooped open in a way that looked terribly uncomfortable. Her hands moved in an odd fashion as she moved the crossword book and pulled over a ledger book. Fool guessed that she'd suffered from severe arthritis before the System and had managed to get that fixed up since.

"One bed?" she asked. "We got a king if'n you want. Otherwise, just one room with doubles. Sauna and hot tub don't work no more. Ain't no ice either."

"Two beds, please. Is there working hot water? I'd love a shower," Fool said. "And do you offer a continental breakfast?"

"We got hot water. You want breakfast? The pub opens at six a.m., they got a breakfast menu. Grocery store's open four blocks down the road. You paying cash or Credits?"

"Cash? Like, dollars? You still take those?" Fool was amazed. With the Canadian government gone, and all the pre-System banking networks with it, he hadn't run across anyone still using actual paper money. System Credits, out of necessity, had replaced everything.

"Course we do. But we can also do that newfangled Credit stuff. Cost you double though."

Fool was tempted to negotiate prices, but when she named the cost for a one-night stay, it was actually far lower than he'd expected. He got the idea that she didn't see a lot of System Credits and thought that she was charging more than she was. He happily transferred over the correct amount for the room, while still acting as if it was a lot.

She handed him the keys to room 214 and went back to her book, and she didn't even look up as they left.

Fool's assumption that the room was on the second floor turned out to be accurate, and the room looked out over the parking lot. They had a slight view of the rest of the town, although the view of the mountains was spectacular.

The room smelled horrendous, as if someone had chained-smoked themselves to death over a hot summer and been left to stew til winter came. A quick toss through the room showed no actual issues though. A quick use of Jackal's purchased Clean spell, applied to a few locations, brought the room up to a serviceable state pretty quickly.

Fool jammed the window open. The sun was still up, and the temperature was still above zero, so he was determined to leave it open as long as possible. It wasn't as though they had any belongings that would suffer in the cold.

Fool fished out the tracking device. Time to find the Princess.

The little ball sat heavily in his hand, the dull, matte finish offering no clues to how it was put together or even how to use it. The only instructions he'd gotten on how to use it were to hold it in his hand. It had already been tuned to the person they were looking for.

The process of attuning it had been complex enough, but Fool had asked for some background on it. He didn't want to be stuck out in the field with something that didn't work as expected or needed emergency repairs that he had no idea how to do.

As soon as he wrapped his fingers around the ball though, he knew.

He'd tested it in the Foundation, and it had been an almost lifeless ball. But there had been something. A small nudge, a tiny imperfection. Nothing he could see, but he'd felt an oddness about the ball.

They'd told him it was linked to the probabilistic potential of a certain future that the Foundation was looking for, and the closer he got, the more pronounced the effect would be. He'd know they'd found the right person by touching them. On contact, the ball would have finished with its task and turn inert.

It twisted in his hand and reshaped itself, and he knew he had to head southeast to find his target. Not too far, maybe two kilometers, but he couldn't tell how he knew that. It was as if the device was speaking to his back brain somehow.

"Okay, we've got her," he said to Jackal. "And it looks like we're going to have to cut through the part of town we're not supposed to go through. Ideas?"

Jackal pinched his nose and looked out the window for a few moments. "Something feels hinky here, and I'd rather get a little better idea of what's going on. I know you'd rather dive right in, but I think we need to get a read on things first. That's my gut impression."

"Yeah, no. That's a terrible idea. I'm betting this Sheriff is planning something unpleasant, and the more time we spend here, the more likely it is that he gets his net set up for us. I don't want to be trapped here. Not at all."

"I get that, and I'm not disagreeing. But we just got here. We break protocol and head off in the direction we were told not to right away? We're gonna get some heat, and that's going to make things more complex. Unless you want to try springing their trap first?"

Fool sat on the bed and looked at the odd device in his hands. "I'm not sure they have a trap just yet. I suspect if we do what they expect—grab a quick meal, hit the Artisans, head for the Shop, and stay in our room all night? I bet we walk out tomorrow morning, and they hustle us out of here right away."

Jackal nodded. "*But.* I hear the *but.* What do you think they're hiding?"

"Not sure. Something. Barnes wasn't just being gruff. He was trying to protect something. I get the feeling he was hoping to snow us, distract us, but he lost confidence and instead just tried to keep his mouth shut. Probably someone told him the best lies are short."

Jackal smiled. "Not everyone has your talents, Fool. It's good advice."

"It is." Fool grinned, then grew pensive. "But now I want to know what's going on. Okay, you're right. Let's check out what's going on before we go hit up the Princess."

"That's not quite what I meant." Jackal paused for a long moment, then added, "Do we really care about what they're up to out here?"

Fool cocked his head and looked at his partner.

Jackal was a giant and the most capable fighter Fool had ever run across. Jackal hadn't started out that way. They'd made themselves into what they were for a reason. Fool knew that reason really well and shared it. The System had a way of teaching its lessons early, and hard. Which meant that Jackal's question was deeper than it seemed.

Jackal didn't just think they were at risk from the Sheriff and his cronies. Jackal thought that something unpleasant was happening in the town, and he knew that if they poked even a little deeper into it, they were going to get more than involved.

If the Sheriff was up to anything that even verged on nasty exploitation, then the two of them would bring him down. But they were on a mission, and an important one at that. So Jackal was asking Fool if they were really okay with potentially letting the mission get derailed for what would be a personal vendetta.

"Of course we do. And not just because I'm sharing the worry you clearly have, but because I'm pretty sure that our 'Contact and Retrieve' mission is going to be a 'Rescue the Princess' mission, after all." Fool smiled thinly. "The Foundation identified this person as important. I have no problem imagining the people in this area recognizing that same potential. Be no surprise at all if the Sheriff has them under lock and key."

"Excellent. Let's smash some evil."

Fool flopped back on the bed and groaned. "Can we just out-think them instead? I suck at smashing."

Jackal walked over and held out his hand, patiently waiting.

Fool let his pout carry him on for another moment, then he took Jackal's hand and let the bigger man pull him up. They headed off to check out the town.

Chapter Nine

The early afternoon sun, at this time of year, added a nice highlight to the mountain range in the town's east. Fool had been raised in Vancouver, and it always gave him a little thrill to see mountains close up and on both sides. The motel was still outside of the town proper, and the road curved to the right after a few blocks, then past a big empty field, but at the end of it was the usual small-town strip of businesses. The downtown core was only a few blocks long and one block deep.

They saw more people moving about as they got closer. It looked like a normal small town—minus the cars, of course. And the random burnt-out buildings.

"They look busy," Jackal said.

Fool nodded. He'd almost say it looked as if people were scurrying. Not the kind of rushing about from imminent threat or to hide something away, but more the weary grind he'd expect to see in the financial district of a major city where it was required to look busy all the time, even on lunch, lest your coworkers eat you alive.

Fool had to bite back the random wonder if that had become a literal truth these days. Likely not, as the System wasn't a zombie apocalypse.

Still, the thought of a business district being turned into a dungeon with a CEO boss monster was amusing enough that he was afraid he might spin off into hysterics. He stuffed that thought down for later. Something to get a laugh out of Jackal with when they were heading back, maybe. Fool also recognized that the mad urge to giggle was a sign of how tense he was.

The kind of rapid movement he was seeing wasn't the sign of a happy community.

They were noticed a few moments later, as they got close to the first shop. A young woman stopped, smiled, and waved at them. "Hi! You folks must be new! Where'd you come from?"

"Prince George, on the way to Vancouver the long way."

Her eyebrows raised. "On foot? I mean, I guess so. Are there more of you? I wasn't expecting a caravan til spring."

"No," Fool said. "We heard there was a regular caravan between here and McBride, but we didn't want to wait. Been long enough. We both have family to get to."

Jackal nodded, already slipping into his more silent mode.

"Huh." The lady shielded her eyes against the sun. "Prince George. I can't even imagine that. There must have been more of you to make that trip safely. They setting up a regular trade route there now?"

"Not yet, no. It's not too bad a trip. We had to Level up a bit to handle it though. It's why we couldn't leave until now. Had to spend some time hitting the dungeons and making raids. You know how it is." He was pretty sure she didn't. He'd taken a quick moment to check out her Skills before they talked. She was a mid-Level Crafter, no Combat Skills at all.

"Wow. I've heard rumors that dungeon crawling was a thing people did. Well, how can I help you? What brings you to town?"

"Just passing through," Fool said. "But we've got some Fire Elk parts to sell. Sheriff Barnes said we might be able to get a good rate."

She brightened up. "You bet! Haven't seen any Fire Elk parts in a while. Sheriff will pay us good money for what we make out of those. You two are gonna be popular. Come with me!" She turned and walked toward one of the shops.

A few people were working inside. The shop was toasty warm and smelled of leather, stale coffee, and pine. It wasn't a small store. The sign in front had mostly been torn apart, probably in the first few days after System activation, but it was clear that the shop used to be the town hardware store. It had since been reworked, most of the shelves and goods removed—probably to another location, if they hadn't been used in rebuilding.

The lady had held the door open for them. "My name's Becca." She pointed at a Crafter working on what looked like a rifle. "That's Irving. He handles most of the outside trade here. Irving! These two got Flame Elk for yah."

Irving looked up from his project. He was a heavy-set young man with a ruddy face, the kind who looked as though his weekends involved his four-wheel and any excuse he could think of to use it. And a truck that probably cost four times more than he could afford. He got up from his seat and walked over to them, wiping his hands clean on his pants before he offered it for a shake.

Fool wasn't surprised that his hands didn't have a trace of calluses.

"Hi, folks. You take dollars for your parts?" he asked.

Fool glanced at Jackal. This was getting weird. "No. Just Credits." He bit back the urge to add more, wanting to see where this would go.

"That's fine," Irving said. "What we can do is write up a scrip, and the Sheriff will exchange it for Credits for you when you leave town."

That brought Fool up short. "Uh… not sure that's going to work. We'd planned to spend the Credits in the Shop. Any reason we can't just get paid in Credits?"

"Oh, that'll be fine. If the Sheriff's giving you access to the Shop, you can make the exchange with Memphis. That's the Deputy at the Shop. He'll make sure you get a good rate."

"I guess. Sorry, this is a bit new to us. May I ask why not just pay us direct in System Credits?"

Irving laughed and looked at Fool as if he was his namesake. "We didn't get any choice about this System thing, but that doesn't mean we need to give up our freedom! We're a free town. The Sheriff came up with a great system to stop us from being tracked by the Corporations. Those big government folks can't control us. Trust me, this is a much better way of doing things."

Fool had a very bad feeling about this. He didn't need to look at Jackal to know the wheels were turning in his head too. Fool had the sense that if he didn't phrase his next question carefully, he was going to get into an argument, and this wasn't the time or the place for that.

"That sounds interesting," Fool said. "I sure haven't heard of anyone else doing anything like that. How do you manage your upkeep and buying System-generated things without Credits?"

"That's easy!" Irving grinned and waggled his finger at Fool. "Sheriff handles it all for us. When we get assigned any Credits, we pass it off to him and he exchanges it for dollars for us. And when we need to buy things, we give him a list of what we need—even groceries if we've got enough extra cash. He can get us just about anything from the Shop. No idea what we'd do without him. I hear how you all get ripped off all the time by scammers in the Shops! We're lucky the Sheriff keeps us safe from all that. It's kinda like having Amazon back, plus they keep the town safe so we can just focus on working. It's just like it used to be, except we don't have to pay EI or CPP or taxes."

"Except the tithe," Becca said. "But that's not really a tax. That's how we as a town pay for the Sheriff and his Deputies to keep up safe. Otherwise we'd have to be like you folks, hunting those monsters all the time just to eat!"

"Right!" Irving said. "It's like everyone else decided to go back to being hunter-gatherers. Makes no sense to me. Why should we give up on civilization?"

Fool was happy for every point he'd spent on Intelligence and Charisma. And Willpower, which he was sure he needed to keep the dumb smile plastered on his face. The situation in town was worse than he'd expected.

"Welp," Fool said, "sounds pretty good to me. Not sure why no one else thought of that first. You folks have got a great thing going on. I guess I'd be happier to take dollars then, but since we have to leave in the morning, I guess we better take scrip. That's a pretty good setup though!"

Irving smiled, and they settled down to negotiating for the Flame Elk parts. Once Fool had worked out the exchange they could expect, it was a very good rate. Fool transferred all his stock over and, with a glance, stopped Jackal from transferring his as well. Best to keep some extra trade goods in reserve. Just in case.

After some more chit-chat about weather and the general state of the world, as well as sharing how things were going in Prince George, Fool and Jackal headed back out. The Shop was only a few more blocks down, but they'd been told the restaurant across the street was the place to go in town and only took dollars.

They stopped in the middle of the street, and Fool pointed at the mountains. Something was flying way above them but heading away. It made a convenient excuse for a quiet conversation.

"Bit of a change from the indentured servitude we've been hearing about in other places," Jackal said under his breath.

"Almost worse," Fool replied. "These folk have no idea how any of it works, and they're doing it willfully. Working for pennies at that conversion rate. Sheriff's playing a tight game. He's screwed if any of these people ever make it into the Shop and see what they can actually get for their work."

"I can see why he's keeping outsiders from coming in. Wouldn't take much to split the whole scam wide open."

"Maybe, maybe not. He's done the right thing in building up the paranoia. Basic cult, almost. And the System is helping, in this case, by being the literal embodiment of the fear all the conspiracy folks had before. I bet these folks would be pretty resistant to the truth at this point."

Jackal nodded. "Wouldn't have been everyone though. Population's not that big around here, but big enough. Some folk resisted. I'm guessing it wasn't pretty for a while."

Fool shrugged and turned to face the restaurant. "Agreed. And I have a bad feeling that the 'Princess' we're looking for was part of that resistance."

Jackal sighed in agreement and followed Fool into the restaurant.

The restaurant was a throwback. Despite all the Shop and the System could offer, the owners had rejected it and insisted on non-System cooking. There were a lot of open tables, and they'd been greeted warmly when they came in, but they'd been seated near the back. All the other patrons of the restaurant were seated there as well, and the reason for it became clear pretty quickly.

The cooking was done on a selection of wood stoves and an actual wood barbecue pit that seemed to have been crudely retrofitted into the back of the restaurant. The stoves were the only source of warmth in the place. Fortunately, they'd installed proper venting with airflow to keep the place from being smoked out. As it was, it reeked of campfire smoke.

And roasting meat. Delicious smelling meat.

"What'll it be for you folks?" The waiter looked to be in his early teens.

Fool figured the town and this kid's parents had decided school wasn't important anymore. Or, he realized with a start, maybe this was the weekend? He hadn't really paid attention to a calendar since even before the System, and he wasn't even sure if people still took weekends off.

They'd found menus waiting for them at the table, but they were oddly not specific about what was being served. There was a "Meat stew, with root vegetables and sage, thyme seasoning" and "Roast, with fresh baked buns and drippings side."

"I'm interested in the stew, but what's the meat?" Fool asked.

The waiter looked off to the side and blushed a bit. "Uh… it's not beef. We can't get that anymore. But it's not, like, rat or dog or nothing."

"I figured, but curious as to what it is? Why isn't it mentioned on that menu?"

The server glanced off to the side again. Fool got the impression that he was looking to see if anyone was listening. It might have also been to look for someone to come and help him answer questions. Fool had never been very good at understanding teenagers.

"It's not polite to ask," the server said. "But it's wild game, whatever the Deputies bring in. Sometimes it's already butchered, so we're not really sure. The butchered stuff sure looks and tastes like beef, so they must get it from someone. Comes in every few weeks. But today it's something that looked like a wild boar? Tastes really good though. Had it for lunch."

"All right, that sounds good. We'll have that, same for both of us. And hey, how long has the Sheriff been taking care of all of your supplies for you? Since the start of all this mess?"

"Kinda, but not really. Took a while for the town to settle down, but the last year? I guess about that long. Some people are a bit sore, but—"

"*Andy!*" a voice roared from the barbeque pit at the back, loud enough to make Fool flinch. A tall, rangy woman tending one of the stoves was the source of the shout. "You leave those men alone with your chatter. Just get their order and get back to work. Now!"

Andy's face turned even redder, and he scuttled back to the woman, who whispered angrily in his ear.

"Be a few minutes for your food!" she said when she saw Fool looking at her.

He nodded and smiled, then he turned to look out the window as casually as he could. Definitely some secrets in this town. He glanced at Jackal. The big man had taken out a notebook and was looking relaxed, taking notes. He was making a pretty good impression of someone journaling thoughts without a care in the world. Fool took the unspoken piece of advice and dug a very worn paperback out of his pocket.

The food, when it arrived, wasn't too bad. Not great, but very passable. The meat had at least been seared first, so it had a pleasant texture. A good, satisfying meal. The only problem was an almost complete lack of any kind of spicing. Which made sense when Fool thought about it. Without the Shop for spices, they'd be relying on what they could scrounge up locally.

It was a completely backward way of doing things, and Fool found himself getting a little irritated. The System had been completely forced on them, and there was no denying it had been a catastrophic event. The entire world had changed, and not for the better. Most of humanity had died, and a big chunk of Earth's history and culture was gone.

They may as well have been hit by a dinosaur-killer meteor, with one key difference—the System had brought tools for survival with it. Survival, even prosperous survival and growth. But you had to accept it.

Fool mourned the lost world as much as anyone, though he had somewhat less reason to do so than most. Life had been cruel to him, and it wasn't likely he would have lived another year or two out on the streets. Probably would have died from some random illness that anyone else would have been cured of in a week or two, but that level of care wasn't available to those who'd fallen off of the bottom rung of social support.

The System had restored life to him. It had given him a second chance that would not have been even remotely possible without it.

Mourning, he thought, was well and proper. Resistance even had its place. Hell, that was, in a roundabout way, the whole mission of the Foundation. The System had been imposed on them with no choice, and there had been some intention behind that. Going to war against that intention?

Absolutely.

But that was a choice for a systematic-level change. Build a new System, force the old System to change. A proper fight for a warrior.

But as individuals and small groups? Resisting the System was insane. It wasn't like being a Luddite and finding more value in life by choosing simpler and more meaningful ways to live. No, this was about as reasonable as a child refusing to go to bed when they were tired.

With sleep, the whole world gets better.

For Fool and Jackal, embracing the System had not only made their lives better, but it had given them new purpose and new tools to be more of who they were meant to be. The System was a path to unlocking the potential that had always been buried inside them.

These folks were choosing to live with their heads buried in mud out of willful ignorance. They'd been offered the chance to do better, live better, and be rewarded better, but had instead chosen to hide away, even building up a false fear explaining it.

That last bit made the least amount of sense to Fool. In some ways, he felt, the world had been so ugly before the System because there were no real monsters to fight. Humans had made themselves into monsters to make up for it. The System had shown them that there were real, physical, threatening monsters all around them.

That was freedom.

When the monsters were all around, why wouldn't you choose to fight them? The moral divide was clear and simpler than it had ever been before.

Now there were dragons. Which meant everyone could be a dragon-slayer. Humanity finally had a single place to focus all their anger and distrust on and let it out.

But instead, there were those who still insisted that the real monsters had to be other people. Even if they had to make themselves the monsters first.

There was, no surprise, another uniformed Deputy in front of the Shop.

This one had a sour face nearly as bad as Barnes's. He held up a hand as they approached. "You must be the new folk I was told about. You sell your stuff yet?"

Fool looked him over. His uniform didn't fit well, and he had all sorts of old accessories draped everywhere. Plate carrier vest, kneepads, two pistols, and what looked like an old military rifle on his back. Fool was surprised he didn't see any grenades, but he wasn't sure that this guy would be able to walk with the extra weight. Still, a quick look at his stats showed he had decent enough Levels and the Skills one would expect of a town guard. Or "Sheriff's Deputy" in this case.

"We did," Fool said and passed over the scrip they'd been given. The lunch amount had been added and signed by the sour owner of the restaurant.

The Deputy took the piece of paper and carefully looked it over. Which seemed like a bit of an overkill since it really only had a few amounts. "How much you want in Credits?"

Fool looked at Jackal, then turned back to the Deputy. "All of it. We're planning on leaving pretty early tomorrow."

"All right. But just so you know, you got a one-time pass from the Sheriff. You want to come back in, you have to clear it with him first. No one gets in without his say-so, understand?"

"Absolutely, officer. We'll make sure to get everything we need."

The Deputy didn't seem to understand the grin on Fool's face, but he looked uncomfortable, nonetheless. After a moment's hesitation, he stepped aside, and Fool and Jackal walked past him into the Shop.

It was in the old IGA, which made Fool smile. It made sense that the Shop would be in the town grocery store, but the grocery store itself had been completely gutted. Not only were all the grocery items removed, but all the shelves and fixtures were gone. The only thing left in the desolate space was the Shop orb. At least no one else was in there.

After a quick look to make sure the door had fully closed, Jackal turned to Fool. The windows were covered in enough dust and debris that no one could easily see in, at least not without being obvious about it.

"What's the plan?" Jackal asked.

Fool thought about it for a moment. "Head back to the motel, wait for night, sneak off to wherever the Princess is and make contact, then talk her into leaving ASAP. Tonight if we can. Make sense?"

Jackal sighed. "How do you want to deal with the Sheriff? The Deputies? How are we going to leave town? Walk out the front gate?"

"Sure." Fool grinned again. "It'll be easy. I'm going to grab a distraction from the Shop. I have just the thing in mind. We should be able to head right out and get enough of a head start to keep them behind us until we get to Tete Jaune Cache. I'm positive the Mountaineers Guild will help us out if they follow us that far, but I don't think they will."

"I'll concede that," Jackal said. "They've got enough extra folk to do some hunting, but I'm not seeing any great concern for the townsfolk from the dear Sheriff. I'd be surprised if they mustered up that much work to chase one person down. Unless it's the Sheriff's daughter. Or girlfriend."

"Ugh. Terrible thoughts. We'll cross that bridge when we come to it. Anything else bothering you?"

"Yeah, one thing. What if the Princess doesn't want to come with us? Have you thought about how you're going to convince a random person you've never met to drop everything and run off with a stranger? I know your Charisma score is pretty high, but I'm hoping you're not relying on that."

"Nah. I mean… yes? Maybe? I admit I was planning on leaning on it a bit, but only when I thought we'd have a few days here. Now that we want to get out as soon as possible, I'm hoping a bit of logic and a chance to adventure will appeal to the young lass."

"You just said young lass, Fool. Getting into the whole 'Rescue the Princess' thing a bit much, aren't we?"

"Once-in-a-lifetime opportunity? You bet! But no, I don't think we'll have to work hard to convince her to come with us. Think about it. The Foundation says she's one of the ideal assets for them. You think someone who thinks like everyone else in town would be that kind of person? My thinking is that she's already pissed off with the way things are running and probably more than ready to get out of here."

"Fair," Jackal said. "But that's another potential issue. You get the hint that not everyone is happy here, right? And that there was some conflict over it? I'm thinking it might be some rather hefty conflict and this Princess-type might actually be involved. Which means we might be getting messed up in something we aren't expecting."

Fool rubbed his forehead. "Fuck. Yeah, hadn't thought about that. Any ideas what we can do in that case?"

"I hate to say it, but I think the usual approach might be our best bet."

"Wing it?"

"Yes. Why not? I really want to argue with you, but the more I look at this, the more I see time running out. The town's been 'friendly and nice', but it feels like a noose slowly tightening rather than a summer vacation on a beach, you know. Let's get this done as fast as we can."

Chapter Ten

When they left the Shop and headed back out, the Deputy at the door wasn't alone. He'd been joined by another Deputy, just as heavily armed but a lot shorter. The newcomer looked up at Fool and Jackal, and it wasn't a pleasant look.

The first Deputy turned back to them as well. "Something's come up. You folks need to head back to your motel now and stay put. It's for your own safety."

"But we were going to grab dinner in a bit," Fool said. He'd made sure to keep just enough cash for that expense. "Is that still okay?"

The newcomer muttered under his breath, pulled out a pad of paper, and quickly scrawled a note on it. "Take this to the pub. They'll prep a dinner for you and bring it to your room. Don't worry about paying, the Sheriff will cover it."

"Oh! Thanks!" Fool said, putting on his most disarming smile. "What's going on? Anything we should be aware of? We might be able to help. We've both fought our share of monsters."

"Nothing like that," the newcomer said. "We just got word that a criminal we've been hunting is back in town, and we're searching for their hiding spot now. They're pretty dangerous, killed a lot of people, so it's safer for you if you get off the streets."

"Good idea, Deputy. We'll do that right away and get out from under your feet. Thank you for your service!"

Jackal was quivering and managed to turn his stifled laugh into a coughing fit.

"And I think my friend could use a drink anyway, so off to the pub we go. Stay safe out there!" Fool added and started back up the road, pulling Jackal with him.

Once they were out of earshot, Fool glanced at Jackal, who wasn't doing a very good job of hiding his grin. He bit back the urge to scold his friend, because honestly, Fool had been trying to make him laugh. He'd just figured the big lunk had more resistance.

"You buy that criminal thing?" he asked Jackal.

"Maybe. I suspect the rebel element is a bit more proactive than we expected. Sounds like the division in the town has led to bloodshed. Bet we get more tonight."

"That's going to complicate our plans," Fool replied.

"Nah. Confusion and noise, isn't that your friend? If we can make a little extra noise out scouting, maybe we can get them chasing their prey and our shadows all night. Tons of extra cover. Maybe we can split up. One of us can head the opposite direction to start and make a little ruckus, then catch back up?"

"Maybe. Let's hit the pub. Bet we can get a better sense of what's going on there."

"Good plan," Jackal said. "And I could go for a beer too. Always nice to relax a bit before a job."

Fool nodded. That was it then. When Jackal said "job" out loud, that was their sign that the planning was over. Things weren't theoretical anymore. It was time to put on their game faces and get to work. After a beer.

It was only a few blocks back to the motel, and another block to the pub from there. A ten-minute walk maybe. In that time, the little town seemed to change almost immediately. The shops they'd passed on the way into town were all closing up. Fool had the idea that if they had shutters, they'd be slamming them shut.

All the pedestrians were gone, and the only people they could see were more and more of the Sheriff's Deputies running about. They were all armed, and some of them were carrying more modern, System-acquired weapons as well. All firearms though. No melee weapons at all.

Fool could understand that. Firearms were lethal. Could kill people at a distance, end the fight long before you could reach the threat. Except, of course, in this new world, where teleportation was a thing. Where the twenty-foot rule became the eighty-foot rule and a good melee weapon wielded right could disarm you—literally—and make your weapon no more than a hunk of metal.

Never mind Class Skills that could literally do that.

But man was a creature of routine and firearms still screamed—to your average Joe—threat. Especially for a town that was clutching hard to the old world.

They opted out of checking back into the motel room and instead went straight to the pub. The pub didn't look like much from the outside, but the inside was strange, with a giant fireplace sort of assembly thing in the middle that made Fool think of a TARDIS. And despite the Deputies rounding everyone up, a few folks were still sitting around and nursing drinks.

Jackal went up to the bar and placed an order with a very pleasant lady for their dinner, to be delivered to their room in a few hours, and grabbed a couple of pints of tap beer for him and Jackal… and a healthy selection of sides as well, since the Sheriff was paying.

If they'd hoped to overhear some conversations and get some more intel on the town from drunken patrons, they were sorely mistaken. The dour faces on the drinkers made sense when they'd both had their first sips of beer.

It was quite tasty and fresh. That was about the only good point. Fool recognized the taste of spruce tips, probably to make up for the complete lack of hops. Which was part of the problem. No hops, because they hadn't sourced any from the Shop and were clearly making do with what they could. Which also meant it was normal beer.

And because anyone with System-boosted Constitution was practically immune to the effects of alcohol by itself, it was effectively tasty water. So no pleasant pre-job buzz to help the mind move loosely. The drinkers were probably folks who lived for the habit of alcohol and had gone through a lot of pain when its effects were reduced.

Thus the dour faces. Fool had some empathy with them.

In a lot of ways, the System had brought about a much healthier baseline for everyone, but at the same time? It hurt to lose a lifelong coping mechanism. At least Fool had had the incredible luck to have someone help with his issues and get him into the Shop to fix things up. With no Shop fix for these folks? That wasn't something Fool wanted to think about. Too many bad memories, too many lost friends and lost years.

"Why are we doing this?" Fool asked. He wasn't sure where the question came from, but once it was out, he felt the truth of it.

Jackal looked at him quizzically, then took a long draft of his beer. He glanced around, but no one in the area was paying any kind of attention to them at all.

"You know why," he said. "Make the world a better place."

"I know, but really, are we making a difference? So few people left, it feels like we're moving through a ghost of the world that once was. And everywhere we go, it's more people like this Sheriff, just trying to crush everyone so that they can make their own share of the pie a little bigger. From what I can tell, it's worse the farther out you go into the Galaxy."

"Stop thinking big," Jackal said. "You look at the patterns you're seeing, you see overwhelming odds against everyone. And that's not wrong, but it's not the whole truth. You and I are a small part of the universe. At most scales, we don't even really exist. Not in any way that matters. Even a mountain has more meaning to the universe than we do, and they'll sure as hell be around long after everything we've ever done is over and gone."

"That supposed to help?" Fool felt a tip happening within him, as if a tiny amount of gravity had shifted and the world inside was just starting to slide down a bit of a slope.

There wasn't any reason for it. The System had cleared his brain of most of what he had lived with for most of his life, but sometimes it still creeped back. His grandfather had joked with Fool when he was a kid, telling him he'd gotten the family curse of being Irish-blooded. *Red rage and black sorrow,* he'd said. It had certainly been true, but in Fool's case, it hadn't really covered the full scope of the issue.

And here he was, about to slide into the black for no reason whatsoever.

"No, it's not supposed to help, Fool. It's just the reality. But it isn't the whole story." Jackal leaned in. "Small things make a big difference. Energy used to flow through the universe, then it started to clump. Those clumps collected and formed quarks and gluons and leptons, and those formed protons and electrons and neutrons, and the whole universe expanded from there."

Fool looked at his friend. Jackal was looking back at him, and his face was earnest, his eyes piercing and dark. Fool couldn't tell where he was going, but the urgent draw in Jackal's voice kept him listening.

"Everything we are, everything we do, comes as a result of the fundamental process that drew those first bits of energy together and shaped them into matter. All of our consciousness, the very way we think, was in some way shaped by the nature of that energy, even before it became matter.

"Look at our world, look at all the people and all the random shapes and patterns we are. The fundamental laws shape us, but they also shape the complexity of life. They make that complexity possible. And the more complex matter is? The more it builds and deepens? The more it acts like energy. In the birth of a star, it converts back and reshapes itself and pours more potential out into the universe. But the sun itself, on one scale, is predictable and restricted in its shape and form."

Jackal paused long enough to take another sip of his beer, then jumped right back in. "That's how our universe works. Things flex and flow between order and chaos, always finding new patterns and growth. As things get more complex, the potential to form into something new is always there. It always, always starts with a single seed. Some singular action that cascades out and explodes into the ignition of a new star."

Some of Jackal's fervor drained away. "I'm not saying that's us. We aren't that crystal, that focus for change. And we might not be around to see the result of what we do. But we're taking steps. Hell, Fool, everything you do adds to the complexity of the world. I swear that's the truth of your god. And it chose you for that reason. The two of you are completely aligned. That's why we do this, to try to fight and make sure that the right seed is the one that starts the ignition, so that we can have a star that shines out and shapes the universe back on its right path.

"Because the System is clawing into it, Fool. It will kill the whole universe if it's left to its own devices. It's alien, and it's wrong. So that's why we do this. Because the universe needs us. It's fighting back right from each atom, and we're the universe. We're its tools, its weapons. And we're small, but not the smallest. It's not just that it matters, Fool. It's that it's our purpose.

"We are here, we are alive, because our universe is fighting for its life. And in the end, that is why our lives matter, just as much as what we do with our lives. So drink your damned beer and get over feeling sorry for yourself, because we have a job to do and some asses that need to be kicked."

Jackal snarled that last bit, almost under his breath, and Fool felt the hair on the back of his neck and forearms rise.

He smiled at Jackal with more than a few teeth showing. "That, my friend, is a deal."

Then Fool's expression softened, and he leaned back. That slide had stopped. Not forever, but for a moment. He wasn't sure he understood everything Jackal had said, not sure he believed it. But having someone believe in him, in their purpose, that was enough.

That was enough, even if it was only for a moment.

"Thank you."

"Fuck that," Jackal said. "We're a team. I'm always here for you. Just like I know you're always going to be there for me when I need you."

They raised their glasses and clinked them together, just in time for the food to arrive.

They wound up spending the rest of the afternoon in the pub. It turned out there was a chessboard, and Jackal had entertained himself by crushing Fool repeatedly in game after game. They'd eventually had their dinner at the table instead of having it delivered. No one had come to check on them, and no one came into the pub to enforce the order to go home, so they pushed it as long as they could.

Eventually, it became noticeable that the sun was getting lower in the sky. A gathering of Deputies stood on the road outside the pub. Jackal and Fool watched them gather for a few minutes, then looked at one another.

"I think that's our sign," Fool said.

Jackal nodded, getting up. "Best be gone before Barnes shows up. I get the feeling he won't be happy to see us up and about at the moment."

They didn't make it far outside the door before they heard a startled "Hey!" come from the gathered group. It was the Deputy from the Shop, who stomped right over to them.

"You two are supposed to be back in your motel room!" he shouted. "What are you doing out here?"

Fool held up his hands to placate the angry young man. "Sorry, we went straight to the pub, and it didn't seem too bad there, so we grabbed a few extra drinks. No harm intended."

"Leave 'em be, Emmet," a voice said from behind Fool.

The look in Jackal's eye already told Fool who it was, even if the put-on accent didn't give it away. His suspicions were confirmed when he turned and found Barnes standing with his hands on his hips. Near his service pistol. It wasn't exactly a subtle threat.

"Again, sorry, Sheriff Barnes. It seemed like a quiet place to be, and we're on our way back to our motel room now," Fool said.

"Good. I'm not blaming you for this, but you'll want to get back to your room. It's not safe out here. We got a terrorist running loose, and if we don't catch 'em, well… lots of danger for everyone, 'specially you folk who aren't local. Emmet shoulda explained that better to you."

Emmet quailed under Barnes's expression.

"No worries!" Fool replied. "Our fault entirely. We'll head back to our room now and be out of your hair."

Barnes held up his hand as Fool started to walk past him to the motel. It didn't quite reach his chest, but it was only a hair away. Fool looked into Barnes's eyes and saw that the civil facade had been stripped away.

The Sheriff leaned in close to Fool and spoke in a harsh, low voice that none of the Deputies would be able to hear. "You be outta here first thing in the morning. I don't know what the fuck you're up to or why you came to my town, but if I see any part of you other than your ass heading south in the morning, you and your girlfriend ain't never leaving this town. You understand me?"

Fool looked him right back in the eye. He wanted to argue. He wanted to be smart, to cut the pompous bullying ass down to size, but this wasn't the time or the place. They still had no idea who they were here to pick up or what they were going to have to do to retrieve them, and until then, the best plan was to play it safe and simple. And bury the flash of rage Fool felt down deep. After they made contact, if there was time, Fool might find a reason to make sure the Sheriff had a very bad day.

He smiled brightly at Barnes. "You'll see my ass first thing in the morning, Sheriff. Just the way you want to."

Fool didn't wait for a response but walked right past. Best pretend not to see the angry red flush coloring Barnes's cheeks. Not the smartest thing Fool had ever done, but he couldn't really help himself. He heard Jackal behind him, and they walked toward the motel.

Fool half-expected to be shot in the back. But Barnes spent his rage on his Deputies, hollering and getting them organized for another sweep of the town.

Fool kept up the laconic pace until they turned the corner toward the motel entrance. As soon as he was out of sight, he sprinted for the door. With a quiet yelp, Jackal took off after him.

Fool didn't stop until he got to their room, and by the time Jackal got in and closed the door, Fool had his face pressed up against the window.

"What the hell was that all about?" he asked.

"Second floor. We can see where they go from here, mostly. Get back out in the hallway and see if you can find some way to get onto the roof! We need to see where they're going. I've got a hunch it's where we want to be."

Jackal didn't wait, just headed back out the door.

Fool kept watching out the window, and almost right away, he saw the uniformed mob walk down the road toward the downtown strip.

They were almost out of sight when Jackal came back. "Found it. Stairs go up, door's locked, but I opened it. Shall we?"

Fool didn't even nod but sprinted out of the room and down the hall to the stairs. He hustled up the stairs. Fortunately, Jackal had had enough foresight to wedge the door open, so Fool ran right over to the edge.

His hope was rewarded. He could just make out the mob, barely visible over the roofs of the surrounding buildings. They went out of sight for a moment, and Fool ran down to the eastern end of the roof, the one that overlooked the large empty field. On the other side of that field was the rest of the town, the residential area. Blocks of homes, all neatly arranged. The place they'd been forbidden to explore.

And sure enough, the posse came into sight again, moving as one across the field. Fool grabbed the tracking sphere out of his pocket and held it up.

Jackpot.

They were heading in the exact same direction the Princess was in. For a moment, Fool had a sense of mental vertigo. He loved being right. But also, just once, it'd be nice to be wrong about something like this.

Things surely had gotten complicated.

Again.

Chapter Eleven

Waiting until sunset was agonizing, but Jackal insisted. Fortunately, the surrounding mountains made sunset happen pretty quickly, and it was dark enough for Jackal to give his grudging consent shortly after.

Even so, it had been almost two hours since they'd seen the Sheriff's posse head off in the Princess's direction. And Fool wasn't sure, but he thought he'd heard at least one shot. He'd wanted to leave right away, but Jackal had convinced him to stay put.

Jackal was right, and Fool admitted that easily. They still didn't really know what was going on in this town, and walking into the middle of what was clearly an explosive situation wasn't the smartest thing to do.

Fool and Jackal didn't have any kind of Invisibility Skill, but their profession had necessitated the acquisition of a good many Stealth Skills and tools, and they readied everything they could for their nighttime scouting mission. The room didn't have a window suitable for climbing out of—and in any case, that would have put them in the middle of the parking lot, which wasn't the kind of stealthy move they were looking for.

At least, as best they could tell, the entire town's collection of Deputies had gone to whatever they were up to—minus the couple on the walls— and Fool and Jackal hadn't spotted a single one coming back. With the rest of the town likely obeying the lockdown order, they should have the streets to themselves.

Fool glanced at the Conditions they were currently wielding, grinning a little.

Geas

Effect: Enforces a mild to serious mental and chemical mental influence on surrounding targets, forcing a specific mindset on the targets. User must also act within the conditions of the geas as well, with cost increasing depending on the geas, resistances and number.

Cost: Variable depending on Geas in effect, number of individuals and cost

Have Faith

Triggers a request to higher power. Effects variable.

Cost: 5 Mana per use

Up on the roof, they attached a rope ladder to the east side of the motel in the darkest spot they could find. There was even a convenient hedge nestled up the side of the building for them to ease themselves down behind.

When his feet hit the soft earth, Fool took a moment to glance around. No one in the area. A quick glance with Jackal confirmed that.

Then they stopped for a moment. A small ritual between the two of them, one last moment of calm before they committed to action. A pause, a stillness that perfectly completed the freshness of the night. It was their little prayer and signal to begin. They wouldn't speak to each other past this, not unless it was necessary.

Jackal took the lead. Both of them had high Perception, but Jackal's was a little more fine-tuned for hunting and reacting. Fool's was better for sensing the overall flow of a situation, so being a little farther back from Jackal helped both of them. Weird how the System had made it easier for them to do that, as though it was lending a helping hand. They both trusted each other to follow any sudden moves or changes in direction.

Jackal didn't seem too concerned about being watched. Instead of bursting out of cover and sprinting across the street to the next bit of shade, he casually walked out of the hedges and into the road behind the motel. Fool took an extra moment to look around, make sure that one had noticed or reacted, but the Sheriff's orders seemed to have been completely obeyed. The town, at least this part of it, was deserted. In the houses all around, the curtains were drawn, and fitful light only leaked around edges, not in open slices that would indicate someone looking out a window.

Not that anyone would see anything. That was something Fool had noted long before the System, being a kid with a penchant for trouble. The nighttime was his friend and his ideal playground. He'd realized that when he looked out a window at night and the lights from the room had turned the window into almost a mirror. And he'd tested that by walking through people's yards when their curtains were open and standing still while they occasionally glanced out.

No one ever seemed to notice.

Once, a man had actually walked up to the window, put a hand in his pocket, sipped his drink, and looked right at Fool. He'd frozen, thinking he'd been spotted, but as much as he looked, the man inside the house never seemed to react. He just looked out, took another sip, and eventually turned back to talk to someone on the couch.

Fool had turned around to look behind him and saw that the house had a view of the distant city, the sparkling lights making a lovely backdrop. He'd been standing right in front of the guy and hadn't been noticed. That was when Fool really fell in love with the night.

The System had taken away a big chunk of that love. The night wasn't his playground anymore, the darkest patches weren't his private hideouts. Now the night was a threat. The dark spots could hold monsters that could kill you in an eye-blink. He'd had to learn, painfully, to fear the night again.

At least he had a bit of reassurance because he was in the company of Jackal, who was probably the biggest threat the night held. It was a comfortable feeling.

He was reminded of that as he watched Jackal move down the street toward their next destination, the open field they'd seen the massed Deputies moving across. Now that Jackal was in stalking mode, the careful "harmless" walk he'd been practicing all day had been dropped as he returned to his normal stride. He stalked the night like his namesake, like a low-slung canine predator on the scent of wounded prey.

Fool kept pace behind, doing his best to be nothing. The night was chill enough that their breath puffed out in temporary white clouds. A gentle wind, lit with the occasional gusts, ruffled his clothing. He'd noticed that wind was enough to dust small clouds of fresh snow across the occasional opening, and he tried to imitate those.

His Geas Skill was active, and he struggled to keep his focus on it. Anyone who looked at him would see him as a brief dusting of snow, nothing that stood out at all. As long as he didn't do anything too outrageous, he could keep up that appearance with only the slightest trickle of Mana.

It didn't take them more than a moment to reach the field. They paused at the edge, carefully looking for any signs of life. Nothing, no one, outside of the homes that ringed the large and empty field.

The snow was crisscrossed with tracks in all directions, and some of them were hard packed from constant use. But there was a clear path where more people had crossed recently, and it matched the path of the Deputies they'd seen from the motel roof.

Kitty-corner across the field was the proper residential area of the town. All they could see in that direction was block after block of houses. There were no streetlights anymore—the Sheriff apparently hadn't spent funds on that upgrade—but most houses had outside lights from one source or another. Between that and the near-full moon, they could see most of the way with no problems.

Jackal seemed to share Fool's opinion, because after a few quick glances to each side, he started across the field in the same direction. Fool wasn't sure if Jackal planned to follow the Deputies' path until he ran across them or to cut off in another direction, but either way, he'd follow Jackal. Just had to trust him at this point.

They crossed the field without incident, and Jackal stopped in the shadows of a small shack at the far end. The road went on past that point, and the rest of the town seemed to be the typical small-town grid of houses. Which meant that every intersection they crossed now would leave them exposed.

Jackal motioned to Fool, and Fool joined him in the shadows.

"Which way?" Jackal asked.

Fool thought about it for a moment, then took out the tracking device to confirm. The device confirmed his hunch. The direction the posse had gone was the same direction as their target. Which brought up some interesting possibilities.

The first was that the Princess was one of the Deputies, and he'd only managed to check direction before when one of the Deputies was in roughly the same area.

The second was that the Princess was a homebody and just happened, with terrible coincidence, to be in the same area that the posse had hot-footed it off to.

Third was the chance that the Princess was in the same house with the terrorist, either a child, family member, or friend.

Fourth was the worst possibility. The princess *was* the terrorist the Deputies were hunting down. That would be fun, because they'd have to somehow get through a town's complete police force to reach her, while that same force had all their attention directed right at their target.

Big fun if it worked out that way.

Big. Fun.

At least it would solve one issue. Shouldn't take much effort to talk the Princess into leaving town with them.

That thought was the most amusing one, since it had the greatest risk, but it did have one fun quirk. He smiled, and the moonlight must have caught the flash of his teeth just right, because Jackal grunted a query at him.

"Just thinking," Fool said. "It's looking like we might actually get to say, 'We're here to rescue you, Princess Leia!' I've been dying to say that."

Jackal snorted. "That's not the line, you know."

"Then what is it?" Fool asked.

"You could say 'I'm Fool, and I'm here to rescue you' if you wanted to be more accurate."

"Well. Whatever. Either way."

They grinned, then Fool looked around. Time for a decision. They could either keep going straight toward the target or work around and try to come at it from a different direction. Starting from here, the town's layout resembled a long rectangle. The direction they needed to go would take them right to the farthest point of the rectangle. The map of the town that Fool had looked at before had placed a school at that point. So they either needed to go to a house right near the school or into the school itself.

Going around would mean skirting the edge of the town and whatever defenses the Sheriff had put up in that area. But it would also mean coming in from the side and maybe getting a better view of what was happening.

Going straight to that corner by following the path of the posse would have a different advantage. They'd come up behind probably the bulk of the Deputies and the Sheriff himself, but they'd also get the best sense of what they were up to and maybe what they were planning.

That decided Fool.

While going the long way might give them a better chance of getting in, going the fastest way would give them a better idea of what the Sheriff was doing, which meant they'd have a better chance of getting out.

Know thy enemy, trip them up with their shoelaces and all that.

Fool gestured with a nod, pointing out the direction he wanted to go, and Jackal started heading in that direction.

It wasn't quite a straight path. Forward one block, then a turn down the next street. After the first series of turns, Fool could see that the town had gone with the weird logic of naming its streets in alphabetical order, descending toward the school, which would be named something that started with an "A." And the avenues were numbered, ascending as they walked away from the start of town. They'd been told not to pass 5th Avenue, and they'd just hit 7th. A quick glance down the avenue showed Fool that they had about two more blocks south to go.

Maybe five more blocks total. Which meant it was time to come up with a plan.

Fool let his mind go into a trance and let his feet take him along. Different scenarios played across his mind. Assuming the worst case—most likely case, honestly. No sense denying it. The closer they got to the end of town, the fewer Deputies they saw walking around or guarding anything, the more likely it was all of them were involved in surrounding whatever property the Princess was in.

Fool and Jackal could sprint right through, move with speed and surprise. It wasn't likely that people focused inward would really notice them in the time it took them to get to the door. System-aided stats were one thing, but the human mind still took a bit to catch up. Add on the fact that Fool and Jackal had System-aided Speed, and everything often came up to a wash.

Unless you were playing with the big boys. Then again, if a Heroic was running around, Fool was going to bend over and kiss his perky butt goodbye anyway.

By the time Fool and Jackal got to the building, the Deputies would notice them, but maybe they wouldn't have time to do anything about it. Still, sprinting close left Fool and Jackal standing outside a door, and what? Knocking?

Maybe walk around the cordon, sneaky-sneak. Look for a place the Deputies weren't watching too much? Might work. The school was on the edge of town, which meant there was a really good chance it would be mostly surrounded by trees. Might be a chance to sneak in that way.

They could try to fight their way through. They'd absolutely have the element of surprise there, and if Fool relied more on his acquired Skills, they'd probably be able to take out most of them.

That surprised Fool when he realized it was true. His steps slowed a little.

It wasn't in him to attack and kill humans like that. But did he have to? He had the chops to run circles around most people his Level or lower, and everyone in this town was, except for the Sheriff. He had a ton of Skills.

Why was Fool approaching this as though he was the same person he had been before the System? Why was he trying to be the best version of who he was, instead of the best version of who he'd become?

His steps slowed then stopped. Jackal noticed and stopped too, but he didn't say anything, just stood quietly and waited for his friend.

Fool's mind was in turmoil. He pulled up his Skill list and really looked at it for what felt like the first time. He reviewed each Skill, one after the other.

Clouseau: *He could change any one physical attribute. He could make himself taller, or shorter, or change his hair color or skin color. Gain or lose weight. Any single thing, one at a time. That could be useful. He'd always thought of it as a party trick, a one-off thing he could use to change his appearance. Now he regretted not putting more points into it, because it would have stacked really well with his other Skills to mimic another person perfectly. But he could still use it. Maybe not right away.*

Have Faith: *He still wasn't ready to use that. Calling on his god for a favor of any kind, in exchange for having to do a favor for a Trickster god? His lowest level*

163

Skill, the first one in his Class, but the one he used the least. Potentially very powerful, but also more risk than he was willing to take.

Talent Scout: *He'd used this to find out what Skills people had and what they were about to use. It was one of his key ways of helping Jackal, and one of the only ways Fool felt even semi-useful in combat. But maybe there were other ways of using it. Something was starting to gel in his head.*

He skimmed the list, running combinations in his head, pairing things together in ways he hadn't imagined before.

I Know a Shortcut, and Location Scout. He'd hardly touched those, but he mentally tagged them, already shuffling himself off to a shadowy set of shrubs by the side of the road. Jackal anticipated what was happening and moved with him, quietly putting a hand on Fool's back to guide him.

Down the road, there was movement.

Fool let his mind rush, opening to these new ideas.

It was all coming together. He'd never really *used* his Skills, he realized. Never trusted them to work at some fundamental level. In his own way, Fool had been fighting the System just like the people in this town. Willfully blind. It'd taken actually being here, immersed amongst a group of similar fools, for it to become clear.

His Skill use had always been for one-off things, used sparingly if at all.

But there was no reason for that. The Mana consumption rate limited how much he could use, but his costs weren't that high, and his Mana refresh rate was pretty good. He could use his Skills all day, nearly continuously, if he wanted to. Hell, his limit was probably his Intelligence score for the total and his Willpower for Regen and thank god he'd been sneaking points into those.

No Fair gave Fool the Ability to alter any single Stat or Ability. He'd used that the best way he'd thought of in combat, to give either him or Jackal a temporary advantage against an opponent. But it was far more powerful than that.

And Pants on Fire? He mostly used that to tell small lies when he thought he could get away with it, but he never really told more of a lie than someone without the Ability could probably get away with. Hell, overall? He'd really survived all this time off of his Stats more than his Skills.

And finally? Geas. He'd used it before. It let him warp reality as long as he obeyed the conditions of that reality. He could make everyone think of and see him as a giant, for example, but the moment he took a step and the ground didn't shake? People wouldn't be compelled to see him as a giant anymore.

But the heart of that Skill was that it compelled people to obey him in certain ways. It was one of his highest Skills, but he'd only used it in one simple way. He wasn't even really sure what was possible with it, but now seemed like the best time to put it to work.

Fool shook his head, coming out of his trance. Jackal was looking at him, with a face full of curiosity.

"I've got a plan…"

Jackal raised an eyebrow in response.

"We're just gonna walk straight in."

Chapter Twelve

"I'm not ready to fight all of them at once, Fool," Jackal said.

"We won't have to. I think I've got a better idea. I've been going about using my Skills the wrong way all along, and I think I can use them in a different fashion."

Jackal nodded. "I'm listening."

"They aren't Combat Skills or Combat spells or Craft Skills or any of the other tools I've been comparing them to. I'm an Acolyte of the Trickster. All of my Skills are a way to imitate what they do."

"Right, isn't that what you've been doing all along?" Jackal didn't exactly look confused. He was watching Fool closely, and Fool got the sudden idea that his too-smart-for-his-own-good friend had probably figured this out a long time ago.

"Yeah. But this is different. Watch," he said. And then Fool walked out onto the road.

Moving down the road was a Deputy clearly doing a patrol. Probably, Fool figured, one of a few who had been sent out to make sure nothing strange was coming up on the posse from behind. Like Fool and Jackal were.

The Deputy raised his rifle butt to his cheek, pointing the barrel toward Fool, and started to shout... but froze, his mouth open, as Fool waved. And then beckoned him forward.

In his mind, Fool ran through his Skills as he activated them.

No Fair to reduce Perception. Geas for a simple twist of reality. Fool was nudging the Deputy to believe he was someone the Deputy expected to see. Fool didn't try to specify who. He'd let the Deputy fill in the blanks.

As the Deputy walked forward, Fool kept updating Talent Scout to see if the deputy had any Skills or Abilities that were firing up to resist. Nothing so far. The Deputy was a low-Level Guard and didn't have any Skills to deal with what Fool was bringing.

Fool casually waved at Jackal to stay in the shadows.

The Deputy walked up to them and nodded at Fool. "Hey, man. Figured you'd be out walking your dog. You gotta get him back in. They ain't kidding about this tonight, okay? Any other one of us might shoot you before talking to you. We cool?"

Fool didn't answer. He didn't know enough about who the deputy was expecting, so he let the Geas fill in the blanks for him.

"All right," the Deputy said. "You have a good night." Then he walked away, looking side to side as he went.

After a moment, Fool turned to Jackal. "Good boy. Ready to go in?"

Jackal shook his head. "Jedi mind tricks? You've done that before. You think you'll be able to scale it up for a more focused group? Thought you said Geas is a fragile Skill."

"It is, but I'm figuring something out. I've been looking at all my Skills as individual bits, not as things that complement each other. I've been using each as a one-shot, but I can get some synergy out of them if I'm careful in their use."

"I've got faith in you. So what's the plan?"

Fool looked down the road. The Deputy looked to have been alone and was still walking away, so Fool nodded off to the side. Best to not be on the road in case the Deputy saw them. They went back into the shadow of the shrub together.

"No need for us to just show up and wing it. I can use Location Scout to see what's going on in the area and where our target is, and then I Know a Shortcut to find the best way to get in. Then when we get there, I figure everyone will be focused on anyone trying to get out of the area. I'll toss up a Geas to have them ignore anyone walking in. They should be most of the way there anyway, and I can use Talent Scout and No Fair as we head in, to actively shut down anyone who might start to resist."

"Huh," Jackal said, and his eyes widened a bit. "So we literally just walk right in?"

"That's the plan."

"And if it fails?"

"Then we go back to the usual and try to fight our way in." Fool grinned.

Jackal rolled his eyes. "All right, whatever. Get your mojo on, and let's see if we can figure this out."

Fool didn't bother to confirm, just called up his Skill Location Scout. It wasn't anything too fancy, basically a grid layout. But paired with the tracking device in his hand, he was able to confirm his suspicions. Their target, the Princess, was a large green dot near the center of what was listed as the town's secondary school. It also looked as though some elementary fortifications had been added.

That was interesting. Those weren't overnight things. This little conflict with the Sheriff had been building for longer than he'd thought, it seemed. And the Sheriff was prepared to end it and soon. The school was surrounded by little red dots of opposition forces, in larger numbers than Fool would have expected from the small town's police force.

But he now had confirmation of where they were going, and exactly where it was, and what they'd have to get through to get there. That meant he and Jackal would have to do a lot less sneaking around.

Excellent.

Next Fool called up I Know a Shortcut, focusing specifically on the Princess. When he'd first planned on using this Skill, it had looked overpowered. Being able to find the perfect route to any location? A cat burglar's dream, really. But it had some big caveats at his Level, the biggest being that it was imprecise. And it didn't promise to be accurate. At all. He was hoping his high Luck would balance that out.

He got the same basic grid map layout, but this time there was a solid black line that went a bit out of town, around the big field that surrounded the school, into the woods that nestled up behind it, and to the back door. Then it went through the halls to the room the Princess was in.

There were also several grey dashed lines. That made him wonder for a bit, so he pinched and zoomed in on those. As he did, a legend for the map flashed up on the side and made the layout much more sensible. The solid black line was for the most efficient path, the one with the least resistance or predicted expenditure of Mana. The dotted lines were alternate paths, and each one came with a listed Mana cost.

That was interesting but made sense. Why wouldn't one Skill know of his other Skills and build off of them? The more he zipped around, the more he realized he'd been using this Skill wrong all along. He'd first chosen it thinking that having a map around would be handy, a replacement for having a map and GPS on his phone all the time.

Instead, this Skill was actually like an advanced project management tool for planning operations. It had automatically updated from Location Scout and was predicting what Skills he might need to pass different obstacles. It was making best guesses as to what each red dot represented. And that made him realize that he should have spent more Skill points upgrading Location Scout. He'd have been able to combine it with Talent Scout to get specific information on each little dot and build up a very precise plan.

He swore quietly. If he'd only paid more attention to his Skills and trusted in them and in himself, he'd have a much better set of tools to use. He put that aside though. No time for recriminations now. They had a job to do. And even with the realization that he could have done more with the tools at hand, he was still in a far better position now than they had been a bit ago. He pinched the map away. It wasn't needed; the details were nice, but they'd stick to the optimal path for now.

"Okay," Fool said to Jackal. "Got a path. We're gonna swing out, loop out of town a bit, circle around to the woods at the back of the school, and head right in. Target's in one of the rooms near the middle of the school."

"So, confirmed the Princess is in the school then?"

"Right. Sorry. Yeah, the Princess is in the school and completely surrounded. It looks like the Sheriff called in some backup too. We've got about thirty people surrounding the school. Pretty sure that's more than the Deputies in town."

Jackal nodded. "Bit more to this than we thought. Sounds like we're putting ourselves in the middle of a little war here. Sure we don't want to get more information about this before we dive in? We aren't even sure what role the Princess is playing in all this. She a pawn, or is she the terrorist? Or a hostage?"

Fool nodded. "Got one more Skill I can use for that. I can get some yes/no answers if I phrase things carefully. You've got the brains here. This is gonna cost a bit of Mana, so just the one. What you do you want to ask?"

Jackal smiled. "This sounds like fun. Fair warning, now that you've told me about this, I'm going to take advantage of it."

"Mana cost, remember?" Fool said, with not a little fear. Jackal looked *way* too excited about the possibilities.

"Sure thing, buddy," Jackal said. "Trust me. Okay, we'll keep it simple. Is our target the person the Sheriff is calling the terrorist?"

Food nodded, then activated his Truth or Dare Skill. It was a simple text interface, so he filled in the question verbatim and pressed the button. A little whirring animation shot up, spun about, and stopped. *Yes.*

Fool watched his Mana drop by a quarter and winced. Ah well. It was there to be spent, and he hadn't been doing that very often. Together with all his other Skill uses in the last few minutes, he realized he'd used up over half of his Mana pool. But even as he noticed that he saw it was already trickling back up. It would be full again before they even reached the woods.

"That's affirmative. Ten-four, good buddy," he said to Jackal, grinning. This, he was finding, was kind of fun. He also felt as if he could be a much more productive member of the team going forward, and that gave him a very warm feeling inside.

"Brilliant," Jackal said. "So less issue talking her into leaving with us. Now all we need to do is break into their little fortress, then break out past all the cops in town and whatever enforcers they brought in."

"Right?" Fool said. "Exciting, isn't it?"

"Very." Jackal let out a short laugh. "This might actually be fun. Shall we?"

Fool nodded, and they started out across the town.

They didn't run across anyone else, and they made good time getting out of the housing area. It was tense when they cut through the giant open field, like a weird little park in the middle of the town, on the other side of the houses. Lots of sky above them, lines of houses facing them with windows lit up, and every step the muffled-loud crunch of snow. And ahead of them was the school. Sporadically lit from inside, the building looked as though it should have been bathed in sodium-light. But those had gone with the arrival of the System and not been replaced.

And there were definitely people milling about in front of it. Pacing, patrolling. Weapons were clearly visible. But all eyes seemed to be focused inside, and Fool kept doggedly following the path that had been laid out for them.

Kitty-corner across the field, at an angle to the school. Next to the school was a big patch of trees that covered half the far end of the field. The half on the left was the school. Their path took them all across the field, then onto a road that actually skirted the woods on the south side. After another ten minutes of walking, they turned left, heading northeast through a barely discernible trail in the woods. It took them another half hour of trudging through snow before they came out of the woods and found a north-bound road that showed no travel at all, just pristine, untouched snow.

Fool paused, looking up and down the road. No signs of anything watching them. Not much longer now. Follow the road about six blocks north, then they'd find another trail going west through the woods, backtracking them right into the rear of the school.

Fool called up his map again and saw that some of the red positions had moved, but the black path was still solid and unchanged. No one watching the back of the school. Not in any meaningful way. It didn't look as though they were patrolling at all. That was odd.

"Hey, Jackal, something weird here. I'm checking the location again, and it doesn't look like they're really covering the back much. I'm not thinking the Sheriff is dumb enough to leave them an avenue to escape from, so any ideas why they're leaving that open?"

Jackal cocked his head. Fool didn't wait for a response but bent into the snow and sketched out a map of what he was seeing.

Jackal hummed to himself for a bit as he looked at the map. "Couple of possibilities. Two big ones though. First is that it's a trap, and he's got some heavy hitters out back. Might be that your theory of them bringing in outside help is right, and they've got some high-Level folks there. Be unexpected. Good trap. Can you use your Talent Scout to check that out?"

Fool shook his head. "Not enough Levels in it for that. Not yet."

Jackal nodded. "Well, we can check when we get closer. Second option is the weirder one and makes me wish we had more time to scout this situation out."

"I'm getting the feeling I'm not going to like this much." And Fool really didn't. Jackal didn't normally stretch things out like this.

"I'm thinking that most folks are out front because they don't expect anyone to try to escape. They expect them to come out fighting."

"Crap," Fool said. He knew what that meant.

"Town divided," Jackal said. "Civil war in miniature scale. Might be even harder to get the target out, in that case."

"Maybe. I think I've got some plans to work with that though. I mean, if the Sheriff thought his folks could win, they'd probably have already attacked. So we're either coming into a stalemate or detente... or someone's got something up their sleeve. Either way? We'll find out when we get in there."

Jackal grinned. "Absolutely. Shall we then?"

"I suppose so," Fool said. "If I'm gonna trust my Skills, then we keep going on this path."

Jackal nodded, and they set off down the road.

The road, being untouched, was surprisingly hard to walk on. The spring heat had started, so the surface powder had melted in the previous days' sun, but since it was still below zero at night, the melt froze back into chunks of ice.

It had been doing that long enough that there was a thick rind of ice on the surface of the snow. Not quite enough to hold them up, so the walk was an awkward series of stepping on the hard shell and breaking through. It was noisy, and if they had been the people they'd been before the System enhanced them, it would have been exhausting.

As it was, Fool found himself rather enjoying it. Stomping through snow wasn't something he'd gotten to experience a lot as a kid. Just one winter, when his family had moved up to the interior for a short-term job. Other than that, he'd mostly had the Lower Mainland experience of thick, wet snow. This was closer to what he'd wanted as a kid, so he let himself enjoy the romp a bit.

When they turned back off of the road onto the trail through the woods that would lead them to the school, the crust went away. The evergreens were thick enough in this patch of forest that the sun didn't cause too much melt, so the snow was still mostly a mix of fine powder and slightly thicker snow. Jackal had taken the lead again, and Fool was amused to note that Jackal looked like a big snowplow, raising plumes of snow off to either side of him as he waded through.

It made it easier for Fool. There was less snow for him to trudge through, though trying to adjust his gait to the length of Jackal's stride was reminding him of just how large his friend was these days. Before long, they came out of the woods and into the back field.

The field was mostly snow but was more heavily covered with tracks. According to Fool's map, the Sheriff's watchers should be on either side of the field and at the corners of the building. They'd have overwatch over the entire field and most of the back of their target, and still have eyeline to posse members at the front for quick messaging.

Jackal was already crouched low, using his built-up Stealth Skills to blend into the tree line. Fool stayed upright but kept himself next to the trunk of the closest tree, blending into its shadow.

Fool took a quiet moment to confirm the locations of everyone his map told him was in the area. It took a bit. The ones at the corners of the school weren't hard to see—shifting, armed figures trying to be still, but looking nervous and unable to contain that energy. The watcher on the south end of the field was better though. Fool hadn't been able to see him until he saw a whiff of steam rising and realized it was someone peeing.

Not the most professional apparently. That was a good sign and would make their access to the building easier.

The last watcher was much harder to spot, and it was actually Jackal who found him, attracting Fool's attention with a soft grunt, and pointing toward the north corner.

Whoever was there wasn't in the wood at all but standing perfectly still in the open. They were so still they didn't even register to Fool as a person until he'd specifically focused on them. Someone far more professional than he'd expected from the locals. Time to put his Skills to use.

Talent Scout was first up, doing a check on the pro. Stealth, a run of ranged Combat Skills... Sniper. Tough cookie, lots of damage potential. A little lower Level than Fool and Jackal, but not by much. The others were the usual run of what he'd expected from Deputies. Crowd Control, Restraint, law enforcement Skills. Lower Levels too.

The three other watchers had low Perception, but the Sniper-build was high enough to be worrisome.

But, Fool reasoned, there was no reason to waste any more time. This was as good as it was going to get.

Talent Scout gave him his targets. He knocked down the Perception of the Sniper-build with No Fair, and put his Geas on all four, commanding them to focus on people coming out, not people going in. He didn't bother to nod or signal to Jackal, just walked forward.

Nothing to see, Fool repeated over and over in his head. *Just seeing what you expected here, folks walking in, not walking out, no big deal, keep looking for a breakout.* He saw a brief spike in his Mana draw and ran Talent Scout again.

The Sniper was resisting, but that wasn't unexpected. He had an Observation Skill that Fool had noted, but figured wouldn't be used unless their Perception triggered it. They were still in the safe zone, but Fool ran No Fair again against the Observation Skill... and was rewarded by seeing his Mana drain return to the expected level.

Fool kept up his regular stride, and Jackal kept pace. Just two normal folks taking a walk, nothing unusual. Nothing to trigger any expectations, nothing to make someone wonder, "who the hell are those two, and what are they doing?"

Everything seemed to be working just fine, and Fool was finding he could adeptly manage monitoring his Mana, updating what people were up to with Talent Scout, and running No Fair to temporarily drop whatever Stat or Ability any of the four might use to resist the Geas. He wasn't sure how he'd do against more than four people, but his confidence was growing by the moment. This was a cakewalk.

The two guards at the corners of the school walked toward each other. They'd meet right in front of the door Fool and Jackal were aiming for, right about when they'd get there.

Jackal swore once, quickly, under his breath.

Fool would have joined him, but he was concentrating too hard. He quickly ran up I Know a Shortcut, and it hadn't changed. This was still the right path.

This was his moment of real trust. Either the Ability worked at some unknowable level and understood what he was trying to do, and was capable of, and updated in real time... or it was still stuck on the original projection. This was the test.

If they failed, they could do what they always did—fight with the best element of surprise they could muster and do their damndest to win. Fool wasn't too worried about beating the two Deputies. Hell, Jackal could handle the two of them almost in his sleep. The Sniper, now behind them? That one might be able to punch Fool's lights out permanently. He might not even know it had happened.

Faith. He had to have faith in whatever sort of twisted intentions his god had for him. And in the Skills he'd been given by that same god.

And this was his first true test.

178

They kept walking forward, and the guards kept up their path toward each other.

Fool readied his Pants On Fire Skill, thinking of the right lie to tell them. Something about how they expected to see Fool and Jackal here and it wasn't worth noting? Or maybe that the Sheriff had sent them?

The options ran through his head as they got closer and closer, and Fool found himself slowing down just a little. It was either that, or all four of them would walk into each other.

The two Deputies stopped an arm's length from each other. Fool paused about the same distance away, unsure of what to do.

"Anything?" the Deputy on the right whispered.

The left Deputy shook his head. "Nothing yet. Been stone quiet all night. 'Cept for that weirdo out on the field. Creeps me right out."

"Me too," Right said. "Don't know where the Sheriff got those mercs from, but I don't like 'em."

"Sooner this is over, the better," Left said, then he turned and looked right at Fool and Jackal. "Huh. Look at that."

Right turned and looked at them as well. Fool froze, all his responses locked in his head.

Right squatted on his haunches, held out his hand, and said, "Here, kitty, kitty. Who's a good kitty?"

Fool looked down and saw the damned cat walking between him and Jackal.

It padded up to the two Deputies, sat in the snow between them, and meowed.

Jackal tugged on Fool's sleeve, and Fool turned to look at him. Jackal nodded toward the door, and they walked again.

One step after another, fifteen more steps.

Miracle of miracles, the door wasn't even locked. They opened it and closed it behind them.

They were in.

"I think I know what to name the cat," Jackal said.

Fool let out a long breath, then turned to look at him with raised eyebrows.

"DM," Jackal said. "For 'Deus ex machina.'"

It was all Fool could do to hold back the maniacal laughter that threatened to burst out of him.

Chapter Thirteen

The school wasn't lit up on the inside, but far down at the end of the hallway they'd entered, they could see what was obviously candlelight coming from some of the rooms. One room had a clear light that indicated a Mana-powered source. There was some source of heat though since the inside of the building was much warmer than the outside.

"Now what?" Jackal asked.

Which was a fair question, Fool thought. He had the tracking device in his hand, and it was clearly letting him know their target was damned close. He guessed the room that wasn't lit with candlelight. But that left Fool with the fun question: Keep walking forward? And maybe surprise what might turn out to be an armed terrorist cell? That didn't seem like too much fun.

"I think we just wait here," Fool said. "They must have heard the door open and close, and if they're expecting to be raided, they've probably just shat themselves, but are going to be coming loaded for bear in a moment. I think standing still and waiting for them to calm down is a good idea."

Jackal nodded, standing upright, and making sure his hands were away from all his weapons. Fool was about to do the same, but then realized he felt silly, so he did the stupid thing.

"Hi!" Fool shouted. "We've come to see the Princess. We aren't with the Sheriff. Can we talk?"

His words echoed down the hall, but there was no answer.

Then a head stuck out, peeking around the doorframe of the Mana-lit room. It looked at them for a moment then pulled back.

Then another head stuck itself out.

Nothing else happened for a moment. Fool was tempted to say something else, but then a third head stuck itself out. The woman walked out and waved at them.

She didn't look like a terrorist. Rather more like a librarian. An older woman, with frizzy grey hair, a full peasant skirt, and what looked like a hand-knit sweater. She smiled and walked down the hall with a businessy hustle.

Fool wondered if this was the Princess. It was possible. Now that he was on a roll of using his Skills, he ran Talent Scout on her. Surprisingly enough, she actually was a Librarian. Interesting. But nothing about her said "Princess" and the tracking device, still in Fool's hand, didn't change at all as she walked forward.

The Librarian walked up to them, stopping about two arm-lengths away. She had a serious expression on her face. Not exactly welcoming, but also not exactly trying to scare them off. "What can I do for you two?"

Fool couldn't help it. "I'm Fool, and this is Jackal. We're here to rescue the Princess."

To his credit, Jackal kept a straight face.

The Librarian's expression warmed up a fair bit, but there was something hidden in her eyes. Fool's stomach flipped with the sure knowledge that things weren't as they seemed.

"Rescue?" the Librarian asked. "Might I ask why? And to what purpose?"

Fool had to think about that for a moment. He wasn't going to reveal the Foundation to just anyone. The Princess, yes, but he didn't know this person at all. He tried to come up with a quick plausible lie, but then remembered... Skills. Pants on Fire. He didn't need to tell the truth.

"We're from the Rebellion. We're here to bring her back to our headquarters so she can lead our forces." It was almost true. Sort of. He had no idea what the Foundation really had in mind for her, or even if they were really "the Rebellion." They were, sort of. But there were some grey areas he hadn't quite dug into yet.

That got a raised eyebrow from the Librarian. "Would have preferred Trekkies to space fantasy fans, but I'm not in charge of the world. Regardless, I'm sure you two have something interesting to say, so I'll bring you to meet the person you're looking for. Small hint though? Don't refer to her as Princess. She doesn't like that." She turned and gestured at them to walk with her.

Fool didn't really have much more to say. He had a ton of questions, but even without her seemingly using any of her Librarian Class Skills, Fool found himself reluctant to speak more. And it was only a few more classroom doors until they hit the room the tracking device was urging Fool into.

It was a busy little room. The terrorists were few in number, and the six people in the room were milling about, prepping a number of weapons and devices. Fool was instantly aware of why the Sheriff called them terrorists and had mustered all his Deputies and apparently hired mercenaries.

The room was an arsenal. Some sort of portal opened into what looked like a giant warehouse, and someone was reaching in and pulling out more gear. The warehouse looked to be a military storehouse. Fool swore he even saw something like a tank in the shadowy recesses of it.

The person pulling equipment out was, according to the tracking device, who they'd come to rescue.

The Princess.

She was in what were clearly military uniform pants, with a heavy utility belt chock full of weapons and gear. She'd stripped off the rest of the uniform, probably for comfort, and was wearing only some sort of tank-top-like garment.

Her enormous muscles rippled across her back and shoulders as she hefted gear back into the school. A trickle of sweat ran down her back, and Fool was completely fascinated by it. It rolled down her back like an emerald.

The sweat drop was clear.

Her skin was green.

And as she turned to look at the two newcomers, she stood her seven-foot-tall self up. Her seven-foot, muscled, green, orc self.

The Princess was a Hakarta.

"I'm Yagnar," she said. "What do you want? And how did you get in here?"

"I'm Fool, and this is Jackal. We're here because we've been told you might be useful to our organization. We can't talk about that in front of everyone else, but given the circumstances, I think we can talk about that later. Obviously, we aren't going to be able to have that talk if you're not around to come back with us. So, can we help? What's the plan?"

Yagnar looked at them for a moment. "I'm not entirely inclined to trust you at the moment. And you didn't answer my question. How'd you get in here? Pretty sure Barnes isn't letting anyone through, and I know he's hired some mercs to help him out. For all I know, you're part of that. Spill."

Fool shrugged. "We just walked in. I've got Skills that let me lie and disguise us pretty well, so we made everyone watching ignore us walking in. Worked pretty good."

"Is that supposed to make me trust you more?"

Yagnar, Fool had to admit, was pretty damned impressive when she stood up to her full height and crossed her arms. It probably helped that her pose made her naturally stare down her nose at Fool. He glanced at Jackal and confirmed that the two of them were not only roughly the same height but also about the same build.

Fool didn't really know what to say to her, except to keep going with the truth. "Yes. It is. I could lie if you prefer, but like I said, our organization is looking for long-term investments in people. Starting that off with a lie isn't a great start. And if you can see my stats, you know I'm good at lying. Can you do that?"

Yagnar snorted. Fool took that as a yes, but maybe she was bluffing. He decided to just take her at her word.

"Great. Then you can see my friend isn't very good at lying at all. Ask him if I'm telling the truth."

Yagnar shook her head. "I'm not any kind of truthteller, but sure." She looked at Jackal. "You two with the Sheriff?"

Jackal gave a shake of his head so small it was barely noticeable.

"Fuck it. Good enough," Yagnar said. "We're not exactly in a good spot, and I don't think the Sheriff is smart enough to send in spies. He's sure as hell not going to negotiate with us. Fucker knows the only goal we have at this point is to wipe him right out."

"He didn't make the best impression on us, so I get that," Fool said. "No problems helping you out with that. But can I ask what's going on? From what we saw outside, we've got time. They look like they're waiting for you to come out."

Yagnar nodded. "It was my plan, so they've figured that out. If it was just Barnes and his Deputies, we'd probably make it out okay too. But Barnes seems to have finally made the alliance I thought he might and got some backup. Made things a bit more difficult for us. So what precisely did you see?"

"Got some paper?" Fool asked.

They did, and with the offered pen, he sketched out a map of the school and surrounding areas. He put little "x" marks everywhere he'd seen a member of the posse.

"Okay," he said. "This is where everyone was last time I checked. We came in the back, through this route." He sketched out their path to the school. "And these three were Deputies, but this person here was something else. Pretty high Level, built like a Sniper."

"And how did you know that?" the Librarian asked.

"I've got a Skill that shows me what Abilities are used, Levels, that kind of stuff. And I've got another Skill that gives me up-to-date maps of places and information about them."

Yagnar sucked in a breath. "Now that's handy. Is that how you got in?"

Fool shook his head. "Different Skill helped with that. Same Skill that might help us get out. But I think first we need to build a plan. What was yours, just so we know where we're starting from?"

"The best I could think of. I've got access to lots of weapons, so I figured we'd load up, wait 'til we hit the lull point in the morning just before dawn, and head out blazing." Yagnar crossed her arms and stared at them.

Fool got the impression she was trying to impress them… or cover up a weakness. He wasn't familiar with Hakarta though, so he wasn't sure if he was reading her body language right.

He rocked back on his heels and sucked on his upper lip. He needed to get a better sense of who everyone was and what they were capable of. And if they had to break out, they'd need to work as a team, so best if they talked through things instead of him just using Talent Scout and figuring it out for himself. Plus, he wanted to get to know them and see who he was going to be fighting next to. Assuming they actually chose to fight together.

"Okay," he said. "Let's back up a bit, get to know each other, and see what we're working with. Yagnar, I'm going to take a wild guess and say you're military? I'm going off the uniform you're wearing and the 'attack before dawn' thing."

Yagnar nodded. "Janik's Raiders. My squad had just cleaned up a lucrative contract, got a killer bonus. We'd also been saving, and we managed to buy a small stake in this new Dungeon World we'd heard about. Real bargain. Figured we'd settle in here, build up a nice, fortified base, and live like kings, hiring ourselves out to Adventurers who needed some extra muscle."

"Valemount?" Fool asked. "You bought Valemount?"

Yagnar nodded.

"So, where's the rest of your team?"

"Dead," Yagnar said.

Fool realized he was really bad at reading alien facial expressions, because hers didn't seem to change at all, but he was aware the room had gone pretty still.

"What happened?" he asked.

"Barnes. We underestimated him. Didn't realize he was building up so much support, and he took us out one at a time. Separated us all on different pretexts. I only survived because of these folks."

Fool looked around. He couldn't read Hakarta facial expressions, but the townsfolk all around, those he could read.

They were pissed.

Fool asked carefully, "If I may? Why did you folks help Yagnar? I mean, Barnes is one of you, right?"

The Librarian answered, and her voice was tight, controlled. "Barnes was assigned here on rotation before the System. And he'd brought some of his cronies along. We only learned about their families after the System, when most of us were dying. Turns out Barnes was part of a racial supremacist group, and they'd been scouting out small towns to build up as some kind of 'centers of resistance' or some shit. Barnes had figured Valemount was perfect, and before the System came, we were just starting to realize that he'd been building up a bit of a camp just outside of town with a few hundred of the bastards. They had a compound and everything. They were infiltrating the town, buying up businesses, taking any job that was open, buying up any house for sale."

She sat down and didn't say anything for a moment. "When the System came, it was bad. But for those bastards? It was tailor-made for them.

188

Swarmed into town almost immediately, and when the monsters came? Those fuckers all holed themselves up in the RCMP station. Shot all the Mounties first of course. They stayed in there for two days while the rest of the town got torn to pieces. Then they came out and killed some of the monsters, enough to get themselves all Leveled up, and anyone who made noise, they shot. Town figured out pretty quick that we had no chance against them, and most folk rolled over and joined up. Strong group in bad times, can't blame us, right? And we figured someone from the government would show up."

Her face got tight, but she kept talking. "Except who showed up was a bunch of green-skinned aliens. Didn't fret me none. Hell, after the System and monsters showing up all over the place? Woulda been weird if aliens didn't show up. I met Yagnar's boss as soon as they landed. Seemed like good people. Methodical, prepared for the beasts. Wasted no time in trying to get people organized and building defenses, offering first aid and food to everyone who looked like they needed it. Sure, they clearly said they were taking over, they owned the place, and we could either accept it or go try our luck out in the woods. That seemed fair, and they seemed like honest folks. Saviors, really. And Barnes and his crew went along with it at first. Of course, it was all a setup. No surprise there for us. Aliens were just another thing to spit on for Barnes's people."

The Librarian walked over to Yagnar. Fool noted how she leaned in toward the big soldier. Some trust and friendship there.

She paused before going on, glancing at Yagnar. Yagnar nodded back at her, and the Librarian continued with her story. "Went great for six months. The Hakarta are tough folk, but they knew what was going on. Some of us even joined up with them, signing on to be mercenaries. None of Barnes's folks though. That should have been a warning sign for us. We figured it was just them being bigots, but the town kept growing. More of Barnes's people, survivors from the System, trickling in. Set themselves up as the police force. Hakarta were okay with that. Thought that being racist about aliens was pretty normal, nothing they didn't expect. After a while though, the humans who'd signed on with the Hakarta started to disappear. Excuses at first. 'Died in a bar brawl' or some other shit.

"It all ended in one night." She looked at Fool, staring into his eyes. "Half the Hakarta were away on a mission, and the Deputies killed all the ones left in town. And anyone they called a collaborator, which was just the old townsfolk. When the rest of the Hakarta came back, Barnes had set up a hell of a trap for them. But they aren't dumb folk and it turned into a hell of a firefight. And it looked like the Hakarta might even win... but sometime in those six months, Barnes had found new friends. Two very scary folks flew on in and pretty much wiped out the rest of the Hakarta."

"Except me," Yagnar said. She put her arms around the Librarian and hugged her. "I figured we were dead anyway, so I rigged our transport and all our gear to blow. Figured I'd go with it. But at the last minute, I saw this dear lady peeking out from a shop that had been mostly blown down. And I realized the attackers were all busy at the front of the transport, with the last of the fighters holding them off. So I took a chance. Set the timer on the demolitions, said goodbye to my friends, and ran. Been on the run since, getting ready to come back."

"Why come back?" Fool asked.

"Because my friends died for this place? Because I'm sick of being a mercenary, sick of being pushed around by the System. This was our dream. We came here with hope and plans. And an open mind. We knew that the people who had just been exposed to a Dungeon World would be raw, damaged folk. We knew the Galactic Council—hell, most of the galaxy—preferred them that way." She shook her head, still clearly full of anger. The Librarian put a hand on her shoulder, and Yagnar smiled at her and went on. "But we wanted to be different. Figured if we came in helpful instead of trying to get our piece of the world, we could build a community that could last, could maybe be a place for other people to get away. Doing that on a Dungeon World made sense to us, because it would be hard. If we helped people survive, then they'd turn out to be hard too. We thought we could become strong enough to fight for a kind of peace."

She looked at the floor for a moment, and when she looked back up at Fool and Jackal, it wasn't sadness that made her eyes glimmer with tears. It was rage. "We had a dream. And Barnes took it. Not just from us, but from these people too. And I'm going to kill him if it's the last thing I do."

Fool sighed. They hadn't really had much of a plan when they came here. Find the Princess, take her back to the Foundation. He'd figured they'd just explain how cool things were and some of their mission, and that would be it. Just take a nice leisurely walk back home.

Then he'd thought they'd be the heroes, swanning in to rescue some helpless young Princess and making a bold escape through the woods.

Plans changed. Even when there hadn't been a plan.

"So," he said, glancing at Jackal. Jackal was already grinning, because he could read Fool's mind. "Let's kill the fucker. How can we help?"

Chapter Fourteen

The cat had somehow found its way inside the school, and Fool found himself idly scratching it behind the ears. It responded with a deep chainsaw purr, kneading its claws into his thighs.

They were waiting in another converted classroom while Yagnar and her followers talked things over. They'd wanted more proof of who and what Fool and Jackal were, but Fool had stuck to his guns about only being able to share information privately with Yagnar.

As a result, they'd been shunted off to the other room to wait.

"Good job using your Skills," the cat said. "About time."

Fool looked down at it.

"Don't stop with the scratches," it said.

Jackal was quietly laughing, and Fool glared at him.

"Why do you do this?" Fool asked the cat. "I mean, this is like some sort of lame sitcom, with you not talking when other people are around."

"I'm not always me," the cat said. "Just when I need to be. Existence isn't as linear as you think it is. I mean, it doesn't need to be. I'm here, and talking, when that's how you make it happen. The sitcom thing is your fault."

"Am I supposed to make sense out of that?" Fool asked.

"Not yet. But you'll get there. Just go with it. You know you want to."

"Fine. Whatever. Why did the Trickster send you? You supposed to be some sort of familiar or spirit guide?"

"Hell no. What kind of god do you take the Trickster for? You wanted that kind of shit; you should have chosen a more run-of-the-mill god. Or, you know, maybe some nice Class that would give you pat answers to everything. Something boring."

"I didn't choose the Trickster. You know that. I wasn't in my right mind back then."

"Weren't you?" the cat asked. "That's your opinion. You know, in some cultures, what you people call illness was considered a gift. Ever consider your mind was right and it was only your society that made you a wreck?"

"Every damned day. That was, like, the essence of my illness. Damn… you are not a healthy creature to be around."

Fool pulled his hand back as the cat opened its tiny mouth to show some impressively long and sharp teeth. "Careful with your words, little human. Don't overlook my value."

"Sorry," Fool said. "So, nothing personal, but what *is* your value? Am I supposed to summon you for interventions or something, or use you to talk to the Trickster? Or are you influencing events by showing up?"

"How much do you know about quantum states, superposition, that kind of thing?" the cat said as it arched its back up in a stretch.

"Nothing," Jackal said. "But I can fill him in later."

"Lovely. Good man. Thank you. Okay, so here's the deal." The cat jumped off of Fool's lap—not without a little pain as its rear claws punched through his normally proof-against-monster-claws armored thighs—and landed on a desk across from him. "As I said earlier, I'm existing only at certain times, from your perspective. From my perspective, and from the universe's, in a certain sense, that's nonsense, but you folks are limited. Nothing to be done about that, but you're going to have to learn to think differently. And part of that is that you have to figure this shit out on your own. I've already given you enough clues. And don't you roll your eyes at me, human!"

Fool froze, because he hadn't been rolling his eyes, but he'd been about to.

"This isn't one of those stupid puzzle things either," the cat continued. "The process of figuring this out is what will reshape your brain and how you think, and that's the point, capiche? Trickster needs you smarter and better. So get on it."

"Nice," Fool said. "Maybe a hint as to how I should start?"

"Meow," the cat said.

And then the door opened, and Yagnar walked in. Fool turned to look back at the cat, but it was gone.

"Where'd the cat go?" Yagnar asked. "I could swear I saw a cat when I walked in here. Do you do illusions, either of you?"

"I dunno. It just does that sometimes. Mysterious mysteries and all that, right, Jackal?" Fool turned to look at Jackal, but his friend was staring at the spot where the cat had been, and his face looked bleached pale. "Everything okay?"

Jackal took a deep breath, then turned and looked at Fool. "Don't ask. I saw… no. No, I didn't."

Fool was tempted to ask more, but Jackal's lips were locked tight. But at least his skin color was returning to normal, so Fool turned back to Yagnar.

"You two are weird," she said.

"We are," Fool agreed. "But we can help, really. Did you make a decision?"

"We did," Yagnar said. "Raised more questions, but it turned out the Librarian was able to pull up some information on you two. Way less than she should have been able to, and no mention of any organization whatsoever, but she thinks there was information that was hidden. But you two look legit, so she voted to trust you. And I trust her, so... here we are."

Yagnar didn't wait for a response but walked over to them and sat on the desk. "So what have you got that can help us out? And can you tell me more about this place you want me to go? I'm not planning on leaving here, to be clear, but I'm willing to listen to what you have to say."

"Fair enough," Fool said. "Let's start there. We're part of a group that, it turns out, shares some of the same goals as you. It's been built up since the System arrived and has some tools for finding out the best way for it to grow. You were identified as one of those best ways, so we were sent out to recruit you."

Fool paused to see how she was taking it. Not well, but the Hakarta gestured for him to go on.

"I have to say, the organization has a lot of resources, and what you're trying to do here is very much in line with what its plans are. If nothing else, if you come back with us, I'm sure we can work out some sort of alliance or partnership. They'd absolutely be willing to sponsor a lot of what you want to do, for sure."

"Lovely. Can you get a strike team sent in here to get all this cleaned up then?"

Fool turned and looked at Jackal, then back at Yagnar. "Well, that's us. We're the strike team."

"That's not funny. Unless one of you is a secret Master Class. You're both Basic Classes, not even Advanced. At least one of Barnes's

196

newcomers is an Advanced. I've got good weapons, but those folks are likely to wipe us out. I've been in this kind of fight before. It's doable if one side outnumbers the other, and right now, the wrong side has the numbers. Unless you've got an escape route, you two are just going to be two more bodies for Barnes to loot."

"Possible." Fool nodded. No point, he thought, in avoiding reality. "But let's not give up just yet. You mentioned weapons, and I saw that you've got portal access to something. Is that something we can use?"

Yagnar puffed out a breath. "Maybe. To be honest? I don't know. I was part of the mercenary outfit, but my specialty is logistics. That portal is a link to the unit's weapons cache, but all of that is pretty advanced stuff. We'd been hoarding it for a long time, thinking we could train up an army. No one here has the training for it, or the Skills, as far as I know. I can use most of them, but I've only got the necessary Combat Skills of a line troop. No Command Skills. How about you two?"

"Think of me as a really good support unit, and Jackal?" Fool turned to his friend. "I don't suppose any of your myriad of weapons Skills apply to long arms, do they?"

Jackal shook his head.

"Ah. Well. Jackal is a formidable fighter, but in a more personal sense. The two of us are pretty good at planning."

"I hope so," Yagnar said. "Like I said, I can handle most of the weapons, but I'm only one person. The rest of those folks back there? They can shoot a bit. And they've made excellent guerilla troops in the few scraps we've had with the Deputies. Craft Skills are quite useful for sabotage of all kinds. But not so great for a siege like this. So tell me about your Skills."

"I can map out precise locations of everyone around us and plan us out a foolproof path to any destination…" Fool paused, because Jackal had made a throat-clearing noise. "Well, not foolproof, but I can plan optimal routes for either escape or counterattack. I can keep up people's moods too. And I can make people believe things that aren't real, within limits. We'll figure out something from all of that."

"That's… not a lot," Yagnar said.

Fool nodded. "I know. But have faith. I've got a few hole cards, worst case. We should move forward without those for the moment, but good to know they're available. Shall we reconvene with everyone else and see about coming up with a quick plan?"

Yagnar looked as if she was swallowing something sour. "Faith. No choice, I suppose. All right, let's do it." She turned to head out, and Jackal followed.

Fool waited a moment until they were gone.

"You should make this quick," the cat said.

"I know. Just wondering… any advice on what to do?"

"Aside from what you hinted? Have Faith? I know you don't want to use that, and that's fair. But don't sweat it if you have to use it. Old Tricky won't always hit you with something hard to pay back. Might even give you a freebie. You never know."

"Last case, I promise I'll use it," Fool said, trying to ignore the foul taste in the back of his throat.

"You still have a Skill point to spend. Now might be a good time."

Fool sagged. Now that he was actually getting a sense of how to use his Abilities, he'd been thinking of holding off on acquiring a new Skill and spending some points on fleshing out the other Skills. But the cat was right.

No point in saving up when you might need the new Skills to survive until dawn.

"Any suggestions?" he asked.

"Feign Death. Just drop dead. Let the whole battle play out how it's going to go anyway, then just get up and go home when everyone's forgotten about you."

"That's not going to happen," Fool said. "Bad kitty!"

The cat glared at him. "Don't even start with that crap. You two chose a name for me. You can use that."

"DM?" Fool asked. "Really?"

"I like it," DM said. "I'll allow it. But you've got two Skills left to choose. Regeneration and Aura of *, so which one will it be?"

"Is that how you pronounce that? I don't think I can make that sound."

"Don't even try. It's not really a sound in any case, just an indicator of a sound-like representative state. Ask Jackal to explain it to you sometime." DM sat back down on its hindquarters and looked at Fool.

"I'm not sure how useful Regeneration would be. I mean, I can see myself getting chopped up into pieces, and I very much would like to recover from that, but it's not going to help everyone else, is it?"

"Maybe you can chop your hands off and throw them outside? Freak out the locals? They seem stupid. Might work."

Fool didn't even bother to answer that. Apparently, DM didn't care much for the integrity of the human body. Or possibly integrity in general. "I guess there isn't a choice then really, is there?"

"Never was, Fool. But cheer up, it's all for a bigger purpose." DM accented its point by lifting a rear paw and carefully trying to pull off a frayed bit of claw with its teeth.

"And what's the bigger purpose?" Fool asked.

"Having fun," DM answered with a grin.

Fool shook his head and rolled his eyes. When he looked back at DM, the cat was gone. Except… maybe… for the briefest second, Fool thought he saw the cat's grin floating in the air.

If copyright was still a thing, that cat was so going to get sued.

Jackal and Yagnar didn't go far, just back to the room they'd first come from. Fool followed and caught up to them as they entered.

"All right," Yagnar said. "Looks like we're working together, so introductions."

She pointed out each person, one after the other. Only four of them were left, the rest having dispersed while the meeting had happened in the other room.

"Emily Crisp, she was the Librarian here and still is. She's got Reference Skills that have been providing most of the weapons and tactics that have gotten us this far." She pointed at the woman who had met them when they came into the school.

Emily waved, looking comfy in the only padded chair in the room.

"George Chan here was an accountant for the Northern Health Authority."

He was the stern-looking fellow, watching them with crossed arms and not a drop of trust on his face. He was wearing normal-looking clothes, jeans, T-shirt, and a tartan-patterned flannel shirt over that.

"Rory Fred is our Armorer, which has been very useful. She's also acting as a Mechanic, which is the only reason the one vehicle I managed to sneak out of Barnes's claws was still running up until this morning. Tried to sneak back into town this morning to swap for a new one. That's when we got spotted."

Rory was a middle-aged woman with pale skin and deep, flame-red hair, which she set off with her black leather motorcycle jacket and ripped black jeans. She'd clearly spent some points on Charisma as well, judging from the pull Fool felt. She had a pleasant, easygoing smile with a hint of a turn at the corners... but that smile did not go up to her eyes.

"Finally, Alex Garret is our HedgeWitch. She's been hiding out with me in the woods for the last bit."

"Hi!" Alex chirped. She was, Fool noted, the youngest person in the room by a long shot and dressed in hunting gear. Armored leathers, many knives all over. Fool thought she looked Gitxsan, First Nations from the northern interior, but that might have just been how she held herself. It brought back a brief flash of memory of an old friend, long lost.

"Armorer. That's probably going to be a first," Fool said. "Assuming you can do a quick repair on our armor? We ran into a nasty monster on the way here, and ours got trashed."

Rory nodded and kept watching them.

"I guess second," Fool continued, "would be the armory. Yagnar, is there armor in there that might be of use to us or your team?"

Yagnar shook her head. "All sized for Hakarta. Might be some that can fit Jackal, with some help from Rory, but it's all pretty specialized. Your own armor might be better. You and Rory can figure that out." She flicked her head toward Jackal at that.

"Right," Fool said. That was one easy gain scratched off. But it made sense. Anything that would be useful for most of Yagnar's folks would have already been spread out amongst them. "I assume you've already spread out any usable weapons as well?" Yagnar nodded, so Fool kept going. "I've a rifle of my own, but we can check if any of your ammo is compatible. So what kind of firepower are we looking at?"

Yagnar took the moment to look over her four followers in the room. She chewed on her lip a bit, then spoke. "Not a lot, but the best most folks can handle. Basic combat rifles for everyone, beamers, aim-assist included. Standard ammunition load-out, armor-piercing and high explosive mixed. Plasma grenades. Everyone has two. I've got an advanced infantry rifle with a grenade launcher. A few rocket launchers I've been trained on. Some mines if we want to go that route. Some heavier ordnance back there, but most of it requires Skills I don't have. Specialized gear. With the help of the Librarian, we'd been hoping to get training and basic Skills for most folk… would have given us the edge we need against the Sheriff, but there hasn't been time. And no time now."

Jackal cleared his throat, and Fool turned to look at him. He made a patting motion against a wall and raised his eyebrows.

"Good point," Fool said. "Have you set up mines as booby-traps around the entrances to the school? To stop anyone from coming in the way we did?"

Yagnar made a sound under her breath that sounded like swearing. "I should have thought about that. Alex, can you grab a few of the others and bring them back here? I can show them how to set up trespass triggers on some of the anti-personnel mines. And before you think I'm a complete idiot, Alex has a Skill that lets her set alarms on locations, so we have warnings on almost all entrances. She rushed through getting all the front-facing egresses covered, and we figured we'd get the back ones done later. Pure luck you two came in before we did that."

"Luck is my middle name," Fool said.

Yagnar looked at him. "What's your last name?"

"So there's enough weaponry for everyone, but not enough to make up for what Barnes's folks have. How many people do you have in total?" Fool asked.

"Twelve. There are some other active folks in town, but they're hunkering down. If we can make a notch in the Deputies here, they'll take the chance on coming out. But I've told them previously that unless that happens, they're to keep a low profile. I don't want them getting killed in a purge if we lose. Always a chance they can find another way to fight later, after all."

"That's… not much of a resistance. Barnes has almost thirty folks outside, and all Combat Class. And it seems like most of the town is on his side, from what we saw."

"Don't believe that," George said, speaking up from his chair. "These are good people, the people of Valemount. The folks you spoke to are probably the ones who came with Barnes, his people. Everyone else is just trying to stay alive, make the best of a bad situation. If we can knock Barnes down, they'll come out and help us. But they've got to think about themselves right now. Not everyone's got it in them to die for a cause. Can't blame them for that."

"Fair enough," Fool said. "So… I guess we need to start with a goal. Can't really build a plan unless we know what we want. Are we looking to get the hell out of here in one piece, or overthrow Barnes? Might as well be clear about that right now. Jackal and I came here to see if Yagnar wanted to come back with us, but…"

He turned and looked at Jackal. He really didn't need to confirm, but it wasn't in him to make assumptions. Jackal nodded once. Firmly.

"Right," Fool continued. "We're not fans of people like Barnes, so we're here to help as best we can. But it's up to you folks what that will look like."

Fool was a bit surprised to realize that he was quite ready to fight the long fight here. It was one thing to plan a daring escape or fight the Big Bad and be heroes, but if Yagnar asked them to stay, sneak out somehow, and help them run a protracted guerilla campaign? It was very much not what the Foundation wanted from them.

Fool was positive that Professor X would be furious at them for doing it. As much as Yagnar was a potential asset for the Foundation, Fool and Jackal were known assets and represented an investment that was not supposed to be spent on lost causes.

This fight would show one hell of a lot more commitment to one person than he usually made. And Jackal was usually far more pessimistic. Yet here they were, ready to die for someone they had just met.

Well, wasn't that a laugh?

Fool sighed and held up a hand. "One sec. Gotta clear something up first."

Dry Hairs for Squids was the name of the Skill, and with a single point spent on it, he could use it on himself and on Jackal. It wasn't a Skill Fool had really used much, and he was starting to realize that he needed to be much more aggressive about it.

Jackal sat bolt upright, and Fool turned to look at Yagnar, who was looking at both of them quizzically.

Fool activated Talent Scout.

There it was. It had always been there, but since it had kicked in the moment he'd seen Yagnar, he'd glossed over it. It was a powerful passive Skill, one that had the effect of boosting loyalty. Dry Hairs for Squids removed mental influence, and clear of it, Fool suddenly had a lot more questions about what he was planning on doing.

"Well, I'll be damned." He made eye contact with Yagnar. "You really are a Princess."

Yagnar Twofang, System Anomaly, Bronze Star Explorer, Slayer of Goblins, Kilums and Brais (Intrepid Explorer Level 18)

HP: 1210/1210

MP: 340/340

Conditions: Shadow Play, First Impressions Count

Scout Notes: Aura effects in play, Royalty

Chapter Fifteen

"Not really," Yagnar said. "It's a hereditary thing. I mean, it grants me that one Skill, but not much else. The Hakarta Noble Family is… rather large. I'm one of a hundred princesses, and even if I was queen? Well… we Hakarta are kind of past all of that. It doesn't really mean anything anymore, not as much as it seems."

"So, passive Skill?" Fool asked. "That's a pretty powerful one."

"No. But sure, I suppose that's an easy way to explain it. Only in the short term though. The effect wears off pretty quickly. It's meant to be a kind of protection, make a good first impression. When I asked my family about it, they said that I should know it, but never rely on it. 'Loyalty has to be earned by actions,' is what my mother pounded into me. I've never forgotten that lesson, not that she ever gave me a choice."

"Fair enough," Fool said. "Give me a moment though."

He turned to look at Jackal, who wasn't looking happy. It really wasn't fun to learn that you'd been turned into a loyal, unquestioning follower with no choice offered. But the look on Jackal's face wasn't a no, just a general sense of anger.

Fool had to review everything he'd been thinking since they set foot in the school. He couldn't find any logical holes in his internal plans. And while he sure as hell wasn't going to hang around and devote his life to Yagnar's cause now, the immediate issue of how to deal with the Sheriff was still something they aligned on. And they all wanted to live.

So they'd keep going with the plan to get out of the school. But if the Princess couldn't be convinced to go back to the Foundation with them? She could go hang, as far as Fool was concerned.

Maybe not. Before he turned and said anything he regretted, he took a moment to consider. She could have warned them of the passive Loyalty Skill, but it wasn't as though she could turn it off. And she'd, for the most part, acted as if it wasn't in effect. He had to give her points for that. If she was going to come along with them though, he was absolutely going to have a talk with her about privilege and points of view.

Some of his anger faded. At the moment, it really didn't matter. And if it didn't matter in the moment, then maybe it didn't really matter that much. Do the job at hand, then see what happened next and deal with that as its own thing.

But there was one important thing he had to do first.

The more he used his Skills, the more he was finding out how useful they were. He wasn't willing to go ahead with any of their plans if Yagnar's rebellion was only following her because they were under the influence of her Princess-Loyalty effect. He knew some Skills could tell you the Status of people, but he didn't have one of those.

What he did have was his Truth or Dare Skill. His Mana wasn't full, after using Dry Hairs for Squids, but it was nearly there. And going from his gut feeling, it didn't seem as if combat was imminent. Barnes didn't seem like the type to press the attack and risk casualties. He'd probably sit outside and wait until they came out. So Fool could afford the Mana cost.

The query was another quick and easy one: Are Yagnar's rebels under the influence of her Loyalty Skill?

The answer came back negative and Fool relaxed. He was pretty aware of how sharp the divide was between his current mental state and where it had been a moment ago. He wasn't about to put people at risk if they weren't in their right minds. It seemed as though Yagnar was being truthful though. It was a short-term effect Skill.

That settled, Fool turned back to the conversation. "Right. So, what's the goal here? I suggest we focus on escape and deal with everything else later. If you have some sort of burning need for vengeance, or frankly, anything beyond basic survival, now is the time to bring it up."

Yagnar didn't answer right away. Instead, she looked at her people, making solid eye contact with all of them. Then she turned and looked at Fool, contemplating him for a moment before evaluating Jackal. And it was an evaluation. Fool could see the wheels turning in her head. They were clearly at risk of losing their lives, but even so… Yagnar was weighing and measuring the worth of the people around her and looking at the potential of the situation. Fool had to admit, she looked as though she had some good leadership skills, in personality if not in Skills.

Finally, she turned back to Fool. "Survival. We need to get out of here, losing no one. I think part of why Barnes wants me is that he wants to get access to the cache."

"Why?" Jackal asked.

Fool figured that was a decent question. She'd just spent some time telling them why an amazing weapons cache was mostly useless to them. It should be the same for Barnes, so either he was unaware of that or was thinking long term. In any case, Yagnar probably had more concrete information than either Fool or Jackal had, and the cache might make a useful bargaining point. If things came to that.

"Something I noticed while I was out in the woods. Caught sight of a meeting. Couldn't make out what was being said, but Barnes was with someone from the Thirteen Moon Sect. So my guess is Barnes is going to sell the cache to them. Or promised them access in exchange for the backup he got."

That got Fool thinking and brought up a lot of questions. "Is that possible? I would have thought the cache was tied to you somehow? Wouldn't it become inaccessible if you died?"

"Not quite. As the logistics officer, I've got primary access to it. But it's actually a sort of limited portal we… got access to. The access point is with me, and I can open it with my Skills, but it's possible to have it opened if someone has the right Skills or can afford to buy access through the Shop. This"—she held up a disc that was hanging from her thick necklace— "is the access point. It's like the lock to the cache. Whoever has this, if they know how, can unlock the cache."

"So, they either need to kill you, take the lock, and figure out how to unlock it, or…"

"Right," she said. "Or torture me for the access code. I believe that would be Barnes's preferred option."

Fool could only nod. That did seem in line with his impression of the Sheriff. "Thirteen Moon Sect? I've heard a rumor about them. Bad news, and a big presence in BC. You think Barnes is working with them?"

"I think he's dumb enough to think that he's got an angle with them," Yagnar said. "George, can you fill them in on what you found for the background?"

The Accountant nodded and leaned forward in his chair. "When we first got things set up, all the town's income, such as it was, was put into a fund that I could manage. One of my Class Skills. Barnes hasn't got the knowledge to lock me out of that fund, even though he's the only one with control of it. I tried to stop what he was up to, but it didn't go well for me. I've been able to see what his expenses are and what's coming in. He's been skimming hard off of everyone and setting up what amounts to a debt-slavery system. The idea didn't come from him."

Fool looked around and noted no one seemed particularly surprised.

"He started with basic grift, but switched to his new system less than a week after he took over. And he got a huge influx of Credit at the same time. When I tracked down the source of that? Thirteen Moon Sect, tied into contracts to run the place for them, then sell it to them lock, stock, and barrel once they're ready to take over. He's already sold out everyone."

"And," Yagnar added, "it looks like they're about ready to take control of their investment. The Sect is about as criminal as things get, and while the System doesn't allow outright slavery, the Sect pushes it to the limit. They hire the worst of the worst to run the places they take over, and they've got eyes on all of BC and the rest of the coast. I know they've taken over Vancouver, Kelowna, Kamloops... we're on the outer edge of their inward expansion on the way to Prince George. When we had originally found out about their plans, we were going to get reinforcements to help us, but that was when Barnes took us out."

Yagnar turned and looked to the side for a moment, clearly wrestling with emotions Fool could only guess. But from the rough set of her shoulders, it wasn't hard. Fool recognized that helpless rage only too well.

"Survival though," she said, without turning back to them. "Everything else can wait. I can't kill him today, maybe tomorrow. So, what's the plan?"

At that, she turned and looked at Fool and Jackal. With her back to them, her voice had sounded brave. Convinced. Dedicated. Fool had expected to see her looking like a committed warrior. The woman he looked at was anything but. As he looked into her purple eyes, he saw only resignation. And from how her tusks were faintly quivering, he suspected she was just barely holding it together. Which made him wonder if hugging was acceptable amongst Hakarta.

No matter, he thought. This was the moment. He'd already made his choice, and her reaction had convinced him. She could have ordered all her people into a heroic last stand, but she not only cared for them, she had the brains to realize that was a dumb idea. And she had the heart to realize that no matter what, her rebels were likely not going to make it out whole tonight. No matter what happened, some of them would be dead in the morning. She wasn't shying away from that, but she wasn't immune to the pain it would cause her either.

Which, to Fool's reckoning, meant she was absolutely the person they'd come to rescue.

And they had to do it right.

Which meant not leaving a mess behind them.

"We'll survive," Fool said. "And we'll get out of this trap too. But Barnes won't see the next down. We're gonna kill them all."

They all turned to look at Fool after that pronouncement. Even Jackal.

"Honestly?" Fool said. "I don't think we have much choice. I might be able to use my Skills to get us out of town. Very likely actually. But then it's a long, hard road back to McBride. We can take some shelter at Tete Jaune Cache, but most of the rest of the road will be a hard go. We can do it, for sure. But do it with Barnes and crew on our back? That's not very likely."

No surprise that nothing he said helped to dispel the doubt on anyone's face. If anything, George looked even more morose.

"If I'm not mistaken, you've just laid out the reasons for him to hunt you down. I think our only hope in this case is to remove Barnes. He's the one fronting for the Thirteen Moon Sect. With him gone, they won't have their easy access anymore. Still going to be a problem down the road, but that's a problem for later."

Yagnar looked almost betrayed by that, but before she could say anything, Emily spoke up. "He's right. I mean, maybe not about the kill them all part, but if we can remove Barnes from the equation, everything gets a lot easier. George, if I'm not mistaken, the selfish ass has tied everything to himself, hasn't he? I can't see him trusting anyone. So any contracts he'll have made will be just with himself, not himself as leader of the city?"

George closed his eyes. His hands twitched, as did his eyes. Clearly, Fool thought, he was one of those people who could use the System interface without using his hands. Fool had to admit he was a little jealous. He also had to admit he'd never really tried that. Something to play with later.

"I can confirm that," George said. "The Thirteen Moon Sect will either need to find a new tool to use here, or resort to force, with Barnes gone."

"Force," Yagnar spat out. "They won't give up. They'll move to force."

"As Fool said," Emily continued, "we can deal with that later. We won't have any chance to deal with it if we're dead, and if we're on the run, there is really no reason for Barnes not to sell the town right away, is there?"

Yagnar sighed and conceded that point with a single nod.

Emily was drawing everyone in with her energy. "So we're outnumbered, outgunned, and outleveled. The enemy has all the advantages, and we have none. Surrender is off the table. We've seen before that they'll just kill us anyway. We've got nothing to lose. As far as I can tell, that's the truth of it, right?"

Everyone nodded. Fool looked at all of them and saw hard determination on all their faces. They'd clearly been fighting to avoid this outcome, but apparently, they'd all come to suspect a fight would be the final road they had to walk.

Emily shifted to sit on the edge of one of the desks. "Let's talk tactics. If we head out the front door, they've got all the guns on us, and we die. If we head out the back, friend Fool has pointed out that there's a high-Level sniper out there, so even if we don't die right away, we get picked off as we run. And then the rest of the posse will be on whomever is left. But some of us might make it out that way. Any other ideas?"

"Roof access?" Jackal asked.

"None," Emily said. "We already thought about that."

"Armor up as best we can and blast our way out," Yagnar said. "I can head out the front first. My combat gear will hold up for a bit, and I can take out some of them. And the rest of you might use that distraction to get a shot in at Barnes before you run for it. That was sort of my plan."

"There's a better way," Fool said.

The discussion was going about as he expected. He had hoped that Yagnar maybe had some cool special-forces-type training or something, but she really did seem like just a line trooper used to team formation combat. Emily had laid the problem out nicely, but the other three looked ready to follow, not contribute.

"We need to break them up first," Fool continued. "Break up their plan before it even starts, but without them knowing. They're clustered around the front of the school with a little around the back. We need to get them moving all around, spread them out. More importantly, we need to get them reacting to us in a way we can predict."

That got a few nods, Jackal glowering as he waited for Fool to get to the point. Jackal always knew Fool had a catch. Came with being an Acolyte of the Trickster.

"You know how you successfully attack a well-defended position? The way they do in all the fantasy books? Attack one side strongly, but it's always a feint, while the real attack happens on the other side. We need to reverse that process. Feint breakouts. We want them to think we are planning to skip out one side, then another."

"Don't you think they'll catch on to that?" Yagnar said. "I mean, you see someone feint to one side, and then to the other. You may not know which way they actually intend to go, but you know they're planning something. And since they've got the numbers, they can just cover the whole area. I'm not sure I can see how this will work as an advantage for us."

"Pretty much exactly like that," Fool said. "We want them to think they've got us covered. We want them to think we're trying to be clever, but they're more clever. We move right, they move right to block, but they keep forces on the left. We move back to center, and they think they've shut us down, made us realize it won't work. That's what we want." Fool crossed his arms and waited, looking smug. Mostly on purpose.

That, of course, got George upset and asking the questions Fool wanted to ask. "So what? What's the point?"

"You know how to trick a clever man? Make him think he's smarter than you." Fool buffed his fingers on his shirt. "As long as they think they're winning, they won't be thinking very hard. And what we're really doing isn't trying to feint them—we're making them move in rhythm.

Once they start thinking they've got us figured out and they move slightly ahead of us? We've got them. That's step one."

Everyone was looking at Fool as if he was crazy.

Rory, for the first time, spoke up. Her voice was quiet, but decisive. "Got a plan to make it that easy, or are you just hoping it will work out? Because if you do it too much, they might just charge us anyway."

Fool really didn't have a plan. Just faith. They'd work it out somehow. How could they not? They were smarter than the bad guys.

Before the System, he'd had the same attitude about things. More often than not, it got him in deep shit. He'd had a hard, hard life, but not from lack of effort or belief in himself.

When it had all really fallen apart and he wasn't even so sure about his own reality anymore? He'd never really lost that sense that if he just trusted himself completely, went with the crazy ideas that popped into his head, and didn't let others talk him out of them? Things might have been far better for him.

On the far side of that life, it was easy for him to look back and see that the problem was his own lack of confidence, which had been built up by his parents.

Fool did have good ideas, but he'd been hammered over and over with the message that he just wasn't going to succeed at any of them. His small successes were always glossed over, and the failures expanded out of proportion. None of it was done maliciously, but out of genuine care.

Being raised by two people who'd only ever felt frustration and failure in their dreams was not an environment that nurtured growth. He'd carried that into his adulthood, choosing partners and friends who would fill in the pessimistic restraining role his parents had done.

No wonder he'd gone crazy.

Rory wasn't asking from the same place, but Fool felt himself responding as if she was, so he took a moment and thought about it.

He trusted himself. The System had shown him he could grow and be more than he'd ever been before. The only limit, aside from being slaughtered by a monster, was how far he believed he could go. And belief was the hardest coin to gain. He couldn't afford to give away even a drop.

So Fool rallied his mind. His life-long habit was to recognize the question was coming from a desire to know what was wrong with his plan, then to search inside himself and find all the things wrong and try to answer all those issues. That just led down a long road of grief though.

What he needed to do was ignore all the voices of doom. Start with the positive, start with what absolutely would work, even if it was just a small part, and build up from there. It was, for him, a relentlessly positive approach, but it still left room for dealing with issues.

But starting from what absolutely would work, instead of what absolutely would not, let him start from a basis of "this will work." It was a way of thinking that had come to him as part of the process of the Shop fixing up his brain, back in the early days.

"I'm not hoping it will work out," he said to Rory. "I'm going to make sure it works. We've a few different paths to get there, so we're all going to have to work on it. Yagnar, have you made any attempts to break out yet?"

Yagnar nodded, a quizzical look on her face as she tried to figure out where Fool was going. "Yeah, almost right away. Tried to sneak out the back but ran into the Deputies there. Fought past them, but the rest showed up almost right away. We were lucky and made it back in without losing anyone or taking any wounds that couldn't be Healed up."

"Just the one? Have you been trying to keep an eye on them?" Fool asked.

"At first. Tried to peek through the windows, but they'd shoot as soon as we did. We had to sneak around and close all the blinds and curtains to hide from them. Tried to peek through the blinds after that. You have to be quick, but you can do it. They shoot the place up as soon as they see a curtain move now."

Good thing none of the Deputies were using any Skills to look through the buildings. That Sniper might be able to do it, in fact. Never mind high-tech solutions. Something to keep in mind.

"That's perfect," Fool said. "Just what we want. Are they able to shoot through the walls?"

"No," Yagnar replied. "School was built sturdy in the first place, and since we had originally planned to use this as our base of operations, some investment in the infrastructure was made. Barring a well-timed shot through the window, it's safe to sneak a peek out a window and duck down." The Hakarta sighed. "At least, we haven't seen them shoot through it. Maybe the Advanced Classes might."

"All right. We're going to start with some testing. We have two advantages here. The first is that they're doing what they think is the right thing and trying to wait us out. The second is that they don't know Jackal and I are in here. If they'd been smart, they'd have sucked up the potential losses and stormed you all right away. Now you've had time to build up some traps... I'm assuming you used those mines?"

Yagnar nodded. "Directional mines set to trigger on the front entrance. You've got some luck on your side. We were just about to rig up the same setup on the back door."

"Luck is always on my side," Fool said. He felt silly adding a little swagger when he said that, but no one laughed, so score another point for his high Charisma. Good for more than passionate arguing

218

apparently. "You should get that set up right away though. I'm thinking they're being cautious for the same reason most people would—they haven't figured out that a siege doesn't work the same way with the System as it did before. It's a lot harder to wear us down with injuries and stress than it used to be. They can still starve us, but that'll take longer than they think. Mint?" He pulled out a box of chocolate mints as he said that last part.

He thought of it as his "grandpa" Skill—being able to produce snacks from his pockets. It probably wouldn't be enough to realistically affect their food needs in any kind of real siege, but it was perfect for keeping up morale. One of the boons of his "clergy," he figured. Always being the guy who had a snack or a drink handy. It was good for the flock, such as it was.

Alex snatched the goodies out of Fool's hand as soon as he offered, which didn't surprise Fool. She looked competent but he still thought she looked a bit young for the group.

"So let's get testing. What we need to do is get some peeking out the windows going on. Get them thinking we're looking to break out and see how they react. I've got a Skill that lets me keep an eye on them, so I'll do that.

"To start, let's just have one person randomly trying windows. Jackal, you're the best on that. Make sure they see you but can't recognize you, and don't get shot, okay? Look timid."

Jackal didn't even acknowledge the order, just got up and walked out of the room. Fool thought about yelling after him, telling him a timeframe to do all of this in, but Jackal probably had a better sense of how to time this sort of thing than he did, so he let him go.

"Right." Fool turned back to everyone else. "I'll keep an eye on our friends, but since we've got a bit of time before we have to do the next bit, let's get a run-down of all your Skills so we can figure out the next best step."

Aside from Yagnar, no one had any obvious "wins" in terms of Combat Skills. They were all Artisans at heart, and the only Skills they had with weapons were from limited usage, mostly in the first few days of the System.

Yagnar had some solid Combat Skills with ranged weapons, but she was weighted toward logistics support. She wasn't quite high enough Level to have any of the really interesting Skills Fool was hoping for, like instant transport or portals or anything fun. She could sure carry a lot though.

Rory was solid. She'd already set to work doing field-expedient repairs to Fool and Jackal's armor. Jackal's main set was still almost completely trashed from the scrap with the Orcabear, and Rory couldn't do anything with that—not in the time they had. But she could Buff up his backup armor, which had been previously damaged and dumped without repair. Jackal had dumped it for his new armor without bothering to have it repaired. Fortunately, it was low enough tier that Rory could patch it right up. Unfortunately, it was also low Level enough to not be all that useful.

Emily and George weren't really going to be of any help, not in the short term.

Alex though… she was looking like a real gem.

HedgeWitch wasn't a Class Fool had ever seen before, but it seemed to align with the historic idea that had been kicking around forever. Her Class Skills were intended to be useful to the community in all sorts of ways.

Making crops better, healing, cleaning or making otherwise unpalatable things edible, and most useful, many connections to the "natural" world. Of course, the natural world wasn't so much so anymore, but it did give her some level of interaction with System monsters that looked as though it might be almost broken if she lasted to the higher Levels. As it was, she provided one perfect opportunity for a distraction that might be the key to the whole thing, especially combined with Fool's final Skill, once he took it.

While they talked, they heard the buzz of energy beam fire, the crack of launched projectiles, and the occasional hiss of something even more exotic. Impacts to windows and walls echoed, even as the stink of subdued fear faded the more they talked.

Good thing too, because he'd need all of them to be calm. After all, the plan was looking as though it would actually work.

Chapter Sixteen

When Jackal finished his circuit of the windows, it was pretty much as Fool had hoped. Jackal's reports of what he'd seen and what the reactions had been matched precisely with what Fool had seen through Location Scout.

The Deputies had responded as expected, getting excited and rushing toward whomever had reported seeing movement, and occasionally firing at whichever window Jackal had peeked through. The Thirteen Moon Sect members were much more professional, staying put. They'd wind up being the real issue.

There were five Sect members, spread out equally around the school. Three of them were basic Combat Classes with fairly high Levels. Two of them were Advanced Classes. One Advanced Class was at their first Level, but the other was ten Levels in. That was the Sniper and clearly the biggest threat. None of them could hope to match him in a one-on-one. They'd be dead, and quickly so.

The other one was stronger than most people, but after some thinking about it, Fool figured Jackal could probably take that one by himself. His Combat specializations would give him an edge. The Advanced Class would normally be more than a match for him, but they'd opted for a more sensible balanced build than Jackal's "kill everything" approach.

Still, tough fight. Not winnable for them in any way, shape, or form if they played it straight.

Good thing that was never the plan.

Fool took a deep breath and pulled himself out of his ruminations. It was time to lay his thinking out for the others. They were all waiting for him, and he took a moment to appreciate that.

His Class automatically dumped a point at every Level into Charisma, and he'd been disdainful of that, but this was the situation where it was meant to be used. It made people pay attention to his ideas. In some ways, it felt like a cheat, but after a life of being ignored? He regarded it for what it was—a necessary tool for his profession, and one to be used ethically.

Maybe Fool shouldn't exactly be as annoyed with the Princess as he was.

"All right. So the first results from the experiment show that they're reacting as expected. As long as we don't get too fancy, we can manipulate the timing of Barnes and his Deputies well enough. If we work the windows and get our timing down… Yagnar, I assume you've got access to coms for everyone, so we can stay in touch and manage this?"

"I do," she said. "When the Thirteen Moon Sect people showed up, I wanted to make sure they wouldn't be able to hack our communicators. I figured the best way to do that was to not use them until the last minute, make them think we didn't have any."

"Good call," Fool said. "I suggest we follow that plan and only start using them when we need to. But if we can coordinate everyone, I'm not seeing any issues with setting up a trap for Barnes. With me and Jackal, I think we've got a pretty good chance of at least killing the Sheriff, then maybe we can pick out the Deputies. We'll see if they still have any fight left in them after their boss is dead."

224

"I suspect they won't," Yagnar said.

"But," Rory said. "Sounds like you've got a big one."

"Thanks." Fool turned his head to look over his shoulder. "I… never mind. Yeah, the Thirteen Moon folks are really throwing a wrench into this. There are five of them, and all of them seem to be more disciplined than I'd prefer. Skills wise, three of them are your generic minions. Basically, no different from the Deputies. Two of them are real trouble though. Advanced Classes."

There was a sharp intake of breath from everyone. No one in the area had an Advanced Class yet, and their presence, by default, meant they didn't have a hope. Not two. Not in a group. They could probably swarm and take down one of them, maybe even both with luck, but most of them would die in the process. That was just a given, and common knowledge they'd all accepted.

"We've got a chance if we're careful and the timing works out. But you need to be aware of those two. One of them, Egon Koll, looks like he just got his Advanced Class, and he's a tough Combat Class, but he's also a fairly generic build. Good at everything, but nothing overwhelming by itself. His one Advanced Class Skill so far is a close-range attack. Stay away from him at all costs. He's on the south side of the school, so we're going to go any other direction."

Fool waited to make sure everyone nodded or otherwise indicated he had spoken before he continued. "The other one is Band Eller, and he's bad news. Stealth Skills, very high Perception Skills, and some weapon mods that would one-shot a tank. I've got a plan for him. That's for Jackal and me to worry about. The rest of you are going to go after Barnes and whatever is left of his Deputies."

Rory said, "That's a nice sentiment, but how do you think all of us are going to deal with him and his deputies?"

"I've got a Class Skill that will reduce their effectiveness and increase ours. And Alex, I'm going to need your help with a distraction. Am I correct in assuming that your HedgeWitch Skill, 'Summon Monster' does what I think it does?"

Alex looked uncomfortable. "Yeah. I try not to use it. It's great if you want to Level and have friends, but it scales with my Level. I thought it was great when it was bringing me low-Level critters I could easily deal with, but I put more points into it and now… it's pulling in things that are more than I can deal with."

"What kind of control do you have over them?" Rory asked.

"None. The only control I get is a sense of what they might be and what Level, but when they come, it's a free creature. It's like a lure they can't resist, but that's all."

"So, might be a problem with that," Fool said. "There was an Orcabear we ran across on our way into town. If you summon that, we're all toast. Is there a way you can tell what you're going to summon?"

"Yeah. I get a sense of type and Strength, at the very least. Give me a minute, let me scan what's in the area…" Everyone stood quietly while Alex activated her Skill. Her eyes took on a silver sheen. "Got something… yeah, something good. Flame Elk. Big one. Alpha. Would that work?"

"Oh, hell yes!" Fool said. "Perfect. How long will it take to get here?"

"About half an hour feels like?"

"Hang tight on that. Yagnar, how much more time do you need to get everyone loaded up with weapons and armor?"

Yagnar didn't even blink or look aside. "Fifteen minutes. They already know the drill, and I've already put aside the right gear for everyone.

226

They've currently got the defensive gear on, so it's mostly just swapping out the close-quarters weapons for battle rifles. Standard Hakarta issue. Pretty much shoots itself, so everyone here can use them. I already changed the safety settings to human standard earlier. You want us right out the front door at your signal, or do you have something else in mind?"

"Front door. Signal will be from Jackal, but… if it works out the way I think it will, then you'll know when it's the right time." Fool stopped and looked around at everyone.

They were all patiently waiting. This was dumb. Fool didn't enjoy taking a chance with other people's lives, but it wasn't as if they had a choice. And he was getting the feeling that every moment was one moment closer to Barnes deciding to storm the place. His previous confidence in having time was slipping away. If that happened, the typical advantage of the defender would mean nothing. They didn't have the numbers. And the Deputies, backed by Egon's Advanced Class Combat Skills, would mow them all down. Anyone who tried to run would be dead meat under fire from Band Eller. It had to be done, and now.

"Okay. We can't put this off," Fool said. "If it's the wrong thing to do, well, it'll be better than waiting here and dying. If there are no more questions, then we need to get people looking out the windows in a pattern I'm going to show you. Meanwhile, Alex and I will work on the distraction… and then we go. Questions?"

No one had any, even though Rory looked pretty sour about it. Fool felt for them. They'd been fighting for months in an on-again-off-again guerilla campaign, only to be trapped this morning. They'd expected to die, then two strangers had shown up and promised to help. But their help was little more than offering them a different way to die. Couldn't feel good.

At least he could do something about that.

He'd only ever used The Show Must Go On, his morale-raising Skill, on Jackal, and only because Jackal knew what it was and approved of it. He felt a twinge of guilt about not getting anyone's consent, but there wasn't time to explain.

"Okay then," Fool said and activated the Skill. "Yagnar, I'm going to give you the perfect path to Barnes for your folks. We're going to end this for you tonight. Let's kick some ass, folks!"

He saw the fire burn in all their eyes as The Show Must Go On kicked in. He felt his hair stand up all over his body as instead of a room of cynical, resigned rebels, they became a room full of predators hungry for a kill. Their motions changed as they moved to their tasks, becoming languid and panther-like, full of physical confidence.

DM was looking at Fool from the corner, smiling widely.

All that energy, it echoed back into Fool. They could do it. These were the right people. They had no chance. The odds were less than zero, but they would win anyway. There was no other choice.

Now if only DM would stop smiling.

"I need a bathroom break." Fool didn't wait for a reply, just walked to the door.

"I think I figured out who you are," Fool said to the cat.

"About time," DM said. "So, ready for your next Skill? It's a good one, and it's the start of your path to your Advanced Class. It's going to be a great journey. You're going to shake the pillars of heaven."

Fool nodded. DM wasn't, in his brief experience, prone to exaggeration. And he'd come to accept that his choice of Class would have much bigger repercussions than he could even imagine. "I am. So how does this Aura Skill work?"

"You open yourself to a touch of the Trickster and show it to the world. It's going to change, depending on what's right. But you already know that, don't you? You already know exactly what it is and how to use it."

"That's not how Skills work," Fool said.

"No," DM replied. "But you've made a pact with the Trickster with your Class. You expect the Trickster to follow anyone's rules? You'll find some information is already inside you, ready to be accessed when you need it, as you progress. For everyone else, going up in Levels is a reflection of how they adapt and can use Mana. That counts for you too, but it's also a reflection of how much more affinity you gain for the Trickster.

"The universe is full of many secrets, and your path is to delve into all of them. When you are at the end of your path, the world will be open to you, and nothing will be unknown. Your only job now is to make sure you are ready for that."

Fool turned away from the bathroom mirror he'd been looking at to look DM in the eyes.

The little black cat looked up at him with a serious expression. Its eyes were flecked with tiny flakes of gold and silver that cycled up and back down from the endless depths of its feline eyes.

"I'll be ready," Fool said. And it wasn't a lie, but it was very much a prayer.

The plan worked to perfection. With careful coordination, the rebels had followed Fool's careful choreography and timing of looking out windows and occasionally opening doors and slamming them shut immediately. The Deputies had worked themselves into a frenzy and kept running back and forth, like drops of milk poured into a hot cup of tea. At just the right moment, before it all swirled into sameness, things gelled into clumps.

The exact clumps that I Know A Shortcut had shown as needed for Yagnar's team to get to the Sheriff, who was still at the front of the school, but now with only three Deputies instead of a dozen.

And Alex's monster was coming.

Fool felt the air change as the Flame Elk got closer, the tension in him building. The deputies were too focused on the school and the imminent outbreak to notice.

Until it stepped out of the woods.

They all felt the sudden shift in attention, the Mana draw. Fool took the chance and looked out a window, and Jackal did the same.

The night was clear, no clouds in the sky, and the moon was near-full.

There is a point when the temperature hovers just around freezing that the air alters slightly, and everything gains an unusual clarity. Distant things seem close, and close things seem somehow sharper, brighter. The stars reach down with their twinkles, and you can almost imagine seeing the worlds that dance around them.

The world froze to silence, and in that clarity, the Flame Elk stepped out.

It was enormous. Fool had seen and hunted plenty of Flame Elk. He'd seen them in giant herds even. But he'd never seen an Alpha, not like this. This was more than Alpha; it was a boss monster of a Flame Elk.

In appearance, it was the ideal image of the perfect Elk, except for the antlers. And its size. It was easily as tall as a house. And instead of the nest of sharp, narrow antlers that the normal Flame Elk carried, these were huge, thick spans of sharp-edged bone, closer to moose antlers.

And they didn't just have a halo of flame like the Flame Elk. These antlers were a deep and morbid red, glowing like iron pulled from the forge. And even across the field and through the window, Fool felt the radiant heat coming off of them.

Next to Fool, Jackal swore under his breath. "It can't be. They're extinct. Were extinct. It's an Irish Elk, Fool!"

Fool didn't answer, entranced by the creature. It was terrifying, but it was also beautiful.

With a hoof, it scratched at the snow, which melted away. And Fool could have sworn that where its hooves touched, the grass underneath sprouted into flowers.

For a moment, time froze.

The power and eldritch beauty of the monster was breathtaking. A ruddy glow from its antlers reflected off of the snow and branches behind the creature, giving it a back light.

The moon, the sparking stars, the red-glowing snow, the trees, and the mammoth beast lifting its horned head to gaze up at the stars.

Fool was transported back in time, to a primitive tribesman, stone-headed spear in hand, hunting for food in the woods and finding instead a god.

"A Maker," Alex said.

231

Fool turned to look at her and saw the wonder in her eyes. Nothing had prepared her for this. Nothing had prepared any of them for this.

The System had brought ruin to the world, had destroyed all that humanity had built. Worst of all, it had forever turned nature against humanity. In becoming a Dungeon World, the sacred unity of humanity and nature had been sundered forever.

But somehow, this enormous Flame Elk echoed into the heart of every human that looked at it and spoke of that ancient pact, that world that had room for hunter and prey to live together, a bond that recognized need but also understanding.

What was lost was not truly lost. The Flame Elk, in that moment, was a promise that the past could be reborn.

Then there was an enormous flash and a crack of super-heated air. A bolt of pure, cyan-tinted energy leapt out at the elk.

Band Eller, the Sniper, was trying to kill it.

He was not having any luck. The horns flared from a deep and ruddy red to a blinding scarlet, and the bolt from the sniper rifle shattered into a scintillating rainbow field all around the Elk that flickered away almost as soon as it formed.

Now was the time, Fool realized. With all eyes on the creature, he activated the Skill that he'd held off on choosing: Aura of *

He felt a crazed energy rise inside him, a connection, maybe even just an awareness of something vast. Something unknowable and alien. Something intently, deeply wrong. An essence of corruption against reality, yet somehow singular even if not sentient. A coalescence of madness and unreality.

And somehow, in some way, it was approaching.

An atavistic fear, so deep it threatened his desire to exist, rose inside him. A surety that he had never felt before, about anything in life, filled his soul and his mind, and his body froze with the unnamable horror of it.

He screamed. And the scream gained weight, a force that reached across the field, and the town, and touched every soul, and they all shuddered with the certain knowledge that a thing was about to cross over into reality.

That a single, ancient wrongness was about to touch the Earth and unmake everything, corrupting all reality for ever.

At that moment, the elk lifted a hoof, and every eye turned to look at it.

And the hoof started to descend.

The Deputies broke. All of them.

Barnes tried to rage at them, but he found his own fear pinned him in place, unable to even breathe. Most of his people ran, except those closest to the Elk, who merely froze. Some of them broke completely. Fool felt their minds snapping loose in denial, shutting down.

Band Eller, Fool could feel, was also entrapped, but actively fighting it with resistances. All the rebels were handling the aura, if not well. They had the advantage of having been warned, and it saved them. Yagnar took the scream to be the signal and was able to use her Loyalty Skill to rally everyone to her as she crashed through the front door of the school.

Fool held on as long as he could, then he released the Aura and felt his mind returning. A wave of nausea hit him—not related to Mana or the Skill, but rather to the flash of memory that had come to him. Somehow, somewhere, he'd experienced this feeling before. The Skill, in this case, had reached into his darkest memories and pulled something out of him... but not something that didn't exist. Fool knew that, down to his core. He'd touched something, and an echo of it had reached out of him.

"Time to go," he said.

Jackal didn't even pause, sprinting out of the room and down the hall. Fool kept up as best he could, pushing himself to the limit. He heard a roar and shaking from outside.

Jackal burst through the same door they'd entered through, out the back of the school, Fool on his heels.

The plan was to have the two of them take out Band Eller, then swing up and deal with Egon. And after that, back to the front of the school and help the rebels wrap up the fight with Barnes.

And that plan went out the window as soon as they exited the school.

The Flame Elk was already there, in a full rage. Band Eller was in mid-leap above it, firing another massive cyan bolt from his oversized sniper rifle, and Egon was charging into the beast at the same time.

Jackal let out a roar and exploded in a prodigious leap toward Band Eller. A giant, two-handed axe was already sweeping up over his head, ready to smash down on the Sniper.

Which left Fool to deal with Egon.

Chapter Seventeen

Fool had no chance against Egon. Not in straight up combat anyway. Egon was a close-quarter Combat specialist, and Fool had only bothered with basic self-defense training. He would have skipped it entirely if the Foundation hadn't insisted on it as part of their initial training. He knew better than to try any of that on Egon.

Instead, he cheated.

Egon was almost to the Flame Elk. He'd come the long way around the school, and Fool had just enough of a head start to intercept him before he got to the Elk.

The heat from the Flame Elk was intense, like being next to a blast furnace. Fool's Health was dropping from it, but not too fast. He wasn't eager to get too close to the beast though. Egon would be enough to deal with.

Fool didn't have a great plan, but there wasn't much choice at the moment. He'd already had his warhammer in hand, so he slid in right in front of Egon and activated his Oh God Don't Hit Me Skill.

It worked. For the moment. Egon slid to a stop in the snow, a momentary, gaping confusion on his face as he looked at Fool.

Egon was built like a grappler. He wasn't human, but he looked almost human. Except that he only had two small slits in the middle of his face instead of a nose, and his skin was a light purple. And there were no irises in his eyes. They were just a uniform green. His shoulders were immensely broad, and he had on a pair of armored metal gauntlets.

Without hesitation, Fool threw his hardest shot at the closest gauntlet. Considering Egon was standing still, and Fool was moving, it landed perfectly. The damage wasn't much, not to Egon. It was all absorbed by the gauntlets. But as Fool had hoped, the blow landed in just the right spot and bent a portion of the gauntlet. Just enough to lock the hand in its open position.

Which was all that saved Fool. For his size, Egon was insanely fast. The warhammer had only just bounced off of the gauntlet, and he had already reached out to seize Fool. His armored hand grabbed Fool by the wrist, but it wouldn't close, so Fool was able to pull his hand free and twist out of reach.

The brief surprise slowed Egon enough that Fool could spin around behind him and quickly activate Geas. He tried something with the Skill that he'd never done before, a simple enough suggestion that made Egon believe Fool was just out of his reach, dodging faster than he could catch.

It was easy enough for Fool to participate in the deception, and he had enough presence of mind to marvel at how it wasn't even a huge drain on his Mana to maintain the deception. Had he chosen something more offensive, that would have been against his nature and likely failed or spiked the Mana cost. He knew his Geas Skill was a strong one, but he'd never imagined this level of use.

As it was, he was pushing the limits of his Perception and Luck Abilities to stay just out of reach of Egon… but that was all he had to do. Fool wasn't the fighter. All Fool had to do was keep Egon busy until Jackal dealt with Band Eller, then Jackal and Fool could work together to defeat Egon.

Unfortunately, that meant that Fool couldn't help Jackal with his combat.

Jackal was struggling against the Sniper. His first shot had landed perfectly and halved Band Eller's Health instantly. That had been one shot though, delivered with all of Jackal's Skills. Once the initial attack had landed, the Level difference between them evened the playing field.

Jackal had an advantage, having already closed in past the optimal range of all of Band Eller's weapons. All he had to do was keep enough pressure on Eller to stop him from increasing that damage.

At least, that was the plan. Band had experience, and that meant more than Levels. As soon as he'd recovered from the surprise attack, he'd pulled out a short, sturdy baton. The first hit he'd landed on Jackal had thrown him for a loop—almost literally. The thing packed a stiff electrical shock, acting almost like a Taser.

Jackal overrode the debilitating effects with his Pain Don't Hurt and Indomitable Will Skills. Combined with the morale boost from Fool's Show Must Go On Skill, he could deal with the second and third hits as well.

The Sniper was fast and used his Stealth to good effect, landing three shots in return for the one surprise shot Jackal had landed. But three shots landed meant three shots of being in Jackal's preferred combat range, and even with the pain and damage, Jackal played a patient game, defending himself but taking the hits in order to figure out the tempo and pattern of Band Ellar's attacks.

By the third attack, he had it down, and when Band tried to withdraw to strike again—only to find that Jackal had maneuvered his axe just right.

Band's wrist was caught in the space between the bottom beard of the axe blade and the haft, and Jackal twisted the axe to lock the wrist.

And launch his Leveled-up One Punch attack with his other hand. He topped off the attack with a shot of Knock Back, which had the effect of slamming Band back into the horns of the charging Flame Elk.

Band screamed as his body was wreathed in flame, then the Flame Elk finished the task by flicking up its horns, tossing the ragdoll form of Band Eller into the trees like a sad, flaming comet of rags.

Fool's Geas finally ran out on him, the Mana cost spiking as he tried to keep an eye on Jackal, Band Eller, and the Flame Elk all at the same time. The split in concentration meant his Skill was having to do more and more work to keep the mutually false reality in place. He kept it up until he saw Band flying through the air, at which point he dropped the Skill entirely. He wanted to keep at least some Mana in reserve.

"*Jackal!*" Fool yelled as Egon finally got a hold of him.

Egon had worked around the frozen gauntlet through the simple expediency of charging into Fool and wrapping his arms around Fool's legs just below the knees. Fool slammed into the ground, and his vision blurred with the force of the impact. Even through the thick snow, his skull still managed to pound into, and bounce off, the hard ground. Everything went black and white for a moment, with a scintillating burst of stars.

By the time Fool got his consciousness back, Egon was straddling him, crushing him, a forearm driven across Fool's trachea slowly choking the life out of him. Fool tried to gasp for air, but nothing could get past the iron bar on his throat. An intense gag reflex rose up as the walls of his throat were pushed flat, and he felt his trachea bending, a hair's breadth away from cracking.

Fool tried to activate Have Faith for one last-ditch call for help from his god, but everything greyed out, and he found himself not caring too much about fighting back or breathing. His vision filled with grey until it was a flat, untextured void, and he felt the immense weight of sleep descend on him.

A flash of white, an involuntary gasp of air, and he was facedown in the snow somehow, gagging and trying to catch another breath. Egon was gone.

With total effort of will, Fool held back the gagging cough and took in a deep breath. He felt his throat knitting itself back together, pulling itself into shape with horrid, wet sounds. He couldn't quite pull himself back up, so he stayed on his knees for a moment, just getting his hands under him and lifting his head.

And tried not to scream as an enormous *crack* slapped into the air around him. Fool's face flinched back and away from the prickling sandpaper burn of the Flame Elk's red-hot iron hooves slamming into the ground centimeters from his face.

And disappearing just as fast.

Fool had the impression of the gigantic body of the beast somehow leaping over him, and he spun around, trying to rise but falling back on his ass.

Just in time to see Jackal dodging under a blow from Egon.

Which was a trap.

Fool saw it in the set of Egon's body, how he held his hands, his knees, how his head dipped. He'd set up Jackal, anticipating him ducking his head. Egon leaned in to catch Jackal's head with his forearm, put him in a headlock, and crush the life out of him, as he had almost done to Fool.

But the Flame Elk hammered into Egon, flaming horns held low, scooping and twisting the grappler up into the air and wrenching him down into the ground with a concussive slap that Fool could feel even from across the yard. The beast followed up with a ringing stomp of a hoof on Egon, then it ground that hoof even farther down as it spun back around to face Fool.

And in its eyes, Fool saw only death and rage. The glorious majesty he'd seen before was gone, and only a killing madness was left. It gathered its hind legs for another prodigious leap, crushing the remnants of Egon, and leapt again…

Into the tree line, in the direction it had thrown Band Eller.

Fool took a deep breath and sagged down. Instead of using his Skill to Heal himself, he pulled out the heavy-duty Healing potion he'd been saving up and chugged it down.

Jackal walked over, glancing at the corpse of Egon with a weary smile. "I guess no experience for that. Too bad we couldn't have enrolled the Flame Elk as a party member."

"Next time," Fool said, collapsing back on the snow with a groan.

Jackal laughed, then pulled Fool up. "We're not done yet. They need us."

Fool nodded. As tired as he was, most of his Health was restored. He hadn't been hurt like that in a long time. He could feel a lethargy, a desire to sit for one more moment, stealing over him, but he knew what that was.

Fear.

He didn't want to get hurt. He didn't want to get into one more fight. Let Jackal handle it. Let Yagnar deal with it. It was their job. He was supposed to be the brains, not the punching bag.

That was the voice of fear, with its icy, lying logic, running throughout him.

All he had to do to beat it was take one step. Which he did. And then another, and neither of those really helped, but now he was moving, and there wasn't anything to do about the fear but let it run around in its own corner of his mind, screaming away.

The rest of his brain had more important things to do.

The front of the school had turned into a standoff.

Barnes was on the street, across from the entrance, and had taken cover with the remaining deputies behind an impromptu barricade built from a few scrapped cars and a lot of snow. Jackal and Fool were peeking around the corner of the school from the parking lot at the side.

Yagnar, Emily, George, Rory, Alex, and the other rebels were holed up just outside the main entrance to the school, and they were using garbage cans and long concrete planters as cover.

The two groups were taking potshots at each other as Fool and Jackal came around the corner.

"How much time we got?" Jackal asked.

"Not long, I don't think," Fool said. "The effects of the Aura have already worn off, so they'll be running on logic and shame now. I suspect Barnes's Deputies will be creeping back in less than ten minutes. If Barnes isn't dead by then, there's no winning this."

Jackal nodded. "I'm guessing you can't use that again?"

Fool let out a sigh. "Not even enough juice for another Geas right now. And I don't think we have enough time. Best I can do is Aziz, Light! And maybe blind Barnes and crew for a moment. Think you can reach them in time?"

Jackal looked down for a moment, thinking fast. "Yeah, I can do that. I'm good for a few more Speed bursts." He looked over the situation for a moment, then came to a conclusion. "Okay, I'm gonna sprint to Yagnar, give them a fast heads-up, then I'm going in. So you wait here, keep an eye on what's going on, and flash them on a three-count after I get to Yagnar. Ready?"

"No but fuck it. Do it. I'll give what help I can." In preparation for that, Fool put away his warhammer and switched to his rifle. He'd be able to put some rounds into anyone who stuck a head up, at least. He'd hold off on firing until after he used his Skill though. No sense in giving Barnes any idea where they were just yet.

Jackal sprinted across the front of the building. Fool took a moment to marvel at that. They mostly used their Skills in combat, so there wasn't a lot of time to really appreciate the advantages the System had given them. Watching now, Fool saw Jackal cover the space in the blink of an eye. It wasn't that his feet moved super fast or that he blurred in motion or any of the other effects Fool had expected to see. Instead, he looked a very large man hustling as fast as he could… like a football player charging, or a sumo wrestler exploding across the dohyō. It just seemed coincident that they somehow covered a longer distance with each step. It was intensely weird, but somehow normal, all at the same time.

Fool counted slowly to three, then activated Aziz! in front of the barricade Barnes was shooting from. It was a utility Skill, not an offensive

Skill, and Fool knew it would only be a distraction. And even at that, only if someone was looking directly toward the front of the school.

Still, it seemed once again luck was on Fool's side, judging from the curses that erupted from behind the barricade.

Jackal was already in motion, and Yagnar was right next to him, firing her combat rifle the whole time. Behind them, all the rebels rose and charged, firing as well.

Barnes and his crew weren't fools though. Even blinded, they fired right where they'd been aiming. Even wild fire is dangerous, and Fool winced as he saw a few of the rebels seemingly trip over themselves and fall after a few more steps. Jackal crested the barricade almost instantly, this time with twin swords in hand, and leapt down the attackers. The gunfire changed to inside the barricade almost immediately, as the blinding effect had already worn off. Yagnar leaped over a second later, and the rest of the rebels were only a few steps behind.

Until a fusillade of cyan energy bolts ripped through them. Band Eller, Fool could see, had somehow survived the Flame Elk and was on the roof, firing into the backs of the rebels on full auto.

Fool saw bolts strike George and Emily, full on their backs. They were Artisans, not Combat Crafters. They had some armor provided by Yagnar, but it was nothing compared to the damage Band Eller could put out. The bolts ripped right through them. For the briefest spark of time, Fool imagined he could see their bodies lit from the inside with the release of energy.

He had no recollection of raising his rifle, of aiming. One moment he was watching two people he'd just met die, and the next he was looking at the strange hatchet face of the alien that had killed them. He hadn't even realized he'd fired until the face disappeared from his scope, and he pulled his head back to try to reacquire his target.

It was only then that he realized that he'd been screaming the whole time.

Fool had no hope that his rounds had done any significant damage to the alien. He'd probably hurt him briefly. But mostly, Fool suspected that he'd just surprised the alien long enough for it to disappear back into whatever it used for Stealth. He'd bought a few precious breaths before it attacked again.

He looked over to warn his friends and saw Barnes die.

The Sheriff was almost holding off Jackal. He was shooting from the hip with one pistol and blocking Jackal's sword with the other. Jackal looked as if was suffering under the effect of some kind of restraint Skill, because his motions were shorter and more limited than normal and delivered with less speed.

Yagnar appeared to have been affected by the same Skill, but it didn't do anything to stop her from pointing her rifle at Barnes and opening up at point-blank range. She emptied an entire magazine into him, as well as a round from what was apparently an under-barrel grenade launcher of some kind.

It looked to be loaded with some kind of anti-armor round, because when the grenade hit Barnes, it blew through him with what looked like a thick laser beam of some kind. Most of the force, thankfully, seemed to be directed away from the launcher, minimizing the damage to everyone else in the vicinity. There was enough force left to split Barnes into two pieces, one raggedly pinwheeling off to the side.

The next cyan bolt hit Jackal dead center. His armor was fried right off of him, and his chest cratered in. Fool saw the disbelieving look on Jackal's face a second before Yagnar slammed into him.

A second bolt ripped through the air where Jackal's head had just been, and for a long, stretched out second, it was as if Fool was standing right next to his friend. Jackal's face was all Fool could see. He saw every plane highlighted in cyan, and even the shadows were tinted with the same shade. The hairs on his friend's face, closest to the bolt, were melting down to the skin, little black balls that would flake off at the first touch.

Things snapped back to normal, but Yagnar and Jackal were out of sight, and for a moment, the area they'd dropped down into was filled with a rain of energy as Band sprayed the area with bolt after bolt.

Fool raised his rifle to take another shot, but Band was no longer in the same spot. Fool lowered the rifle, looking with his eyes, but even with his enhanced Perception, he saw nothing. Band must be reloading and using his Stealth to find a new stoop to fire from.

A wave of despair rolled over Fool. The Sniper was too good, too experienced and high Level, and knew how to use his Skills perfectly in this environment. He was absolutely capable of killing everyone if Fool couldn't find a way to stop him. Fool refused to believe that Jackal was dead, but he knew he was pinned down by fire right now. No one could risk sticking their head up without losing it.

Another cyan bolt ripped through the night, and one more rebel died. Fool couldn't even see who it was as he flashed his eyes up to the roof of the school.

There. Band had only moved a few feet over. Clever, as the expectation was that he would have gone to the far side of the roof.

Fool activated No Fair, shutting down Band Eller's Stealth field.

The Sniper was already moving, leaping through the air again. Once again, Fool's vision narrowed into a fuzzy tunnel, and all he saw was Band Eller. The sniper was almost floating through the air, knees drawn up, approaching the syzygy of his arc, rifle pointing down.

Fool struggled to raise his rifle, but it was slow. So slow. He'd never be able to raise it in time to have any effect on Band. And Fool's heart froze, slowing the world down even more, as he realized what the Sniper was doing.

He'd leapt to get the angle on Jackal. He'd be able to shoot Fool's friend and finish him off. Probably Yagnar at the same time. The mission, as Fool watched helplessly, was failing in front of him, in painfully detailed slow motion.

He felt the leaden thud of a single pulse of his heart, the ragged start of a breath creeping into his lungs, for a futile scream of warning that could only come too late.

They were all going to die, and there was nothing he could do about it.

Except one thing.

Time slowed to a stop, but even at that, he saw his Mana plummet.

Have Faith.

His first Class Skill, the one he hated to use more than anything. The prayer to the Trickster god for aid.

Time stopped.

Fool's consciousness expanded, flowing outward. It was achingly slow, and timeless, and it felt as if his mind reached out to infinity in less than the space it took for a photon to transition from one quantum to another.

And he was one with his god.

Laughter filled his mind, and a calming sense of reassurance.

He was the Trickster, and the Trickster was next to him.

"Your friend will be fine," the hazy, smoke-like figure said next to him. "We should do this more often, you know. This Skill isn't really meant to be used just in emergencies. I wouldn't have made it available at Level 1 if that was true. You should be calling on me when you feel the need."

"You probably already know why I don't," Fool said. The twist of reality, the otherness… it was a tearing echo inside Fool of what he had been at his worst, when he'd had almost no self to be.

"I do, but that's why I chose you," the Trickster continued. "You might not think of it this way, but you survived the worst. You came out of it on the other side. The System gave you tools to deal with your mind in a more relatable way, but you already had most of the tools. Had you been born in any other era, you would have been a treasure to your community and known a more peaceful and fulfilling life. I'm here to help you realize that potential."

Fool didn't answer, because he knew the conversation was already over, the presence of his god fading, even as it reached into the world and altered fate. And Fool felt the hooks of the Debt settle into his soul.

The Skill cost far more than Mana. It always required that he fulfilled a Debt to his god in return for the favor. And now he was carrying two Debts.

But now Band Eller had to deal with the consequence.

Chapter Eighteen

The Sniper was frozen in time, tracking his rifle down, towards Jackal's head. Fool felt the tension returning to the scene as time rolled back to normal.

Band Eller's finger tightened on the trigger. Good shooters knew to squeeze slowly, calmly, and let the shot be a surprise.

And this time, it was the biggest surprise of Band Eller's life.

The trigger went back, closed the loop of the electronic ignition of the ammunition in the rifle. Each round was a compact disc of metal that fed into an ignition chamber in the rifle. The barrel was a dense weave of super-conductors, possible only with Mana, that contained the small fusion explosion that happened in the firing chamber, and sent out a bolt of nearly pure plasma, wrapped in a cocoon of Mana to retain its shape. The shape allowed it to maintain enough cohesion to maximize damage. It was tunable as well. Band Eller could adjust the size of the bolt all the way from a shotgun-like blast to a fine needle, allowing it to penetrate the toughest armor. Without the Mana containment, the plasma would blast out of the rifle like water from a hose, spraying out wider the farther it traveled.

But the Mana had another function as well. The physics of what happened when a disc of exotic particles underwent fusion meant that a tremendous amount of energy was released, in many forms. Most of it went out as super-heated plasma, but the remainder was mostly hard radiation. When the rifle worked properly, that radiation was a feature, combining with Mana to recycle back into the weapon and helping to power the next shot.

But if the bubble of powerful magnetic fields and Mana were to be somehow disrupted? If, say, a Trickster god nudged apart the immensely strong fields by altering the level of attraction and repulsion by a tiny, miniscule amount? Miniscule in degree, immense when one was talking about the power levels being wielded.

Well, then the plasma "round" wouldn't form correctly. The fusion would still happen, but it wouldn't be able to fall into the planned shape, wouldn't be able to be propelled down the barrel and into the target. Instead, all that energy would boil up and bubble inside the ignition chamber, building and cascading on itself, until a miniature sun came to life inside the gun.

Of course, a sun so small wouldn't be stable. It was dense enough and energetic enough to momentarily warp space and time around itself. It might have, if circumstances had been right, briefly self-sustained. Had it done so, Valemount would be lit from one end to the other, daylight echoing back from the surrounding mountains with a slap. It would have come with a sleet of hard radiation combined with a wild storm of Mana that would have sterilized the entire valley.

But the interference had been coldly calculated by a vastly intelligent being, and instead of sustaining, in a space of pico-seconds, the miniature sun tore itself apart. Its own warping of space-time could not contain the explosive force of its central ignition, and it blew itself apart.

The explosion raced out ahead of the shell of the dying microscopic sun with a wave of radiation that crossed the internal vacuum of the ignition chamber, and it struck the super-dense, exotic matter of the walls, dumping all its energy into them. Here, the potential danger was even greater, as the power of the fusion-driven particles striking the exotic matter started a chain reaction of fission. The resulting nuclear explosion would still be powerful enough to destroy the town, but System-enhanced buildings and bodies might at least be able to survive that.

A Trickster god might not care about the result of his minor meddling. Thankfully—or perhaps, cunningly calculated by said Trickster—another System was in play. One that swept through the chamber, made a minor adjustment in the Mana and the world it was already bending to suit its need.

In the end, the chain reaction fizzled out. In the end, only a miniscule portion of the exotic matter underwent fission. No more than one would expect to see from a normal chemical reaction.

In the end, the result of the cosmic forces rending themselves into potential lethality in the rifle's chamber was nothing more than a fizzle, a comparatively weak sparkler where a chest-shaking firework was expected.

Band Eller felt differently.

Fool watched as the rifle exploded in a sudden sphere of light, the pressure of the light so severe Fool swore he felt it against his chest. The actual pressure wave hit a moment later, then the sound, but by that point, he'd closed his eyes and hunched over.

The echoing, roaring *bang* tumbled and blew everyone away from the center of the explosion, but by some miracle, none of the rebels were seriously hurt. The front of the school was rocked, all its windows shattered, and the System-enhanced structure was nearly pushed to failure. It held, but the cracks wouldn't Heal until morning.

Band Eller absorbed the brunt of the blast at point-blank range. He had the armor and protective devices to stop him from being instantly vaporized or shredded, but the kinetic energy of the explosion was still transferred directly to him. He blew backward at nearly the speed of one of his own bolts, across the school and into the woods beyond.

Silence descended, broken only by the residual ringing that was slowly fading from Fool's ears. He touched his ears, wondering at the heat that seemed to come from them. His hand was wet, and when he pulled it back to look at it, there was blood on his fingertips.

He was overwhelmed with gratefulness for his System-enhanced body. Loud bangs were something he'd been exposed to before—asshole teenage kids loved to throw fireworks at the homeless. He knew what it was like to temporarily lose hearing, and he really didn't want to even imagine what life with ruptured eardrums would be like.

He slung his rifle back over his shoulder and ran Location Scout again to see if any bad guys were still up and about. All he could see were markers for good guys. Either Band was dead, or he'd been blown out of the small perimeter of Fool's Skill. Fool figured that was the most likely outcome and reminded himself to check again in a few moments. Someone like that, who'd shown a knack for coming back at the last minute, wasn't someone Fool wanted to forget about anytime soon.

That taken care of, he made his way over to the barricade where he'd last seen Jackal and Yagnar. Location Scout had shown markers for them, so he knew they were alive, but he had no idea what condition they were in.

Fool's damage was Healing, and his Mana was slowly creeping back to normal, but he felt too weary to clamber over the cars and snowbanks, so he walked around them. When he got to the far side, he saw Yagnar leaning against the far car. Her gear and most of her clothing had been absolutely trashed by the explosion. She was cradling Jackal in her lap, and he was in even worse shape. All he had on were his boots and some charred black scraps of cloth.

It gave Fool a bad moment, seeing Yagnar holding Jackal like that. For the briefest second, he thought his friend was dead. Jackal certainly looked as though he was, with his exposed skin showing blacked patches of skin, split down deep enough to show dark red, coagulating blood.

And he still had the hole in his chest.

But that was a relief for Fool, because he could see the hole was closing rapidly. And the deep, wide cracks in Jackal's skin were also closing. Fool smiled, grateful once again that his friend had chosen Regeneration as a Class Skill.

Yagnar, on the other hand, was not Healing quickly. She was holding Jackal in her lap with one hand, and the other arm was held awkwardly at her side. Dislocated shoulder for sure, Fool thought. And a broken forearm too, judging by the bone sticking out.

She looked up at him as he walked closer. Her face was worn and weary.

"Status?" Yagnar croaked.

"Good," Fool said. "All good."

Fool walked up to her and started Healing her. His Class Healing Skill was labeled as "Kiss It Better" and he was once again glad it wasn't a literal description. Not that he'd mind, but Yagnar didn't look as though she was in the mood.

"Bad guys look out of commission for the moment. No one in the area. Stay put, let me check on everyone else." Fool stuck his head up over the hood of the car they were leaning against.

The remaining rebels were pulling themselves up. Alex waved at Fool, and he nodded back. Rory was helping someone to their feet.

Fool stepped back and squatted next to Yagnar and Jackal. "Everyone who's moving is up and moving. Alex and Rory are checking in on everyone. Do you need a Healing potion? I've got a few."

Yagnar shook her head. "Already Healing up. Just need time. Wish I had some Healing spells right now, for your friend. I'm supposed to be part of a team. Always had someone else who had the spells."

"Don't worry about him," Fool said. "He's got a Regen Skill. Uhm... that doesn't cover clothes though. I don't suppose your Skill can conjure up some new clothes? Or even a uniform that might fit? He's a bit self-conscious about being naked."

"Really?" Yagnar said, looking at Jackal as the fighter started to stir. "That's a... shame. Yeah, blankets. Have to get back to the supply depot for uniforms, but I'm sure we can find him something later."

"Perfect," Fool said. "And don't let him fool you. He's already awake. He just likes it when pretty ladies hold him."

"Screw you, Fool," Jackal said. "I hurt and I'm really not in any rush to move just yet." The effort of talking shook something loose in him though. He started to lift himself, but then curled over and hacked up an enormous lump of something bloody, with bits that looked as though they should be inside. Jackal looked at the pile. "Yeah. No. Gonna stay put a bit. Bad guys?"

Fool ran Location Scout again. Nothing. He ran it again for the farther part of the woods, out toward where Band had been blown... and found him. Right at the very edge of detection and moving away fast. "Clear. Band Eller looks to be booking it out of here. Thankfully."

Jackal made a grunt of agreement.

"In that case, we shouldn't have to worry about him," Yagnar said. "He was contracted by Barnes, and now that he's dead, he'll probably decide this is a lost cause. We can get George to confirm that though. Pretty sure his Skill…" Her voice faded away as she saw the look on Fool's face.

"Band," Fool said. "Emily too. It was quick, at least."

Yagnar turned her head up to the sky for a moment, and Fool waited for her.

"Okay," she said.

Her arm was mostly back in its socket, and Fool's Healing Skill was reknitting the bones in her arm as well. She carefully used that arm to push herself up. Jackal complained, but only for a moment, then he sprang up to join her. He was almost Healed, dead bits of skin falling off to reveal new brown skin underneath. He'd been chugging extra Healing potions since he could get his arms moving. She reached out into some sort of space that her Skill provided for her and pulled out a large blue blanket that she handed to Jackal to cover himself.

"Let's get all those Deputies and finish this off," she said. "After we get everyone all together. And deal with…" Her breath hitched, and Fool nodded.

"We'll move George and Emily to somewhere more sheltered, just while we deal with the rest," Fool said.

Yagnar nodded and turned to walk back to the remainder of her rebels.

Fool turned to Jackal, who was wrapping the blanket around his waist. He quickly made a small knot of two ends, then folded some pleats together in front and back, tucking them. He made a few adjustments and stood up straight.

"I haven't done that since I was a kid visiting relatives," he said with a bit of a bashful grin. "How's it look?"

Fool took a minute to appraise his friend. His injuries were almost fully Healed, and even though it was still freezing, Fool knew Jackal would be fine in the cold. He had more than enough Constitution to deal with it.

You couldn't really tell Jackal had just been on the brink of death. He looked, Fool had to admit, magnificent. Broad shoulders, well-defined musculature, and perfect posture. Jackal's build was more in line with the heroes of antiquity. Not quite the triangle of modern superheroes, but with a thicker midsection that spoke of real power. And the sarong-like garment he'd fashioned for himself really accented it.

"You look like Rama," Fool said.

"If my skin was blue, you'd tell me I looked like a Smurf," Jackal said, but there was a grin on his face.

"Smurf Hercules," Fool said. "Smerfcules. Ha. I like that."

Jackal smiled and looked around. Just over the barricade, they saw Yagnar talking with her people.

"Time to finish this off?" he asked.

"Not just yet," Fool said. "Give them a bit to take care of their fallen."

Jackal nodded and watched as Yagnar and the remaining rebels carefully covered up the bodies of those lost, including Emily and George. Then Fool and Jackal walked over to them, and they all stood together at the front of the school, looking over their friends.

Yagnar stepped forward and turned to look back at them. "Round up all the Deputies. Knock on doors as you go. Get everyone up, get them helping you. We end this tonight. We take back the town, in front of everyone. Don't kill any Deputies, don't even hurt them. If they resist at all, put out word for me and I'll come and deal with them. Don't take any shit from any of Barnes's people though. Once we have the town together, we will, as a group, decide how we're going to follow up."

There was a chorus of nods, and the group quickly split up and headed out into the town.

Yagnar turned to look at Fool and Jackal. "You two with me?"

They nodded their agreement.

"Thank you. We'll talk more about it later, but I figure the least I owe you for all of this is to talk to your people. Once we've got the town settled, everyone's got a plan. That okay?"

"More than fair," Fool said.

"Great," she replied. "Now let's go see if anyone is dumb enough to fight us."

Her tusks shone in the moonlight as she smiled.

Waking the town turned out to not be much of a problem. The firefight had woken everyone in a few blocks, and the more massive explosion had shaken everyone out of bed. Some of the nearby homes had lost windows, but there hadn't been much damage beyond that. The group of rebels moved in a slow spread, and Fool watched them collecting people for the first few blocks.

The division of the town was showing itself. Barnes had apparently physically separated his newcomers from the older town residents by moving the older residents to the outskirts, which was the area closest to the school. Most of those folk were not only awake when the rebels came

257

to get them, but they were fully dressed and armed with whatever weapons they had. One woman was angrily holding a wooden spoon and a kitchen knife.

Before long, it was a rolling posse of its own. Yagnar kept Fool and Jackal close to her and didn't try waking anyone. She just kept up a slow, steady march and clearly had a destination in mind. Her eyes were focused on the town to the north. After any interruptions to answer someone's question or to wave at someone, her eyes went right back to that location.

The first resistance didn't happen until they were almost to the main road, back to the part of town that Fool and Jackal had been allowed to rove through. But the resistance did use any gunfire or Skills. Just some angry yelling that turned into shrill screaming about rights being violated and consequences when the Sheriff heard about this.

Fool let himself have a grim little smirk when that screaming ended sharply, most likely because the news of Barnes's demise had been delivered. Fool hadn't been surprised to learn that Barnes's folks hadn't just been content to occupy the town and take away all the opportunities from those who had lived there before the System, but they had also taken the opportunity to bully everyone not connected.

It was the usual small steps of fascism. Separate people into "Us" and "Them," then work to slowly but steadily dehumanize Them. Even on this small scale, the engine of evil was still rolling into high gear. Given another year, Fool figured, the real nastiness would have started. Of course, if the rumors were true about the Thirteen Moon Sect, then that nastiness would have arrived a lot earlier.

The first Deputy was found in his house. Rory had kicked open his door when no one had answered and found him cowering and sobbing under the coffee table in his living room. His family had run out as soon as he'd come home screaming. He was quickly tied up and dragged along with the rest of the group.

Before long, they were back at the main street of Valemount. It had looked like a nice little small-town main drag a few short hours ago, when Fool and Jackal had wandered along it. Now it was just empty. Even the Shop no longer had any guards, and some of the rebels took the chance to dart in and resolve some overdue business.

"Not going to hit the Shop?" Fool asked Yagnar.

She'd been, from earlier discussions, on the run for a while. Fool figured she probably had a bit of catching up to do. She was still staring down the road though.

"Later. I'm pretty sure I know exactly where all the rest of them are hiding out." She nodded with her tusks down the road.

Fool turned to see which building she was indicating. At first, Fool thought she was pointing at the motel, but then he realized it was the building closer to them than the motel, set back a bit from the road.

The old RCMP station. Made sense that the Deputies would hole up there and would have dragged all their cronies and families along with them.

Yagnar was already walking toward it, not waiting for Fool. Jackal was right next to her, which Fool thought was crazy. He figured Jackal would have at least taken a moment to purchase a new set of clothes, if not armor. But he was striding along next to Yagnar. Sometime in the walk, he'd summoned up one of his maces, a big heavy thing that he used rarely. When he was angry. Fool took one last look at the Shop and realized he really didn't need anything either. It was time to end this.

Yagnar was in no rush, so the rest of the trip took them about ten minutes. In that time, the rest of the town had turned up, and most were following along behind Yagnar. Some folks were coming in from other directions.

Fool was astounded to see no torches or pitchforks, so grim was the emotional energy rolling off of everyone. But the near-full moon and stars were lighting everything nearly as well as the Mana-fueled streetlights that had been bought for the town. And instead of angry mutters, the crowd moved with a silence that was even more frightening.

Fool had been in some bad places in his life and suffered a lot. But he'd never experienced what these people had—the slow, steady removals of their freedoms, and the steady rise of fear of what their future might bring. It was one thing to fear the changes the System wrought, but another to see your fellow humans exploit you and set you up to be carved up and sold, or worse.

And yet, Fool hoped they weren't about to do the worst.

Years ago, back when he'd been young and whole, he'd had a girlfriend who played bagpipes. She was a competitor in an archaic form of pipe music called *piobaireachd*, and she'd played her favorite song for Fool once. It was called "Padraig Caogach" or something else hard to pronounce. It had a wild, wailing feel that called to something dark and sharp, and when Fool had asked her about the name, she said the full name of the song was the "Flame of Wrath."

The way she'd told it, the composer's brother had been murdered by a rival clan, and in revenge, the piper had waited until the clan was in church, barricaded the front door, and set fire to the church. He'd then composed the song on his pipes, playing it while watching the clan burn to death. The story, if true, had stuck with Fool, and he had found himself ruminating over it for months, thinking of the legacy of horror the song carried with it.

A crime paid back with a worse crime, and a taint added to someone's soul forever.

It was something he didn't want to see happen to the people of Valemount, and he was very worried he was about to see a new song of wrath composed.

Chapter Nineteen

The townsfolk gathered surrounded the RCMP station in silence. There would be no escape for those inside. That done though, no one took any other action. They all stood, waiting for Yagnar. Rory and Alex were at the front with a smaller group of followers, and they looked up expectantly as Yagnar approached them.

"All of them in there?" Yagnar asked.

Rory nodded. "Yep. Sent out runners to check every other place. They're all inside as best we can tell."

Yagnar turned to Fool. "Do your thing. Let us know how many people are in there?"

Fool gritted his teeth, a knee-jerk reaction to being ordered to do anything. He bit back his instant denial though. Yagnar had lost a lot of people close to her and was on the verge of wrapping up a lot of emotions. Fool figured it wasn't the best time to bring up his own issues.

"How many do you expect to be in there?" he asked.

Yagnar didn't even pause to think. "Forty-three. Including children."

Fool nodded and activated Location Scout. He looked at the status screen, which helpfully noted the relevant locations of everyone inside with steady red dots. He had to count three times before he was sure.

"Forty-three exactly," he said. "Almost all of them are in the basement. About a dozen on the top floor, mostly looking out the windows. No one is near the doors at all."

It looked to Fool as though they were hiding in fear. That was to be expected, but something about the arrangement was rather pathetic. There was no defiance in it, just what looked like abject surrender. He looked up at the building and saw a face looking at him through the blinds before quickly pulling back. Their eyes held only a morbid fascination and a sense of despair. They were all resigned to dying.

Fool looked at Yagnar. She was staring into the building but didn't say anything. Around them, the citizens surrounding the building muttered in low, dark tones. Yagnar noticed that as well.

"Rory, Alex?" she asked. "Thoughts?"

The two women moved over next to her, and Yagnar pulled them off to the side. Fool couldn't hear what they were saying, but Alex's voice was cut with anger, while Rory's sounded more steady.

Jackal moved over next to him. "Trust."

"I'm trying," Fool said quietly. "I'm not going to be a part of murder though."

"You don't know what they've been through," Jackal replied. "And it's not our place, not our town. But we walk if that's their choice."

Fool looked up at him. Jackal's eyes were locked on his, and Fool had no problem reading the question in his eyes. *Yeah, friend, I'll be okay. Just hurt.* And Fool agreed with the unsaid part of what Jackal was saying. If Valemount, and Yagnar, went all vengeance-happy, then the Foundation would do without her. Professor Xi would have to find someone else.

The discussion ended. The trio walked back over to Fool and Jackal.

"The numbers match," Yagnar said, "but we need to make sure. Fool, are you able to use your Skill to see if they're all Deputies and the other folk? No Thirteen Moon Sect folk in there?"

Fool shook his head. "I can check them one at a time from out here, but it's using two Skills at once, and that will take a long time."

Then he stopped, because DM had jumped up on Jackal's shoulder and was looking at him.

"Right. Sorry. I forgot I do have one other Skill I can use. Truth or Dare. Real simple. I can just ask my god a yes or no question. Or his avatar, I guess." Fool took a deep breath and looked the cat in the eyes. "Are there any Thirteen Moon Sect members in there?"

The cat looked at him for a moment with no reaction at all. Then it shook its head. No.

"There you go," he said to everyone else. "Any other questions?"

Everyone was slowly backing away from Jackal and the little black cat on his shoulder, except for Alex, who was looking at the cat with a quizzical expression. DM ignored all this, adjusting on Jackal's shoulder and lifting a paw to lick it. Jackal winced, since the action caused some of its claws to dig into his shoulder.

"Oh. Okay." Yagnar looked a little curiously at the cat, but not too much.

Fool took that as a sign that his arrangement with the Trickster god wasn't all that unusual in the greater galaxy, with its long-term exposure to the System. He made a note to ask Yagnar about that later.

"Right," Yagnar said. "So we're going to talk them into surrendering. As angry as we are, most of them didn't do anything all that illegal. Just unethical. Being a bully isn't illegal, but we sure don't want them in town anymore. Not sure where they're gonna go, but we're taking our town back. So one of us has to go up there and start negotiations. I figure that's my job, so unless either of you have any clever suggestions?"

Jackal shook his head as Fool paused. Then he realized he really didn't have anything to add. After all, they'd only been in town one day. They'd helped with the fight, but this wasn't any business of theirs. For sure, it looked as though McBride and the Foundation would want to start up a mutual agreement of some kind, but that wouldn't have any effect on what was going to happen now.

"We got your back," was all Fool said to Yagnar.

She nodded and walked over to the station, then knocked on the front door.

It all ended rather anticlimactically. The Deputies were more than willing to accept any conditions and only wanted to make sure their families weren't caught up in any kind of retaliations.

The only real sticky points were the merchants that Barnes had set up. They'd been making a solid profit by edging all the residents of the town into their own form of wage slavery/indentured servitude, and were, to say the least, indignant about giving up their incomes and position in the community. Once they were past the fear of being instantly killed by a raging mob, they turned back into immediate bullying.

That had turned a large part of the community back in the direction of becoming a mob, but Rory had stepped up and taken control of the dialogue at that point. She'd pointed out to the business owners that the Deputies who'd supported their business model would be banished shortly, never to return. The business owners either had to agree to abide by the laws of the new town council, which they were going to form in the morning, or be banished along with the Deputies. The same applied to the Deputies' families.

All agreed to abide by the new laws, and once they'd made up some binding short-term agreements, with the aid of the System and one remaining Lawyer, everyone called it a night. The Deputies would stay in the RCMP station overnight, watched over by guards, but not locked in the cells like most had wanted.

Fool and Jackal finally found themselves back in their barely visited motel room and ready for a night's sleep.

Which, Fool thought, was not that far away from sunrise. He didn't even bother to undress before he dropped on the closest bed and fell asleep.

He woke to the wonderful smell of bacon, eggs, hash browns, and coffee.

And the hard, sharp punch of claws into his full bladder.

He shot partway up with a loud "Oof!" and looked down into the adorable eyes of DM, looking all completely innocent as it kneaded into his bladder with its cute little paws.

"Good morning!" Jackal said. He was far too cheery for a morning.

Fool muttered something about the unfairness of higher Stamina and less need for sleep and hauled himself upright to relieve the pressure on his bladder. Afterward, he thought about heading back to tuck into the heaping room service that Jackal had somehow arranged, but opted to take a quick shower instead, grabbing his backpack as he went.

The quick shower stretched out a bit as the heat sank into his bones, and Fool let the events of the previous day play over in his head.

The arrival in town, the quick poke around, the decision to sneak out, and then one hell of a fight. He winced at the recollection of meeting Emily in the school's hallway. The easy smile on her face, the kindness that rolled out of her, all blended with the sudden cyan flash that took her and George's lives. He shook his head under the water, trying to put those memories somewhere deeper inside himself. Something, he promised himself, that he would pull out and review later, when life gave him time.

His mood turned a little as he did that, because the process reminded him of how many other times he'd had to do that. Lost lovers. Friends. Sudden deaths in the small communities he'd found himself part of. The brief moments of happiness and connections and shelter pierced through with the dull shock of recognizing that someone just wasn't going to take a breath anymore.

The System had given him back his mind, but the pain of everything he'd gone through was still there. And the System had brought with it a world that was almost as bad as his previous one. There was always going to be more pain, more loss. He needed to find a better way to deal with his emotions.

Fool turned the tap to cold, and the sharp icicles of water burned his mind clear. He focused on his breath, slowing down his heart rate, forcing the shivers to stop, until the water felt almost normal again. Then he turned the heat back up and soaked in it for a few minutes until the heat made his muscles relax again.

He dried off quickly with the provided towels, then changed into his other set of clothes from the backpack he'd brought in with him. Feeling almost human again, he opened the bathroom door and headed back into the main room.

Jackal was in the process of feeding a piece of bacon to DM, and Fool thought about scolding him for that, then decided against it. DM was an avatar of some kind for the Trickster god. Maybe that came with improved digestive properties. In any case, it wasn't like they had a litter box to change.

Jackal jerked his head toward the single desk in the room, which still had a completely useless flat screen TV over it. By some miracle, the heaping plate of breakfast foods was still somehow steaming hot, and Fool sat down and ate until he was full and then some.

He licked the last bit of ketchup off of his knife, then put the cutlery on the empty plate, grabbed the cup of coffee, and turned in his chair to look at the other two. "We all ready for what the day's got planned?"

"Indeed we are," Jackal said. Sometime in the morning, he'd replaced his gear completely. He was wearing a rather nice new outfit of black jeans and a T-shirt of an eighties... seventies band that Jackal was far too young to know about. He must have hit the Shop while he was out getting breakfast.

"That's actually a bit before my time, you know," Fool said.

Jackal looked down at the shirt, pulling the bottom out so he could look at the image, which was a collage of photos with splashes of color all over it. "Really? I thought they were a big eighties, sort of post-punk band."

"They were, but that album was mostly their stuff from the seventies. But I have to admit, I loved that album. Have you actually managed to listen to it yet?"

"Not yet," Jackal said, sitting back down on the bed. "I figured I'd wait until you were up and moving about. Didn't want to wake you. Is this one I'll like?"

Fool had to think about that. Jackal had been a fan of eighties music when Fool met him, a taste picked up from his parents exposing him to it. But he'd mostly been exposed to the pop music of the time, and Fool had been gradually introducing him to some of the rarer cuts.

"Some of it. Some of it you may not like. It's a bit toward the 'noise on purpose' end, supposed to make you not be happy. But it's pretty engaging."

Jackal leaned back on the bed and pulled out the music player he'd bought from the Shop. A fancier version of headphones, the little device projected full surround sound directly to the listener at their preferred volume, but could also act like a pair of speakers, pumping out the tunes to the rest of the space at a reduced volume. "It's not going to be as bad as 'The Ideal Copy', is it?"

"It's still art punk, but more to your taste," Fool said. "Crank it up, I'll catch up on my reading. Nothing pressing for us out there?"

Jackal shook his head and fired up the music.

Fool shoved the chair back, moved the empty plates aside, and put his feet up on the desk. He'd bought himself a nice little book reader from the Shop on their last mission, and he had some sci-fi to catch up on. He'd always loved nothing more than a full belly, some leisure time, and a good book to read. They'd been hustled off on this mission not too long after returning from their last one, and Fool thought maybe it was time for a bit of a break.

They had individual quarters in the Foundation, and Fool had come to realize having a regular little place to call your own was nice, but what he really craved was a home. An actual house with a yard and maybe a basement. Some place where he could pile junk, and with a fence that would require maintenance. Maybe even a garden. And some bookshelves. Maybe, he thought, Jackal might want to be roomies. They could probably find a nice place in McBride.

Content in their chosen worlds, the two of them let the next hour slip by. They often did this on missions when the stress got to be too much. It was their way of staying on top of rattled nerves, and a mutual admission that things had gotten more tense than either of them preferred.

After lunch, there was a knock on the door. Fool got up to answer it and was unsurprised to see Yagnar waiting in the hall.

She skipped the greeting. "I'll be heading back with you. Town took a vote this morning. Put Rory in charge. Drafted up a new settlement agreement pretty quick. So I'm free for the next bit. When do you want to go?"

Fool stepped back and sighed, then looked up at her. She was tall enough that she'd have to bend down to get through the door, and he was struck for a moment by the alienness of her. He supposed at some point he'd get past seeing aliens as weird and different, but for the time being, he was still having to consciously fight his reactions. Sometimes they flared up more than others. He forced himself to look at her and judge her with his reactions put aside. And when he did, he found he had some questions.

"We can go anytime, but…may I ask why you want to go now? It's only been a few hours, and you've been fighting to get back here for some time."

Yagnar lowered her head and looked off to the side. Fool had no idea about Hakarta body language, but he felt as if she was uncomfortable about something. In his experience, sometimes the best thing to do was be quiet for a moment. It didn't take her long to wrestle with whatever was bothering her.

"I fought to get back here. I fought to avenge my fellow soldiers. And I fought to bring back the dream we had when we came here." She looked off to the side again. "But it doesn't feel right anymore. I'm not… happy. Some part of me still rages, and I don't think that's the best way to build this community back up. Maybe it's time to admit the dream is dead as much as my fellows are. I'm not sure. But I think maybe it's best if I let the people here build themselves back up. They are strong enough now to survive on their own for a bit, but…"

"But not for long?" Fool offered.

Yagnar nodded.

"And you can't handle it all for them. Barnes kinda screwed them over, didn't he? Left them too short of Combat Classes to survive for long, and it's risky to let them Level up Combat Skills in this area. Too high Level overall, and while there are lower Level monsters, it'll be tough finding them without getting squished. Before long, they'll get crushed. So you need to recruit new immigrants?"

"I am conflicted," Yagnar said. "I have my own feelings to think about. If I stay, maybe I can help them Level up. We could also advertise for new immigrants in the Shop, but that, too, is a gamble. But mostly… they will be fine for a few weeks. And I think it's best that there be some space between us, so that I can come back on more equal terms. They need to have more sense of their own worth before we can work together. And I think maybe your organization might be the best source of the aid we need."

Fool nodded. "Absolutely. The Foundation will be willing to help. That said, I think we might be able to find some closer support for Valemount. Have you thought about reaching out to the Guild at Tete Jaune Cache?"

"Tete Jaune Cache?" Yagnar looked confused. "That's just a fort. When did a Guild move in there?"

Fool took a deep breath and blew out a sigh. "I suppose Barnes kept that a secret. Figures. The Mountaineer Guild has bought up the Fort and is moving it toward a full-fledged settlement. At least, they're adding new buildings to it. Not quite sure how all that works, but there're lots of them and they seem a cheery bunch..."

Yagnar's brows had gone up as soon as she'd heard "Mountaineers Guild." She nodded. "Yes. They have a reputation for being very crazy, climbing peaks with no Skills and their Abilities reduced to a universal standard. But they are also known as a high-Level Guild, one that adventurers retire to. What luck that they are so close by!"

"Luck seems to happen when I'm around," Fool said with a wink.

Jackal seemed to be listening to the conversation, judging from the loud, disbelieving snort that came from the room behind Fool.

Fool turned and looked at him, then turned back to Yagnar. "Right. Let's go."

Chapter Twenty

Yagnar still had some gear to pack, so it wound up being almost two hours later before they met at the entrance to Valemount. Jackal and Fool used the time to hit the Shop one more time and refresh all their consumables, as well as use some of the Foundation's Expense Funds to replace their shredded armor and other gear.

At least, for the trip back, they'd be back up to full snuff. A bit better off than they had been when they arrived at Valemount, not counting the experience they'd gained. Fool hoped they wouldn't need it all before they got back to McBride, but the trip down had been bad enough. Not even thinking about the Orcabear, which he sincerely hoped would have moved back into the mountains.

When they finally made it to the gate, Yagnar was waiting for them, but she wasn't alone. Alex was with her, and DM was curled up in Alex's arms, being petted into a drooling sleep by the HedgeWitch.

"Made a friend?" Fool asked, nodding at the cat.

"Managed to Level up during the scrap last night," Alex said. "Chose my next Class Skill as Familiar, and this little devil popped right up. Sorry if I stole your cat. I didn't even really expect it to be a regular cat, didn't think there were any others around, but here we are."

Fool tried to pull his jaw back up, but he couldn't really hide the surprise. "I... regular cat? Are you sure?"

"Well," Alex said, "not regular anymore. The Skill is giving me certain perks, and since she's connected to me, she's got the ability to share some of my Skills. We can also communicate at a certain level. And she'll Level up with me! Isn't that great? I mean, for me. I suppose if you want your pet back... well... I dunno. Not sure how this works."

Fool shivered and felt a chill. His obligation to the Trickster god had shown up in the form of the presence of the cat. Well. *Whatever*, he thought. Cats and gods, they have minds of their own, and that's what I get for agreeing to be an acolyte of one of them.

He debated letting her know that DM wasn't a common house cat at all, but rather an Avatar of the Trickster god, an actual representative extension of the being made manifest, but... how was he to know what it really was now? "It looks to me like DM has found the home she wants. Just take good care of her, okay?"

As he said that, two notifications popped up. He scanned them quickly and was only slightly surprised to find that his two obligations from his use of Have Faith had been marked as fulfilled. One was a slightly delayed one, for recognizing the nature of DM, and the other... for letting her go. Fool internally shrugged at that. The Trickster had said that the obligations were something he was supposed to be using more frequently and to not be so afraid of the cost, and it seemed the Trickster was showing that now. And honestly, the cat hadn't been much of a burden. Just a mystery that had nagged at Fool and annoyed him. And his first obligation to the Trickster had resulted in his connection to the Foundation, so it seemed that the Higher Being did have a plan for him.

Best to go along with it. For now.

"All right," Fool said. "I guess we're off then. Alex, enjoy the cat, and hopefully we'll see you again."

"Actually," Yagnar said, "she's coming with us. She asked to come along, and I agreed. I hope that's okay?"

Fool turned to look at Jackal, to see what he thought. Jackal, as expected, didn't say anything, but he raised an eyebrow and glanced at the two, directing Fool to look at them again. He turned back and looked them both over again.

Yagnar was dressed for travel in a clean new uniform, with a small pack and a cluster of small arms rigged all about her on a tactical vest and hanging from her utility belt. She had a new, nasty-looking battle rifle on a strap on her shoulder.

Alex was looking… bright, young, and eager. Which, on closer look, Fool saw wasn't quite so true. She was bright and eager for sure, but she had tiny hints of lines around her eyes and a narrowness to her jaw he hadn't noticed earlier. Along with her clothing choices of snug black pants, oversized boots, and scarves and wraps everywhere else, he'd tracked her as being in her late teens. But now he realized he was an easy decade light in his assumption. She was, he figured, in her late twenties or early thirties. Not a kid. And there was a touch of iron in her eyes as well. And a certain… vulnerability?

Then he looked back at Yagnar and saw the same look. And then noticed how close they were standing to each other.

"Oh," Fool said.

Alex and Yagnar looked at him.

"Uh, never mind. Sure, more company is welcome. Happy to have you come along. Have either of you traveled this way before?" Fool asked, changing the subject to work around his oversight.

"Not since the System," Alex said, and Yagnar just shook her head.

"All right, so the next stop is Tete Jaune Cache. There is a nice, safe fort there. It's a little too far to make today. We'll be camping overnight. Shouldn't be any problems between here and there, it's a fairly empty stretch. We'll hit Tete Jaune Cache tomorrow afternoon and probably stay there for the night, catch up on any changes. After Tete Jaune, the next leg is to Dunster for a small fort, then on to McBride. Be a couple of days, and we have to take it careful for that stretch. Last time, we ran into two different kinds of giant spiders, and both have their own dangers. We'll need to keep an eye open in their territory, and since there are four of us, we'll probably sleep in shifts and keep a watch. All cool?"

The two of them nodded, but Alex held up her hand. "What kind of spiders?"

"One is like a jumping spider, but really big. Like cube-van size. The other looks like the kind of spider you'd find in your house, shining dark brown, and they're between dog- and pony-sized. Those aren't really aggressive. You can walk past them without any issues, but they will eat you if they come across you sleeping or if you wander into a web. So keep your eyes open and you should be fine."

"And what are you holding back?" Yagnar asked. "You keep glancing to the side, toward Jackal. What should we know?"

Caught out, Fool replied, "I'm not really trying to hide it, just kinda hoping we don't run across it on the way back. There's a massive, really bad boss monster out there. An Orcabear."

"Orca. Bear?" Alex asked. "Like, a bear with an orca head?"

"No," Fool replied. "More like an orca with bear legs, only still hairless, and it has six of them."

"Are you sure it's not a giant tardigrade? Six legs? Waterbear?" Alex asked.

"Nope, definitely an orca," Fool replied. "Got the fins and black-and-white coloring and everything."

"What is an orca?" Yagnar asked. "And how many kinds of 'bears' does this planet have?"

Fool bit back the funny reply to that and replied as truthfully as he could. "An orca is a kind of predatory whale. It's sometimes called a 'killer whale' because they look sort of like a giant scary shark, and they hunt seals, amongst other things. They can make some impressive kills out where people can see them, so they got a bit of a rep. Not deserved really. Well, I guess it is these days, but still…"

"Why is a whale in the mountains?" Yagnar asked. "I know the System works in mysterious ways, but this is a bit of a stretch. Is it common on this world?"

Fool didn't have an answer for that, but Alex did. "It's some bullshit is what it is. The System colonizes almost as bad as white folk." Her voice was a little angry as she went on. "It's probably an Akh'lut. An Inuit legend, the wolf-whale. Shapechanger whale that could walk on land. System probably figured this was First Nations' land and didn't really pay attention to whose land it was."

"Probably for the better." Fool suddenly realized who Alex reminded him of, but he stomped down on that sudden pain, fast. That memory was from the coast though, not the interior. Still, he remembered quite a bit. "Better than a Sisiutl, maybe?"

"Ha!" Alex nodded. "Be almost as bad though. But this is Simpcw land. I'm not even sure what would come from them. I never asked. Rory might know."

"Well, in any case," Fool continued, "we tangled with it on the way here. Would have killed us if the folk from Tete Jaune hadn't shown up just in time. And even with all of them, they were only able to drive it off. I'm hoping it took its licking and went somewhere far away. Like Wells Gray park or something. Nobody's likely to go anywhere near that for a while."

They all nodded, and there didn't seem to be any other questions, so with some last waves at the new townsfolk guards on the walls, they left Valemount, finally on the road back to what Fool and Jackal were calling home these days.

Fool tried not to think about the Orcabear.

The rest of the day and the first night passed with no issues at all. Conversation had slowed, since Yagnar and Alex spent most of their time looking all around. Fool had asked about that, since they hadn't seemed so paranoid in town. It turned out that the area south of Valemount was actually much more densely populated with low-Level monsters than the area north, where they were. While Yagnar and Alex had been hiding out from Barnes and his cronies, they'd faced nearly constant nuisance attacks. It had at least allowed them some solid Leveling up, far more than anyone in Valemount.

They arrived at Tete Jaune Cache right on schedule, just after noon. Fool's heart sank a little when he saw how many more roving patrols were out, compared to when they had been there a few days before. The whole Fort looked to be on high alert.

When Lexi ShiningMoon came out to greet them, she filled them in on the reason. "It's back. We lost an entire group of climbers yesterday. Some heavy hitters are coming in to help, but they won't be here for another three days. I don't think we can hold out that long. We got lucky on the first encounter. It's much stronger than we thought. We need every bit of help we can get."

Fool's stomach turned to a tiny icy ball and dropped about two feet down. Until Lexi had confirmed the Orcabear was back, he'd been able to hide his fear of running across the creature again. The image of Jackal, nearly torn to pieces, flared back up in his mind, and he could almost feel again, the hot breath of the beast as it closed in on him, bits of flesh hanging from its teeth.

He turned to look at Jackal, and to his amazement, the man was actually smiling.

Lexi looked surprised by that as well. "Jackal? I'm guessing from that smile that you've got a plan for a rematch?"

Jackal didn't say anything, but he reached up to pull something from his Inventory. He pulled out a spear, and Fool belatedly recalled that Jackal had had a bit of a smug expression when they'd exited the Shop in Valemount.

The spear was an unusual-looking weapon. It had a wide cutting head, but the center of the spearhead was a cut-out, instead of a solid piece. Overall, it was shaped like a long, wide leaf with an oval missing in the middle.

The reason became apparent when Jackal stroked a small stud on the side of the spear, and the hollow center flared into a glowing, ruddy ball. The blades of the spear immediately glowed, and a ripple of heat flared out from the spear.

Yagnar sucked in a breath. "Plasma spear. I haven't seen one of those in a long time. That must have cost you a small pile of Credits."

Jackal only grinned and turned off the burning spear before returning it to his storage.

"Got any more of those?" Lexi asked.

"We only have a limited" —Fool almost said budget before he realized that would reveal too much about him and Jackal to people he really didn't know that well— "stash of saved up Credits, and Jackal thought this would be a prudent use of our funds."

It was close enough. The discretionary funds they had did have a limit, and funding weapons for other people was outside of the budget, explicitly.

"Shame," Lexi replied. "But good call. We confirmed in the Shop that it's vulnerable to heat, but we hadn't been able to generate enough heat to really affect it. How did you two figure it out?"

"I guess you missed that part," Fool said. "Just before you rescued us, I managed to hit it with a plasma grenade and took a sizeable chunk out of it. Didn't affect its Regeneration, but absolutely hurt it."

"Uhm, how tough is this thing?" Alex asked. "Fool only mentioned it in passing, but this sounds pretty bad."

"Sorry," Fool said. "I was hoping it would be gone. It's big, does a lot of damage, and has a very fast Regeneration. Poison bite too, so it slows down your Healing and Regeneration. Plus, it's got a high level of armored protection from a thick layer of blubber. Plus, it's mean."

"That about sums it up," Lexi said. "You two from Valemount?"

"Sorry, yeah," Fool said. "Allow me to introduce Yagnar and Alex Garret. This is Lexi ShiningMoon of the Mountaineers Guild."

"Pleased to meet you." Lexi waved at the two. Then she squinted at Yagnar and tilted her head. "Huh. You're one of *those* Hakarta. Never met a noble before. When we deal with this Orcabear, some folk back in the Guild will be happy to buy you a drink, if you feel like satisfying some curiosity."

Yagnar chortled. "Not much to say, but happy to drink if they're buying."

The hollow in his belly was starting to bother Fool, and one thing he'd learned in the last few years was that the best way to deal with fear was to not let it fester. No thinking, just action. Not action without planning, but the sooner he could do something, the better he'd feel.

"What's the plan then?" Fool asked.

"We think we know where it's coming from," Lexi said, "but it covers a lot of territory. We were hoping we could find its lair, but the best we can do is predict where it'll be. It seems to hit the same hunting trails, so we'll go out tonight and try to ambush it. Four teams, to cover all the routes. No real plan other than to pin it in place, surround it with ranged fire, and bring it down. If you've got any ideas, we're all ears. We've got about another six hours before we head out in teams."

"I can try. I've been working on my Skills, and I think I can help narrow down the routes for you. Maybe we can outnumber this thing more thoroughly. Won't be able to do that until closer to the time though, so we've got time to work it out. But Jackal and I are going with the team that has the best chance of catching this thing. That okay?"

"Absolutely. You've got the experience and the Levels. We want you with us where you can do the most good."

Fool turned to look at their traveling companions. "You two didn't sign up for this, so you can hole up in the Fort overnight. If we don't make it back, I'm going to send a message up to our people, and they'll send down a squad to escort you the rest of the way."

Alex shook her head and glanced at Yagnar, who'd crossed her arms and was just staring at Fool.

Fool looked at them for a moment and said, "You really don't want to tangle with this thing, but it's up to you."

Yagnar shook her head.

Alex smiled. "We might be more help than you think. So" —she turned to Lexi— "can we have a tour of your Fort? I love the look. Tell me more about it!"

Fool could only shrug. He looked over at Jackal, who didn't have anything to add either. So be it, Fool figured. Maybe it wouldn't be as bad as he remembered.

The whole area was in a bit of an uproar, and after a while of tagging along behind Lexi to see if they could be of use, the Valemount group was politely shuffled off to the same restaurant Fool had enjoyed the meal with Lexi in. Lexi promised she'd be along shortly to catch them up and work on a plan to fit them in, but for the moment, she was too busy getting the basics organized.

While they were waiting for their delayed lunch, Fool took the chance to ask Yagnar about something that had stood out to him when they'd arrived. He hoped he wasn't about to ask something rude. "So… Yagnar, what did Lexi mean about you being one of 'those' Hakarta? I'm not that familiar with Galactic things. Is it something you can share?"

Yagnar, to Fool's immense relief, smiled. "It's not that big a deal. It's the Princess thing. How much do you know about Hakarta? Just the usual,

I expect? I've heard 'Space Orcs' before and had to look that up. Not the nicest comparison, but you seem a bit more urbane."

Fool smiled and took a drink of water from his glass, then leaned back in his chair. "Honestly, not much. Just that your race tends to be mercenaries, specializing in what we humans might consider 'modern' arms—range weapons, things like that."

"That's true," Yagnar said, "but also not true. Many Hakarta, probably the majority that you will meet, fit that stereotype. We have excellent schools, and a long history of the kind of warfare that makes us particularly good at those skills, but… would you consider fitting humans into a simple summary like that?"

"Right. Sorry, I'd like to say that non-humans are new to me, but I'll admit I let my biases get the better of me. I'm listening. I'd love to hear more about your people."

Yagnar didn't acknowledge that with more than a brief nod before she continued. "Hakarta are an old people. We've been around the System for long enough that the homeworld is something most of us never see. But our homeworld wasn't all that different from yours. And we had as many nations and people as you humans do. Our cultural history goes back a long, long time, and if you're really interested, you can find probably millions of books in the Shop. My particular culture was one that stuck with the traditions of royalty long into the Hakarta modern age— somewhat akin to your English, but on a smaller scale. We also kept fairly neutral in wars and political maneuvering, so we were considered the best choice for banking and other concerns that were best served in the long term by being removed from nationalistic concerns."

"A Swiss Princess!" Alex said. "Oh, my god, I'm dating Elsa."

It took until a few moments after their food arrived for the humans to stop laughing and explain the humor to Yagnar. She took it in stride with humor, but her raised eyebrows at Alex hinted at later retaliation.

"Anyway," Yagnar said, "moving on. Yes, my extensive family has a good many princes and princesses. It's not considered a big deal amongst us Hakarta, but for some reason, the family gained a certain bit of Galactic fame when one of my great-aunts wrote a book. And our family is noted for our distinct features, so it wasn't too surprising that Lexi recognized me."

Fool looked at her, as when Yagnar mentioned "distinct features," she had tilted her head, as if to showcase what that feature was. For the life of him, Fool couldn't figure it out. He'd always had a bit of face-blindness, and it seemed to be worse with non-humans. He made an appreciative face, the one with the pursed lips and the nod and the raised eyebrows. It seemed to be the right response. Yagnar gave him a very tusky smile, and they all dug into their food.

Chapter Twenty-One

Lexi arrived as their dessert was arriving, and she ordered a large meal of her own and another round of pitchers of beer for everyone.

"Okay," she said, "the teams are sorted, weapons and armor for everyone. We sorted teams into the best combinations of Skills and equipment, so each team should stand a pretty good chance against the Orcabear. We've decided that the best case is to load up one team with the strongest people and hold that team back to act as a reserve for whichever team contacts it first. You four will be in that team, along with me. So what's this new Skill you've got?"

She snuggled right up to Fool, crushing him against Alex. Clearly, he realized, she'd rather enjoyed their evening together. He had the crazy urge to put his arm around her, but he was feeling a bit shy in the company of others. Lexi had no such shyness and was rubbing her shoulder against him affectionately. He couldn't help but smile. He was suddenly feeling not only more positive about killing the Orcabear, but was also really looking forward to getting it over with and coming back to the Fort and to Lexi's quarters…

"Not so much a new Skill," he said. "Just a way to use an old Skill better. It's a pathfinding Skill, but it's smart enough to take into account tactical goals, so I should be able to use it to find the best path to reach the Orcabear, considering the group we're with. I can then use Location Scout, my other Skill, to have a look at the actual place where the first Skill says we'll meet it, which will let me see what sort of conditions are in that area. The Skill won't tell us what to do in that location, but it will tell us the best place to be. It's up to us to figure out why."

Lexi nodded. "That's... pretty useful. And I can see why you said it wouldn't be too useful until we get closer to the time. I'm guessing it's got some time and distance constraints?"

"Yup," Fool said. "The closer the better, but for our purposes, about an hour is best. Do we have an idea about when and how far from the Fort we might run into the beast?"

"Absolutely. It's been hitting us just after dark. Right after sunset, it comes to us. If we send out teams to catch it, it picks them off later in the night. But if we stay put, just after the sun goes down. So about three hours from now. But we never know what direction it will come from."

"I think I can help with that. And if we're already in the right area... hmm... one moment."

Fool activated his I Know A Shortcut Skill and let it reach out. He had a good image of the Orcabear in his mind, and a path to it showed up almost right away. It was a good distance away, to the west.

"Okay," Fool said, "we're in luck. I can see where it is already. It's almost directly due west, which means it's probably up on one of those mountains. So it has to come down to get to us. We can plan on being hit from the west, and I can check in every half hour or so until I'm certain which way it's coming. Do you want to try to get it outside of the Fort, on the way in, or here at the Fort?"

"I'm tempted to say here at the Fort, but if all we can do is wound it and it runs away again, we're just going to keep having the same issue. But I have to admit, even knowing which way it's coming? I'm not entirely confident we can kill it."

"Can I make a suggestion?" Fool asked. Lexi nodded, and he continued. "Let it come to the Fort. Fill up the perimeter as if you intended to defend the Fort but keep most of your teams outside. We'll pin it against the Fort and kill it once and for all. It's a tough beast, but we've got the right people to take it down."

He stopped and looked at everyone. He'd started with his usual flippant tone, but he felt himself committing to the plan as he spoke. There was no doubt in Fool's mind that they could kill it, but at what cost? Was he willing to risk his friends' lives? Was he that confident? He looked into all of their eyes, one at a time, and realized it wasn't a question of believing in himself, but rather of believing in his friends.

"We're the right people," Fool said, dead serious. "We can do this. We will do this. We've got what it takes to kill this thing, together. I believe in all of you." His voice raised and he grabbed his mug of beer. "Let's kill us a monster!"

When the sun went down, Fool's confidence faded with it. The cold night air rushed in, and he shivered. They were outside the Fort proper, away from all the buildings. As best he could tell from his updates, he was away from the path the Orcabear was taking to the Fort.

He held back a shudder of fear and checked his I Know A Shortcut Skill one more time. It was closer. Much closer. Right on schedule, right on the predicted path. And according to the plan, they were in the right place. They wouldn't be seen by the Orcabear. The whole team was hunched down in a short gully just outside the Fort. Fool felt brutally exposed, but if they hunched down, they would be invisible from the Fort. But only from the Fort. If the Orcabear came from any other direction or deviated at all from its predicated path—or hell, just walked around the Fort before attacking? They'd be completely exposed.

The wind was blowing against them as well, which added a cold, sharp bitterness to the night. But it was one more element that added to them being in just the right place. All they had to do was hold tight and wait.

"Still coming?" Yagnar was belly down next to Fool, her rifle out and ready to be drawn into action, braced against the small rest she'd made for it in the snow.

"Still coming," he replied. "Right on schedule. Won't be much longer."

Yagnar took a moment to roll over on her back and stretch out her arms and shoulders. "I'll say one thing about your world. It's got a lovely view of the stars."

Fool tucked in beside her and looked at the sky. The night was still young, but it was true night. A faint hint of dark amethyst-purple on the horizon was all that was left of the twilight glow.

The Milky Way split the sky, and for the first time he could remember, Fool could clearly see why it was sometimes called a road across the sky. It ran across the sky with a fuzzy white glow, and each star shone pinprick-bright across the remaining bowl of the sky.

Orion was rising high, and the nebula was bright and easy to see. Fool turned to his right and looked and saw the Sisters and their attendant constellation twinkling merrily. He smiled and turned back to Yagnar.

"Didn't use to be able to see all the stars like that," he said. "We had enough bright lights that you could almost count the stars without a problem. Even out here, in the boonies, we'd still be seeing fewer and fewer stars. Guess we can thank the System for that too."

"Only in the short term." Yagnar gazed at the sky with a faint smile. "Once civilization gets its hooks in, people will care less about things like being able to watch the stars. And since no one likes the night anymore, the System helps them put in more and more lights. We once ran ops on a world where the sentients had spent a good chunk of their income arranging a near-perpetual light over all the settled portions of their world."

Fool had a hard time imagining that. For a sizeable chunk of his life, nighttime had been a time of relative ease and relaxation. Most of the rest of the world would shut down and hole up for the night, which meant less hassle for him, fewer people and their stress to avoid. Daytime was for getting out of everyone's way, preferably by finding a dark place where no one looked. With his world changed, he still preferred the quiet of the night, even if he found fewer and fewer opportunities to explore it.

"Lot of worlds out there, I guess," he said.

Yagnar nodded. "Many. More than any of us could see in a lifetime."

"I think I'd like to try," Fool said, not even realizing it was out loud until he heard his own voice. He chuckled softly. "When I was a kid, we'd only just landed on the moon. I loved to read science fiction and dream about making trips across space. But then the years rolled on by, and it looked like space was just going to be another place owned by people who only cared about buying and selling and being in charge. And I accepted that reality as a bit of a hard lump I had to swallow, that no one in my lifetime was ever going to really be a space traveler. I guess I was wrong."

They sat for a bit more in companionable silence, watching the stars twinkle and dance in the sky.

"You can, you know," Yagnar said. "Still lots out there to explore. Alien worlds. The System makes getting out there possible. Not cheap, but not too expensive. Dangerous though. Very dangerous. But lots of explorers. Even some who try to reach beyond the System and see what lies out in the vast of the universe."

"Now that," Fool said, "sounds like my kinda retirement. I guess I'm gonna live a lot longer than I thought I would, so maybe once I've done what I can here, I might see if I can go out there."

"Maybe look me up when you do," Yagnar said. "I had an uncle who was a barbarian throwback. Liked to use all kinds of optics to watch the stars at night. Gave me a bit of taste for the wonder of it all."

Fool grinned at her. "Sounds like my kinda guy. Deal. If I get the chance, I'll let you know."

Yagnar grinned and flopped back down on her back, arms crossed behind her head.

"Hey now," Fool said, "don't get comfy. Monster's coming."

"Soon?" she asked.

"Now." He stood as the first notification from a scout flashed across his vision.

Just in time for the air to be split by the ear-splitting, howling, mournful roar of the Orcabear.

"Stay down," Jackal said, and Fool glanced at him. Jackal was crouched low, hiding behind his own berm of snow. "Remember the plan."

Sheepishly, Fool dropped back down. He'd forgotten about that. And it might have been the biggest mistake he'd made, as he could already see the trees on the other side of the clearing, behind the Fort walls, rippling with the approach of the beast.

He didn't know how good its eyesight was, but if it had seen him bolt up, their careful plan was ruined. It was, however, the perfect time to put his lessons learned to use. He turned to look at Jackal.

Fool said, "Have Faith." And bolted back up.

The plan was to have the Orcabear attack the Fort while the troops inside kept its attention on them. But Lexi had some worries, because the walled portion of the Fort was now only part of the soon-to-be-settlement. They'd already started to build outside of the walls proper. For the evening, everyone had been taken inside, if they weren't part of the scouts or other teams. But their hard work was exposed and likely to be lost if the Orcabear rampaged through.

Fool had to admit, at least to himself, the plan was a little sketchy. After all, why would the Orcabear only attack the Fort and not prowl around outside, if the people in the Fort were only defending? They'd kind of skipped the whole "bait" part of the trap, but no one had come up with a plan other than assuming that the natural aggression of the beast would lead it to attack any gathering of people.

In a flash, Fool had realized he had a perfect solution. He had to admit, part of his thinking came from seeing how easily the creature was plowing through trees as if they were grass in a field. In their previous encounter, he hadn't truly been able to understand the size and Speed of the monster. But as it came barreling through the trees, he finally understood the scope of the threat.

With that understanding, he'd also realized that nothing was stopping this beast from going all the way south to Valemount in the space of a single night and rampaging through that town as well. He couldn't let that happen.

Not when he could do something about it.

Fool was a terrible fighter. He had no Skills for doing damage, or making weapons hit harder, or removing armor, or any of the other Skills.

But he was distracting. And he knew, if he put his mind to it, he could be annoying.

Annoying enough to be the perfect bait.

He darted forward as the beast broke through the tree line.

It was so much bigger than he remembered. Or it had grown. In any case, it broke through the trees like a whale breaching the surface, trees falling around it like green shoals of water. Fool could see it clearly now. The giant orca head, looking big enough to bite a bus in half, and head extended back to where the fins would normally have come out. Now that area had been transformed into thick shoulders leading down into pillar-like legs that looked to have come from a gigantic hairless grizzly, still mottled in the black-and-white patches of the Orca. And its dorsal fin still crested above the trees.

Its final two sets of legs were smaller, but still thick and muscular. Behind them, the short, powerful tail with its flukes was snapping up and down. As Fool watched, the creature made a half-turn and the tail snapped a fir from its base, sending the tree spinning through the air.

Fool had either forgotten to be afraid or had somehow moved through the fear. He felt something roaring up inside him, but it was beyond any emotion he'd ever felt. It was more of a strong sense of momentum and purpose, and there wasn't a heck of a lot of thinking going on with it.

He charged at the Orcabear, vaguely aware that he was yelling something. And his Skills were going full bore—Have Faith paramount among them. The Trickster had told him to use it more frequently, so he was letting it rip, adding it to his already prodigious Luck. He could feel the small bargains flying: Make sure no one decides to follow me. Make sure I don't fall on my face. Let the Orcabear see only me. A host of other small things, piling on.

And he used Geas as he never had before, latching right into the skull of the Orcabear with one simple message: The man running at you is your mortal enemy, and you want to kill it more than you want to breathe.

All of his Skills were for helping others. Low value. Ever since he'd first seen what they were, what the path of his Class Progression looked like, he'd resigned himself to being a second-rate character, an NPC that the real heroes would come to rescue. He'd worked hard to not rely on any of his Skills and learned to rely on his equipment and on his friends.

Now Fool knew better. In this heady rush, in this moment of throwing his life on the line in the stupidest possible way, he knew he was the hero. He was the Trickster.

He didn't need weapons to win. All he needed to do was actually have faith and trust in his Skills. And to embrace that he was meant to be the luckiest sumbitch alive.

The Orcabear blazed across the clearing, moving so fast it was literally plowing waves of snow on either side of it. Its mouth gaped open, a banshee wail of hate blasting out of it, and in a flash, Fool and the Orcabear met and clashed in the middle of the field.

Or would have, if the beast hadn't stumbled just a little. If Fool hadn't skidded to his knees in the snow.

The gaping mouth, full of vicious fangs, passed just over Fool. He felt a brief tug as a thin wisp of his hair caught on one of its teeth.

He slapped the whale on the belly of its chin as it passed over him, and in rage, it snapped its mouth down to savage him. Its snout caught in the snow, and the shift in its center of gravity was enough for it to stumble.

It started to cartwheel forward, and for a brief, shining moment, Fool saw its great white belly leaping over him. He couldn't help himself and reached up a little higher, just grazing the belly of the beast as it tumbled over him.

"Be free…" he whispered as a maniacal burst of glee came over him.

The Orcabear tried to balance itself, thrashing about in some ancestral memory that told it to spin about when leaping in the air. It was just the wrong reflex at the wrong time, and for the briefest moment, the watching team was treated to the astounding sight of a gigantic monster perfectly straight and balancing on the tip of its nose.

Then momentum took over, and the tremendous mass of the creature completed the tumble, a bouldering ball of thickly armored flesh smashing through the clearing.

Right into the waiting team.

All of whom managed to scatter in time, with a chorus of yells and screams.

The Orcabear slapped to a stop flat on its back. It spun back to its feet and shook itself like a dog, letting out another rage-filled, mournful howl.

Yagnar fired her weapon into it point-blank, and everyone else opened fire. Fool saw Jackal charging at it with his plasma spear.

It ignored all of them, even as chunks of its flesh were blasted off. The Orcabear only had eyes for Fool, and its beady black eyes glared into Fool's like black holes from the edge of the galaxy, promising eternal doom with no escape.

Fool turned and ran. He had no hope of reaching the entrance to the Fort. Even if he could manage it in time, they wouldn't open it for him. They knew better.

Still, he had no other plan.

His skin crawled, even while doing a full-out sprint, as another piercing wail ripped out behind him.

He felt the ground shaking and pushed himself, faster, right at the wall of the Fort.

For a moment, Fool glanced up and saw a startled pair of eyes looking down at him from a parapet.

He tried. He really tried. He'd seen videos, before the System, of parkour folks who looked as if they could run up walls. He'd obviously never tried it, but the System had enhanced his body, and he thought... maybe.

He ran right at the wall and, at the last second, leapt up and reached out with one foot.

Have faith, he thought.

For the briefest moment, his foot stuck to the wall, even as momentum bent his leg and brought his body toward the wall. He kicked his other leg forward, and his head turned to the side.

As the world slowed to a crawl.

Out of the corner of his eye, so close Fool could almost reach out and touch it, was the giant beady eye of the Orcabear.

Its mouth rose up under him, and he was reminded of how it had savaged Jackal. Again he saw the nature documentary clips rolling in his mind's eye, and he could almost read the brain of the creature.

Its mad little mind was firing on all cylinders, a red, rabid glee filling it as it could almost taste the pleasure of gripping the puny human in its teeth and whipping its head up and down, tossing its body up again and again, until it was nothing but little morsels to swallow.

Its mouth opened, head arching back and up.

Fool's foot slipped off of the wall, and his stomach leapt up into his heart as he started to drop down.

Right onto the rising nose of the beast.

His foot caught between two of the wickedly pointed pegs the creature had for teeth, and in a panic, Fool kicked down and away and felt a mad twisting as he spun with momentum...

...the Orcabear's jaw and head lifting, to grip and tear...

...and the forces all adding up just right to fling Fool into the air.

And a little forward, enough that he flew up in an arc and cleared the top parapet at the apex of his arc.

He landed and instinctively bent his knees and squatted to remove some of the momentum. And then stood. A near-picture-perfect landing, all the forces of momentum and gravity conspiring in his favor. In front of him was a quick and unpleasant drop down to the ground inside the Fort. He turned to his right and saw an astonished Lexi.

He smiled.

"Hi. Thought I'd drop by," Fool said, raising an eyebrow.

Chapter Twenty-Two

He almost fell as the wall shook. Lexi didn't say anything, just raced to the parapet, leaned over, and fired.

Fool started to walk toward the wall, but it shook again, and the screams of the Orcabear battered against everyone's ears.

When he finally reached the wall, he looked over. Then rapidly pulled his head back and heard the wet snap of the Orcabear's teeth slamming shut where his head had just been. He rushed back to see the Orcabear dropping back down. Fool would have sworn the wall was too high for it, and he had to see how it had managed.

He saw it land and glare him as its skin was peppered by heavier and heavier weapons and spells. It backed up in rage, then gathered itself into a slightly smaller shape and leapt again. Fool leaned his head back and noted the beast had gotten almost enough height to get a claw on top of the parapet. That wouldn't be good.

He glanced off to the side in time to see Jackal barrel into the side of the beast. His Plasma spear carved a swath through the side of the beast, and it screamed in rage.

Fool's Mana suddenly dropped to nothing, and he hurriedly shut off the Geas. Clearly, he was not even close to the biggest threat to the Orcabear anymore.

He was suddenly exhausted. He'd never used so much Mana at once before, never burned through it so intentionally and willfully. It was up to everyone else now. The beast was in the fight, and they had it where they wanted it.

Hopefully, it wasn't too much for them. Fool pulled out a plasma grenade and looked over the wall again. It was the only thing he had that could help in the fight, but he couldn't see a way to use it without injuring his friends. He kept it in hand and split his attention between watching the fight and watching his Mana creep back up enough to where he could be of use.

Yagnar was battered aside, having gotten a little too close to the beast's tail. Alex screamed and ran after her, and the creature snapped around and bit a Guild Member who'd jumped down to help in half.

Lexi swore but kept steady fire with her rifle, sticking to the plan.

It took Fool a minute to find Jackal again, in between the flashes of gunfire and spells. They'd figured out that fire was the element to use against the Orcabear, but the Mountaineer's Guild didn't have any Fire Mages on hand, so the Spellcasters had been resorting to a mix of other spells to get the same effects. It seemed to work. The creature's Health was dropping. Slowly, but still dropping, even with its Regen in effect. The biggest damage had come from Jackal's first hit with the spear, but he didn't seem to be next to the monster.

Then he was. Jackal must have been knocked aside again, because he was charging in from the side, and his armor was once again in tattered wreckage.

It was a bit like déjà vu. Fool knew what Jackal was going to do. He was going to use his favorite Death From Above Skill and leap on the Orcabear with the spear, for a big chunk of extra damage. Only last time he'd done that, he'd been nearly ragdolled to death by the beast.

No time for thinking. Fool had to be quick, and he had to trust he had enough Mana left.

"Have Faith," Fool whispered and activated the Skill. Then he tossed his plasma grenade right at the Orcabear's mouth.

He must have remembered to set it for impact, because it went off right as the creature raised its head to snap Jackal out of the air. The grenade went off with a brilliant flash, and Fool was close enough to feel the flash of heat.

Jackal's leap brought him to just behind the head of the beast, and Fool could only watch in horror as the last of the ball of plasma scorched his friend's exposed flesh.

It didn't stop Jackal at all. Gravity had little truck with things like feelings.

With a roar, Jackal plunged the burning spear into the skull of the Orcabear. The raging plasma head of the spear tore through the thick blubber, hesitating only slightly on the reinforced bone of the beast's skull, and plunged into its brain.

Jackal screamed again and threw his weight backward, causing the plasma spear to twist about in the brain of the Orcabear.

It died without even a shudder.

The celebration lasted through the night, and it was only when the sun came up people drifted off to bed. Fool and Jackal had both Leveled up, which surprised Fool. He hadn't expected to get as much experience as he had, but apparently, he didn't need to nail kills for experience. In fact, from what he could see, he would gain even more experience for using his Skills constantly and actively.

He'd mentioned that to Jackal, when they'd had a bit of time alone, and Jackal had posited something that made sense when Fool thought about it—experience comes from using Mana, not from killing. Fool had sort of known that. Artisans and Crafters had to Level up somehow, after all. His Trickster Class didn't really seem to fit into any of the roles he'd been told were normal though. He wasn't a Crafter, and he equally sucked at Support and Combat. He'd always assumed he just had a bit of a bad Class and had done his best to alternate between Support and Combat roles.

And Fool had done damn well at it, all things considered. Hitting Level 40 the hard way spoke well, he thought, of his overall capability. But now that he saw what the results of using his Skills were? Level 50 didn't seem all that far away, then he had a whole slew of potential for his Advanced Class Skills. He'd thought that would take years, but now?

Maybe a year. Two at the tops. The hard part was going to be finding ways to use his Skills on a daily basis.

Trickster.

If Fool was going to burn through enough Mana to Level up at the rate his Class seemed capable of, then he had to make sure he used his Skills constantly. Not just in battle or on missions, but daily, hourly. And in order to do that, he needed to come up with all sorts of reasons to use them.

Well, he thought, my friends are smart and tough. It's not like they can't put up with a bit of daily reality-altering. Besides, it would be good for them. Make them more open to the surprise and chaos that life in the System was sure to bring them. And doing it with loving care would take the sting out of it.

The possibilities had been running through his mind when the festivities finally caught up to him, and at some point, he'd clearly fallen asleep.

He must have, because otherwise why would he have woken up with DM on his chest?

Fool's eyes were crusty, and from the light filtering in, it was later in the afternoon. He had no idea where he was.

DM's bright green eyes blinked at him, and he felt her little paws kneading steadily on his chest, pointy claws cycling in and out of their sheaths.

"Good morning," Fool said.

The cat purred.

"Where am I?" he asked.

DM didn't say anything, but she stopped clawing at his chest, turned around a few times, and flopped down on him. She was on her side, but she made sure to flick her tail up, so he had a view of her butt.

"Oh. Lovely. Thanks," he muttered, then froze when he heard someone muttering in their sleep next to him.

His brief panic faded when he realized he was still fully clothed, but then came back a bit when he further realized that he wasn't in his bed... and he was wedged between two other people. Fool turned to his side, slowly looking. He was wedged on his right side next to a giant shoulder in short sleeves, with green skin. Yagnar.

That would mean on the left... yup, curled up on her side, squinting at him with one eye open, was Alex.

"Shuddup," she said. Then she closed her eyes and went back to sleep.

Yagnar let out a mighty snore, and DM shifted, standing. Somehow, her little claws got even pointier, and she managed to stab them repeatedly into Fool's bladder while purring.

The pressure was too much to deal with, so he slowly pulled himself up. It was a careful operation, because he didn't want to wake everyone else, but sitting up just put more pressure on his bladder. At least DM had obligingly hopped off, stomping over to Yagnar, and curling up on her thigh.

The room was dim but lit enough for Fool to see that it wasn't his room. And Lexi was in here too, as well as a few other Guild members. All fast asleep, in chairs or on the floor. It must have been the after-party room. Fool had a vague recollection of spinning his way along with a flow of departing people and sitting down for a moment before heading off to his cabin. He'd also been somewhat subtly trying to follow Lexi to see if she maybe wanted a repeat of their previous evening.

He managed to lever himself up and carefully put his feet down without waking anyone, then he made his way to the door. The room looked to be in the main building and didn't have an integral bathroom like the cabins did. When he opened the door, he saw a bathroom just across the hall.

Something nagged in the back of his brain, and he turned around to look at everyone. They looked so comfortable, all cuddled up and dreaming peacefully. It didn't seem fair that the pain of his full bladder had pulled him away from all of that coziness.

A little, evil lightbulb went on his brain. He could make it fair.

He whispered, "Have Faith" and went out the door.

His bladder was mostly empty when the first frantic banging started on the door, and he tried not to giggle as he saw the experience notifications pop up.

This was going to be fun.

With only a little use of Mana, everyone found their bladder pressure fading to more expected levels, and the line of people lost its frantic edge. Alex was giving him the stink-eye, which meant that at least one person had figured out what had happened.

He brought some temper back to everyone by burning up more of his Mana and using his Mint? Skill to offer a small cup of coffee and a granola bar to everyone, which the humans enjoyed, and the aliens took with a wary glance. More trickle of experience. It wasn't much. He'd need ten years to gain one Level at this rate, but still... every little bit counted. And Fool didn't have to stretch his thinking much to see that he enjoyed this. It was fun to play a little harmless prank on people, and even more fun to treat them afterward. Sure, they all would have enjoyed sleeping in, but now they were awake, fed, and still had a good bit of the day ahead of them. Win for everyone.

Jackal strolled in to the room a moment later, looking shiny and fresh. "There you are! I thought I'd let you sleep in, but you took a while to find. We still planning to leave today? We can still get a head start, camp overnight."

"I suppose so," Fool said. "Yagnar, Alex, and Lexi are up. Might as well get them ready to go."

"One step ahead of you," Yagnar said.

Fool turned, and she was standing in the doorway, travel pack in one hand. Through the door, Fool saw Alex tossing her pack on as well.

He looked back at Jackal, who luckily didn't have his pack on him, or Fool would have felt very bad. "I suppose it's as good a time as any. I'll grab our gear if you want to coordinate with Lexi on our escort?"

"Already done!" Lexi yelled from inside the room. "Who do you think was sleeping in here?"

That rang even more bells for Fool. Thinking back on it, he did recall someone saying something about them having to leave early, and all crashing in the one room to speed it up. That was less fun and salacious than his first memory, so he figured it was probably the more accurate recollection.

"All right," Fool said. "I guess I'll just grab our packs then."

"I dropped them off by the gates after breakfast," Jackal said.

Fool glared at him. Too much efficiency going on. He'd have to do something about that.

He had to admit though. The bustle of sudden activity, the little bit of sleep, the recollection of the party last night? He was feeling pretty damn good. Life could be worse.

Lexi hadn't agreed to provide them an escort just to get past the spider infestation, but rather because she thought it was time to make contact with McBride and maybe get some sort of mutual defense and trade negotiations going with the other town. They'd already dispatched another group to Valemount after speaking with Yagnar the previous day.

They traveled without stopping all afternoon and made excellent time. They stopped briefly for a meal at sunset but decided to push on through the night. After all, they'd slept in enough, and a quick round of various energy-boosting substances gave them enough juice to push through. They were making a bit of a gamble that they wouldn't run across any of the giant Jumping Spiders. Lexi had done some research while Jackal and Fool were in Valemount and found that the giant spiders were a bit on the cowardly side. As such, they were likely to be off hiding from the Orcabear. They'd be an issue later, but for now, they weren't likely to be a problem.

The False Widow spiders were another issue altogether, and not a bad one at all. For all that they looked identical in every way, shape, and form to the terrestrial *Steadota Grossa* spider, they were actually an alien species of telepaths. They'd emigrated at some point recently, but Lexi hadn't been able to find any information on that.

They were an enigmatic species. As others had noted, they wouldn't eat conscious, moving sentients, but if you were asleep, they considered you fair game. That issue aside, they were also amenable to trade, and their silk was considered the premium raw material for certain kinds of armor and other products. Lexi figured the local communities could really benefit from the spiders' presence, as long as they kept the spiders confined to the wilderness. The females had a habit of seasonal migration and setting up nests in settlements, which could result in rather tragic circumstances. A simple upgrade for settlements could be purchased in most Shops and would send out a psionic buffer that kept them away.

It also explained why other spiders were showing up. The Widows used other spiders almost the way humans used livestock... or pets... the information hadn't been precise. Or it was so precise they'd need a damn degree in extraterrestrial biology, sociology, and anthropology to understand what they were talking about.

Sometimes, asking the System for answers could backfire really easily. Be careful of what you wish for, writ large.

Fool wondered what kind of fool had wished for the System? He'd probably have to kick him in the ass. Then kiss him.

In any case, the spiders had a Class in their race that could mutate other spiders to larger size.

Yagnar and Lexi had developed a plan to work to reduce the impact of that, as part of their negotiations.

Said negotiations took place just before dawn when they ran across a nest of the Widows. Negotiations went smoothly, as the Widows were interested in being good neighbors. They had some truly alien concepts of what that meant, which made things difficult. After a few hours of talking, and some judicious help from Fool and his Skills, a basic treaty was worked out.

They made it to Dunster in time for breakfast.

Balvinder was a bit surprised to see Fool and Jackal with company, but she got the sparse troops of the Fort to set up a small feast for everyone. It was a tight fit for all of them around the tables in the lunchroom, but they managed.

"Mountaineer's Guild?" Balvinder asked Lexi, who was snugged in next to her. "I thought it was called the Adventurer's Guild?"

"Yup, that's us! And no, we're much smaller than those Guilds. We actually had to negotiate a bit with them. Nestled in between Robson and Wells Gray, Tete Jaune Cache is a pretty good location with lots of potential for high-Level spawns not too far away. But for some reason, the other Guilds pulled out at the last minute. Something about opportunities coming up elsewhere. In the end, we got a pretty good deal. And the mountains really are beautiful here!"

"They are!" Balvinder said. "It's what brought my family here in the first place. My dad worked in logging camps when he was younger, and he said the mountains here reminded him of home more than anywhere else in the province. So he moved Mom and all us kids up here. So tell me how you climb these peaks! Do you have a special Class and Skills for that, or is it all equipment?"

Fool leaned in to answer. He was still fascinated to hear how they did it. "Nothing. They do it bare. Primitive-style."

Balvinder raised her eyebrows and looked at Lexi. "For real?"

Lexi nodded enthusiastically. "It's a sacred bond between us and the mountain. We still use pitons and hammers and stuff that's almost identical to what you humans used, but using Mana to help us in any way is considered cheating. We even take potions to reduce our Attributes down to baseline."

That got Jackal involved. "You're kidding! That's... I mean, really. Suicidal. Never mind the mountains themselves, those peaks are crammed with high-Level monsters! How do you deal with them with no Skills?"

"Oh, monsters don't count," Lexi said. "Although some people can be really hardcore about even that, but even the crazies will usually bring along spotters to keep any stray beasts away. We hardly lose anyone to monsters. Just to the mountains. The way it's supposed to be."

Jackal shook his head. "I thought Fool was nuts."

Fool didn't like how loudly everyone laughed at that. "I'm not crazy enough to climb a mountain without gear." He wasn't able to keep the indignation out of his voice.

"Right," Alex said. "But you'll scratch the belly of an Orcabear like it's an oversized dog!"

That got everyone laughing again, and when they slowed down, they saw the bewildered look on Balvinder's face and started up again. They eventually calmed enough to tell the story, and Fool found himself unable to get a word in edgewise as everyone recounted their recollections of his part of the fight with the beast.

"Are you kidding me?" Balvinder practically shouted. "He *Free Willy*'d it? I would pay for a recording of that!"

"I bought one!" Yagnar shouted. "So worth the price. I knew I had to get one or no one would believe me. I knew as soon as I saw it! You humans are nuts!"

Fool groaned and dropped his head on the table as Yagnar collected Credits from everyone, transferring the System-collected clip of the fight to everyone. The table dissolved into excited exclamations and play-by-plays, and Fool was just about to use his Geas to sneak out of the room. He was stopped by a hand on his back and a warm, breathy voice in his ear.

"That was very brave," Balvinder said. "I like brave men."

He had a hard time stammering out a response, and his blushing turned even darker when he saw Lexi looking at Balvinder with a certain calculation he'd been intimately familiar with earlier. Balvinder caught the look and smiled at the diminutive alien.

Fool almost made it out of the room before Jackal snagged him.

"Where are you going, buddy?" Jackal said. "We're in no rush. Why don't we stay another day here?"

"Great idea!" Lexi shouted, looking over Balvinder. "If we've got time, I can think of a local peak I wouldn't mind trying with the right company…"

"Sounds like a plan," Yagnar said. "I wouldn't mind doing a bit more hunting. Alex and I could use some more Levels, not to mention a few more Credits for when we get to your big city."

"I'm in!" Jackal said. "Fool, you can escort Lexi on her peak climb."

Fool groaned and turned around to see Balvinder and Lexi smiling at him.

It wasn't that he objected so much to the idea of what they had planned for him; it was just that he was having a hard time seeing how it wasn't going to be really awkward.

Ah well, he thought. Maybe he'd get some experience points.

The End

Epilogue

The road up to the house was still neatly tramped down snow. It was just compact enough that you couldn't really make out how many people had come in or gone out. The driveway was long enough, and steep enough, to need a switchback. Even without that, the house was hidden from the road.

Fool smelled the tantalizing aroma of hot butter and flour and something sweet baking. The first few times he'd come back to the Foundation, he'd assumed that Gramma, all their iterations, had some special Skill that let them predict when someone was arriving. Either that, or the Foundation had far more surveillance gear around than Fool thought.

Eventually, he found out the truth. The posting was a bit boring, so the assigned Grammas had started baking to keep themselves occupied. The results had been popular enough to keep it going, and they were always working on new recipes.

Yagnar smelled it about the same time as Fool, just before the house came into view. She left her nose up and gave the air a deep whiff. "What *is* that smell? It smells... good."

Jackal smiled, leaving the answer up to Fool.

"Don't know yet, but I don't smell cinnamon, so it'll be a surprise," Fool said. "A good surprise."

Yagnar raised an eyebrow, and a few moments later, they were at the entrance to the house. Jackal and Fool stomped the snow off of their boots in the entryway and showed Yagnar where to hang up her outerwear.

Yagnar hadn't been sure about how she was going to fit into, or if she'd agree with, anything the Foundation had to offer, so they'd avoided telling Alex about it as yet. Instead, they had talked Alex and Lexi into shopping and talking to the McBride Council.

Gramma opened the door to the foyer with a big smile and started to greet them. Then she paused. "My, not quite what we expected." She glanced at Fool and Jackal, then back at Yagnar. "Do you like blueberries?"

Yagnar looked down at her, a quizzical look on her face. Neither Fool nor Jackal had really thought to explain to her what to expect from the Foundation, but this probably wasn't something she'd have expected.

"I've tried them," Yagnar said. "They are pleasant, but I'm told they are better when in season and not frozen."

Gramma smiled. "Well, I've just pulled some turnovers out of the oven, so you can—" She was interrupted by Fool and Jackal bulling past her to get to the kitchen. Gramma cleared her throat and said to Yagnar, "I'll make sure some are left for you. Actually, why don't you head upstairs? There are some folk waiting for you up there. I'll bring up turnovers for you. And some drinks. Everyone else will be having coffee. I've also got Earl Grey tea in one of these cupboards, if you prefer."

"Coffee will be fine." Yagnar smiled and shook her head as she watched Fool frantically sucking air past his burned tongue and Jackal carefully blowing on the end of a turnover, while he delicately passed it from hand to hand. She pointed at the stairs at the end of the living room, heading up. "I assume those stairs there?"

"Those are the ones," Gramma said. "Go right on up and say hi. I'll be along in a few moments."

Yagnar nodded and headed off to the stairs. Gramma let out a little sigh and headed over to the kitchen, which was just to the left of the entry.

"You boys better take those to go. Professor Xi is waiting for you in the Rumpus Room."

Fool stopped trying to work his way into a safe nibble of the turnover and glanced at Gramma. "Downstairs? Are we in trouble?"

It was unusual for the Professor to come into this part of the house. He was usually quite busy in the main part of the Foundation, involved in some sort of esoteric research.

"No trouble," Gramma said. "At least, I don't think so. Not sure what you two have been up to, but he seemed in a good mood. I wouldn't keep him waiting though."

Fool nodded and looked at Jackal. Jackal had yet to actually take a bite of his turnover and was reluctantly putting it back on the cooling rack.

Fool sighed and walked toward the same side of the house Yagnar had gone to. While she'd gone up the stairs, Fool and Jackal went around to the other side, where the stairs down were tucked under the other stairs.

The basement wasn't really the usual kind of basement. The house backed up against a good, steep slope, so the rear wall of the basement was underground. That was what allowed them to have the secret entrance to the Foundation, after all. But the front of the basement was sloping glass, running from the ceiling almost to the ground. In spring, there was a lovely garden outside the door to the side. In winter, the glass helped keep the room warm. As it was south facing, the sun shone right in, and it kept the room at almost greenhouse temperatures. And indeed, a long brick planter box had been built right up to the windows, and a variety of plants grew in it.

Professor Xi was sitting in a chair near them in the sun. He had his favorite plaid blanket in his lap and a steaming cup of tea on a side table next to him. He looked up as the two came down the stairs and put aside the book he'd been reading.

"Welcome home," he said.

"Thanks," Fool said as he and Jackal walked up to the old man.

Gramma appeared to be right. Professor Xi didn't look angry at all. In fact, if Fool had to guess, he would say that the old man was just about to drift off into a nap. Fool couldn't think of anything they'd done wrong on the mission, but he still felt his stress level dropping.

"Good to be back," Fool said.

"I gather you found the Princess," the Professor said. "Tell me how the compass worked."

"Pretty much as expected. Took us right to her. No complaints about that at all. It fit into my hand without any issues and was pretty nondescript. About the only improvement I would ask for if we use that again? Would be nice if we could not have to hold it at all. Maybe if it could put up a notice in the System interface instead?"

Professor Xi nodded. "I believe they're already working on that as an improvement. The team will be looking for a full debrief from you shortly. I'm sure they'll grill you thoroughly and will be happy with any suggestions you have."

The old man sighed and looked out the window. Fool and Jackal waited patiently. It was easy to think of Professor Xi as an old and forgetful man, but he was as sharp as a tack and never missed anything. Finally, he turned back to them.

"Impressions of the Princess?" he asked. "We've gotten much more substantial data on her and how she'll work with our plans. Every step you got closer to her, the more time the compass spent next to her, the more refined our information became. That part of the mission was a sterling success, but I'm interested in your impressions. What is she like?"

Fool glanced at Jackal out of habit. He knew Jackal wouldn't volunteer any information unless directly asked, but the glance back was an almost subconscious tic that Fool had developed. It also gave him a moment to think, somewhat like glancing at a clock, back in the old days.

"I think," Fool said, "that she'll be a good fit. She's not what we expected. Capable though. Not a warrior, but she can handle herself very well under stress. Cares about her people. A lot. Some interesting Skills. She's got a knack for making people loyal to her, and while there is a System aspect to that, I don't think she realizes how much of it comes from her personality. I think she's an asset and worth bringing into the Foundation, if possible."

"If possible?" The Professor tilted his head at that, inviting more information.

"Loyalty goes both ways. She's built a strong connection to Valemount, and she may not be willing to give that up, so I'd suggest any overtures keep that in mind. She's also not a free agent. She has a partner, in addition to her obligations."

"What are the odds of Valemount self-sustaining?" The Professor clearly didn't ask that lightly because there was a touch of steel in his voice. The Foundation might have resources to help Valemount, but those resources were limited. The Foundation had to look at the bigger picture, and if that meant cutting loose a potential resource in the short term, then so be it.

"Good, I think," Fool said. "They were being pretty heavily exploited by a rogue element, but it didn't last long enough to really kill their spirit. They've suffered pretty badly in terms of having any sort of fighting element, but they've got some strong Crafters and a good stockpile of resources. Given that they now have good neighbors acting as a firewall between them and the high-Level monsters in Mount Robson Park, they've got the opportunity to grow."

The Professor looked at him and raised an eyebrow. "I'll ask about those neighbors in a moment, but I'm sensing an inherent downside to that 'opportunity' you're hesitating on?"

Fool pursed his lips together, hesitating for a moment. "A group sent some mercenaries to help oppress Valemount, and it looks like there was a bit of a conspiracy in play to sell the town to that group. We wound up killing one member of that team and injuring another, who managed to escape. I think it would be wise to expect some follow-up from that."

"What's the group?" the Professor asked.

"Thirteen Moon Sect," Fool said.

"All right. We'll look into them and take that into account. I take it the neighbors are that Adventurer Guild we heard about?"

Fool shook his head. "No, turned out we were mistaken about that. It's the Mountaineers Guild. Solid folk, but an odd Guild. Not too far off from some of the old Alpine groups I heard about back before. They lean toward mountain climbing with no System aids."

"Interesting!" The Professor actually leaned forward at that; Fool was amused to note. "We should look into making contact with them, see if their goals might fit our long-term interests… Jackal. You look like you swallowed something sour. What is it? What did you two do?"

Fool looked out the window. Carefully. No eye contact. "Ahh… I might have initiated contact already."

Jackal was unable to hold in a quick, snorting snicker, but he managed to stop the guffaw he clearly wanted to let out.

The Professor looked at Fool and sighed. "I hope… that you left a… *positive* impression at least? Nothing to clean up?"

"No, sir," Fool said. "Actually, one of the Guild Members is currently in McBride. Came back with us."

"Good. Try to maintain a positive relationship. We'll look into those avenues later."

The Professor looked out the window for a while. Fool had the impression that the older man probably thought this was a companionable silence, but Fool and Jackal were still standing awkwardly. Finally, the old man turned back and looked at them with a measured stare.

"I see you both collected some good experience, but Fool… something's changed. You look… a bit more together than usual. What changed?"

Fool tried not to look startled. He'd grown a lot in the last week, and he wasn't even really sure how much. It wasn't anything he'd thought the professor would notice though.

"Nothing much, sir," he said. "I guess I'm just starting to understand what my Class is all about and getting more in touch with my Skills. I've been trying to work around them, and now I'm learning to work with them."

"About time," the Professor said. "Edwards figured you'd be another year making that jump. I thought you would have done it months ago.

Good for you. I'll make a note to have more details on that taken in your formal debrief."

Fool groaned internally. He understood the value of the debriefs, but they could sometimes take a day or two, and that was a long time to be answering questions about stuff you would sometimes prefer to forget. Like the first run-in with the Orcabear, and that feeling that Jackal was going to be gone for good, and thinking he had no way to stop that from happening. Those were memories Fool would prefer to leave lost in his mind forever.

He snapped his mind back to the present as he saw the Professor said something else.

"And on that note, make sure you both get some rest and recovery going. It looks like we've got another mission coming up for you. Nothing concrete yet, but we may have found another key person for our plans. We've got some sources of information in the area, but nothing too detailed yet. Potentially though, a key leadership figure. But something really strange is going on. As best as we can predict, this person might be the lynchpin of all of our hopes going forward. But at the same time, they might be the thing that can bring all of our plans crashing down. So we need you two to go and evaluate in person. You should expect to leave before the end of the month, if things go well. But be ready by next week, because you'll need to make it all the way over to Prince Rupert."

Both Jackal and Fool started at that.

"Is that even possible?" Fool blurted. "How are we supposed to get there? The only safe way would be to… well… *is* there a safe way to do it? Can we get transport? That's a hell of a long way on foot!"

"We'll see about transport," the Professor said. "But I know it'll be dangerous. It's either going to be a long loop around the most dangerous parts, or tough it out through a few high-Level wilderness areas. We'll tackle that when we know more. There are a few assets we haven't used yet, and if the projections solidify, we'll pull out all the stops to help you succeed. We're calling this 'Project Pendragon' for the moment, and that should let you know how important we think this is."

Fool nodded and crossed his arms. "The One True King returns, you think? Isn't that a bit much? I know we have wizards and dragons these days, but that's still a lot of fantasy weight to put on things, isn't it?"

"All fantasy has a basis in reality," Professor Xi said. "It's just that a lot of that reality was hidden from us before the System came. So get yourselves ready. Because you're either going to have to save King Arthur or kill him."

Fool and Jackal will return in Book Two

Fool's Bond

www.starlitpublishing.com/products/fools-bond

Authors Note

Hey reader. Hope you enjoyed reading about these two heroes, because we've got a lot more in store for you. As I write this, the next book is done and I've already gotten it back from the loving hands of my editor, red lines and all. Re-writes are on the way, and the final book of this trilogy is being drafted at the same time. I expect to have it done and edited before the end of this year.

Fool and Jackal have a rough road ahead of them, but it's for the best. How else can we really know what's in the heart of a character if they aren't pushed to their limits? At the same time, we should also seem them finding real joy, because the hardship has to have a payoff. Real life is like that, but we need to really reach to find the joy when the rough stuff punches us down. But it's always there.

There is a fair amount of me in Fool, and some in Jackal. I've lived long enough to have lost everything…more than once. And I'm still young enough to be aware it could happen again. And yet, I find I'm in the best place of my life. Not because I'm in a secure place or have tons of savings or anything like that, but because I'm finally doing what I've always wanted to do.

Writing.

A writer isn't anything without readers. I finished my first novel because my wife insisted I write her something to read, every day. Now I'm writing for all of you. You are part of my process, and I can't tell you enough how much I appreciate you. The only way I can really show my appreciation is to give you more to read, so…

See you in Fool's Bond, and in Fool's Last Dance.

- *David, from the mountain village*

About the Authors

David R. Packer has been a full-time teacher of historical European swordplay, a high-tech wizard, and a security professional. For a few years he was a for-pay bad guy working in police training, which once had him on the run from the entire police force, across the whole city.

Aside from that, he lives a cozy life with 2 cats and a real-life she-hulk for a wife. He has many books and likes coffee far too much.

You can find out more information on David's books by visiting his website: https://boxwrestlefence.com

Tao Wong is an avid fantasy and sci-fi reader who spends his time working and writing in the North of Canada. He's spent way too many years doing martial arts of many forms, and having broken himself too often, he now spends his time writing about fantasy worlds.

For updates on the series and other books written by Tao Wong (and special one-shot stories), please visit the author's website: http://www.mylifemytao.com

Want updates on upcoming deluxe editions and exclusive merch? Follow Tao on Kickstarter to get notifications on all projects. https://www.kickstarter.com/profile/starlitpublishing/created

Subscribers to Tao's mailing list to receive exclusive access to short stories in the Thousand Li and System Apocalypse universes.

For more great information about LitRPG series, check out these

Facebook groups:

- GameLit Society

https://www.facebook.com/groups/LitRPGsociety/

- LitRPG Books

https://www.facebook.com/groups/LitRPG.books/

- LitRPG Legion

https://www.facebook.com/groups/litrpglegion

About the Publisher

Starlit Publishing is wholly owned and operated by Tao Wong. It is a science fiction and fantasy publisher focused on the LitRPG & cultivation genres. Their focus is on promoting new, upcoming authors in the genre whose writing challenges the existing stereotypes while giving a rip-roaring good read.

For more information on Starlit Publishing, early access to books and exclusive stories visit our webshop: https://www.starlitpublishing.com/

You can also join Starlit Publishing's mailing list to learn of new, exciting authors and book releases.

Glossary

Aura of *: Area effect mental attack Skill that's not really defined. More specifically, it has the effect of making the targets feel increasingly uncomfortable and out of touch with reality. It builds a feedback loop off of whatever the target initially interprets this as, and rapidly spikes it up into overload.

Aziz: Yeah, I'm a huge "Fifth Element" fan.

Beau Geste: Classic 1939 Gary Cooper film about the French Foreign Legion. The actual fort in the film is Fort Zinderneuf. Fort Whisky is the fort that gets swamped by bugs in the "Starship Troopers" movie. Did you know there is also a book called Starship Troopers, and it is also good? Probably someone will make a movie out of it someday.

Blue River: Blue River is too small to be a village.

Cariboo Mountain: Next door neighbours of the Canadian Rockies, and contain the Selkirk, Monashee, and Purcell ranges. These were my stomping grounds as a kid and the reason I get confused when I go to other places and they refer to hills as "mountains."

Clouseau: Inspector Clouseau was of course, the master of disguise. This skill makes Fool almost as ingenious as the great man himself.

CPP: Canada Pension Plan. You get money when you decide you are just too damned old for dealing with people's shit. It't not much money, though, so it's best to suck it up as long as you can.

Dry Hair is for Squids: Jack Deth is cool. Cooler than you. "Trancers" is amazing.

Dunster: They have an ice-cream social once a year!

EI: Employment Insurance. In Canada, a part of every paycheck goes into a fund. If you lose your job, this fund is used to pay you a portion of your wages until you get a new job. It's usually six months worth, but it can be extended if you are taking the right kind of classes, or working part time. Super handy.

False Widows: Steodata, generally Grossa. Big black shiny spiders that might live under your sink. These are great spiders. They will eat Black Widows and Brown Recluse spiders, as well as all the other pests in your house. They also stay put, so if you see one, you can safely ignore it and it will always be there doing it's job for you. Don't try to touch them, their bite stings like a hornet.

First Nations: The people living within the Canadian legal boundary called British Columbia. Despite popular misconception, most of this land is still completely owned by them. They have a serious issues with squatters. Please note that the author is not First Nations, and everything he has to say related to First Nations people, practices, and namings is not to be trusted or assumed correct. Hopefully this encourages you to go and find more reliable sources, as there are many. Here's a great place to start: https://www.bcafn.ca/

Fool's Warhammer: Not really a warhammer. The head is based off of a museum piece, but the whole thing is closer in weight and usage to a Hungarian Fokos, which is kind of a walking stick with an small axe head or hammer head on one side. Lightweight, fast, and real handy for troll smashing.

Foundation: Professor Xi chose the name because he is a giant nerd.

Friston: Karl Friston. Jackal is trying to explain how Friston's Free Energy principle might apply. You can look it up. It's a deep rabbit hole of very hard to understand stuff, but will give you a better sense of how the world works.

Geas: I've been afraid to say this word out loud since I was twelve and got my first D&D set. I still have no idea how to pronounce it. I guess I should listen to the audiobook. Narrators research this kind of stuff, right?

Gitxsan: Coastal First Nation that no longer lives on the coast. Sort of like the Canadian version of Normans, who were descended from viking raiders that thought "oh gosh, wouldn't this be a nice spot for a winery. Let's learn to make croissants!" Alex is not Gitxsan. Fool is really, really bad at faces but really good at assumptions.

Halkomelem: One of the First Nations in the BC lower mainland area.

Have Faith: Fool can ask the Trickster for a favour. Any kind of favour. In exchange, the Trickster will ask something in return from Fool. The Trickster doesn't need to really be asked the question, though, since he always seems to know what Fool needs. And Fool never has any idea of how the request will be fulfilled.

Hoary Marmot: Squeak!
https://www.youtube.com/shorts/WC5NnBFvfdw Seriously, Marmots are very cool. They will truly ignore you, to the point of walking right over you to get to something else, unless you bother them. Then you get to see a whole different creature.

Jumping Spiders: Did you know they make good pets? Very playful! So cute!

Maker: Alex is a nerd, and likes the book with sand and giant worms.

McBride: A tiny village in the Robson Valley. Has a pretty good coffee shop, and a town's worth of facilities. Really. It's quite strange.

Opilione: I am one of the few humans to have been bit by one of these. It hurt. Very pinchy. I also had the terrifying experience of crawling through a quartz tube (abandoned small gold mine) waaay up in the mountains when I was a kid, and looking up at the ceiling and realizing it was a few inches thick mat of these guys. I got over the fear eventually, which is good because these things are seriously weird and fun to look at. They are probably the most alien looking thing that you can see commonly, and probably ignore.

Orcabear: I used to dream about this thing. Brrr.
A monster with top half of an orca and the bottom half of a grizzly bear.

Piobaireachd: Traditional form of bagpipe music. Also called ceol mor or "big music" as opposed to ceol beag or "party tunes." It starts with a simple melody that is repeated, and then gets more complex variations added. This was the first music I learned to play on the pipes. Sounds great echoing off of the mountains…if someone else is playing it, because I suck.

RCMP: Royal Canadian Mounted Police. Sometimes called "Mounties" but only if you're buddies. Militarized FBI with horses and cool dress uniforms. Most police in Canada are RCMP, and they go through substantial training. They are expected on occasion to be the only law enforcement for a very, very large territory.

Sheriff: You rarely see or hear of Sheriff's in Canada. They have strictly limited duties, and no political connections at all. They occasionally provide extra security, but mostly they only handle prisoner transfers and courtroom duties. A Deputy Sheriff is someone who only works in the court system, so the usage of "Deputy" in Valemount is incorrect, but is the sort of thing some Canadians would think is right because they spend all their time watching American TV and have a hard time figuring out which country they live in. Sheriff Barnes is one of those people.

Simpcw: First Nation that also has ownership of the area this book takes place in. First Nations don't use the same border system theory that the settlers did, and this caused a lot of confusion for people try to assign ownership to things because it makes them sleep better at night.

Sto:lo: Fool's pretty off-base here, as are most of the people. Sto:lo is used in the lower mainland, and the usage of this word has spread a bit, but where Fool is located it would be slightly more proper to use either the Dakelh word: Lhtakoh, or the Tsilhqot'in word: ʔelhdawox. Locals use this word currently, anglicized to "Eldako" for some areas, but never to the river for some weird reason. Fool is Metis, but he was raised without any real education of his ancestry, so while he has a keen interest in First Nations lore, what he knows is spotty and often wrong. He sure tries, through.

Sunbeam Ecological Reserve: You can see this from McBride. It's lovely. I haven't been up yet because I don't own a 4x4.

Talent Scout: Fools most used skill, but it's not that great. Probably could have bought a basic identify spell from the Shop that would replace this.

Taxes: We pay these in Canada in the hopes that the CBC will eventually find a new comedy group as funny as Kids in the Hall. Or even SCTV. Someday.

Tete Jaune Cache: Local's sometimes pronounce this "Tee Joan Cash." Tete Jaune means Yellowhead, as in the Yellowhead highway. Or "Blondie's road" if you are feeling catty. Tete Jaune was the nickname of a Metis scout in the area when it was "discovered." It's very pretty. Don't take my word for it. You should visit it sometime.

Tom Cody: "Streets of Fire" If you haven't seen it yet, you're in for a treat.

Valemount: You go through this on the way to Jasper. If you want to save money on Jasper hotels, you stay here instead. Cheaper hotels but still overpriced restaurants.

To learn more about LitRPG, talk to authors including myself, and just have an awesome time, please join the LitRPG Group! https://www.facebook.com/groups/LitRPGGroup/

Made in the USA
Las Vegas, NV
08 November 2023

80433821R00201